THIS BOOK IS PART OF ISLINGTON READS BOOKSWAP SCHEME

Please take this book and either return it to a Bookswap site or replace with one of your own books that you would like to share.

If you enjoy this book, why not join your local Islington Library and borrow more like it for free?

Find out about our FREE e-book, e-audio, newspaper and magazine apps, activities for pre-school children and other services we have to offer at www.islington.gov.uk/libraries

MISSION LONDON

Alek Popov

Translated from the Bulgarian by
Daniella and Charles Gill de Mayol de Lupe

First published in 2014 by
Istros Books
London, United Kingdom
www.istrosbooks.com

© Alek Popov, 2001, 2014
First edition in Bulgarian: Zvezdan Press, Sofia, 2001

Artwork & Design@Milos Miljkovich, 2013
Graphic Designer/Web Developer – milijkovicmisa@gmail.com
Cover photo @Anthony Georgieff
Typeset by Octavo Smith Publishing Services

Edited by Christopher Buxton http://christopherbuxton.com

ISBN: 978-1-908236-18-0

Printed and bound in Great Britain by CMP (UK) Limited | www.cmp-uk.com

Supported using public funding by

ARTS COUNCIL ENGLAND

This book has been selected to receive financial assistance from English PEN's
"PEN Translates!" programme, supported by Arts Council England. English
PEN exists to promote literature and our understanding of it, to uphold
writers' freedoms around the world, to campaign against the persecution and
imprisonment of writers for stating their views, and to promote the friendly
co-operation of writers and the free exchange of ideas. www.englishpen.org

"Even if we achieve tremendous successes in our work, there is no reason to be complacent and arrogant. Modesty helps people to advance, while vanity pulls them back. This is a truth we must always have in mind!" – Mao Ze Dung, Greeting to the delegates of the 8th National Conference of the Chinese Communist Party

1

Kosta Pastricheff was counting the aeroplanes flying over South Kensington. It was a delicate spring morning only slightly overcast. The forsythia in the corner of the garden was covered in bright blooms. Kosta was sitting on the stairs, barefoot, in just jeans and a jumper. An empty bottle of Becks lay at his feet and between his fingers a forgotten cigarette still burned. Planes were flying overhead about every two minutes. The drone of each lingered until it merged with the noise of the next flight. He had counted over twenty. The sound reminded him of the wash of the sea. The windows of the house were wide open and a strong breeze carried with it the fragrance of old fags, swirling the thin curtains around like the veils of a drunken actress. In the dining room on the ground floor, there remained the detritus of the previous night's party. It was getting on for eleven but Kosta was in no hurry to tidy up. He had the whole afternoon at his disposal.

Meanwhile, another three planes flew over.

A persistent ringing brought him out of his blissful equanimity. At first, Kosta told himself that there was no power that could make him open the door. Then he softened, realizing that such moods are bad for one's curriculum vitae. He pushed the fag-butt into a gap between the tiles and unwillingly dragged himself to his feet. As he trundled across the foyer, the enormous crystal mirror balefully reflected his figure as if hurrying to expel his scrawny reflection from its gold-plated frame. The ringing began anew – this time shorter and faster.

"Coming, coming..." muttered Kosta and thought to himself, Fuck you!

A tall gloomy gentleman, wearing a greenish raincoat, suitcase in hand, jutted from the doorstep. Behind him, a black-cab was executing complicated manoeuvres to get out of the narrow little street. For a few seconds they inspected each other suspiciously.

"Who you are looking for?" asked Kosta in Bulgarian.

A bitter smile lit up he gentleman's worn face.

"I am the new Ambassador," he said, gazing at the bare feet. "And who are you?"

"Umm, me, well…" stuttered Kosta. "I'm the cook". (The ex-cook – the painful premonition transfixed him.)

"Very well," nodded the Ambassador. "Might I come in?"

Kosta mechanically moved out of the way; he felt an inexplicable chill as the man passed him. His faint hope that this was a practical joke arranged by the Bulgarian immigrants he had been hanging out with recently, slowly started to evaporate. The man put his suitcase on the floor, looked around and raised his eyebrows in disgust. The cook felt he had better say something first.

"We weren't expecting you for another two days." There was just a hint of reproach in his voice.

"It shows." The Ambassador's response was cutting and followed a glance into the dining room.

"If we'd known you were coming today…"

"I changed my plans."

Then blame yourself thought Kosta.

From all those many years spent around the dining-tables of his so-called superiors, the cook had developed a special psychological intuition. Instinctively he knew that his new boss belonged to that extensive and many-branched cretinous family of jobsworths. Yet, there was something else, something behind this man's idiotic glassy look, which made him unpredictable and dangerous. Suddenly, Kosta realized that this guy intended to settle here. Even more, this was his home now and he – Kosta – was about to become his servant. And that seemed infinitely unjust to him.

At that moment Kosta's little son crawled up the stairs from the basement, which was occupied by the cook's family. The child had escaped his mother's attention and he was jubilant. Mumbling his baby talk, the child stood up and waddled adroitly towards the little table beneath the vast mirror. A frail object on the table had been annoying his primitive instincts for a long time. Kosta had unfortunately lost his former agility, gained through the practice of various sports in his youth. The little one grasped the table's corner and quickly tilted it, whereupon the little porcelain basket, inventory number 73, crashed to the floor with an apocalyptic tinkle.

"Ding-ding" mumbled the little one happily.

"I'll give you a ding-ding!" Kosta growled, suppressing his instinctive urge to bash him on the head.

The Ambassador looked on with a poisoned face.

"Child's play," muttered the cook unconvincingly. He grabbed the child with one arm and leaned over the balustrade. "Nora!" he shouted. There was no answer. "Norraaaa!" he repeated. "Come here at once!"

"Get stuffed up your shitty ass!" a harsh voice replied.

2

The Mayor of Provadia energetically turned on the hot and cold taps and let the shower pour over him from head to toe. The water slapped his wide Tartar face, smacked his massive, hairy chest and bounced over his titanic belly. The Mayor of Provadia was in a tip-top mood, despite the slight hangover-haze wrapped around his brain. With the completion of his mission his self importance was in full flood. He had visited that mystic, faraway island that had once controlled a third of the world. He had done the museums and the shops. He had seen how the people over there lived. He had drawn the necessary conclusions and could bravely declare that he now had an idea of how the reforms were progressing in that developed western country. He was pleased that he had not lost his mind amidst the splendour and vanity of Oxford Street.

But what made him even happier was the fact that today he was going back to his hometown, Provadia – a town with a glorious history and fertile land.

"Ola-la-la," he sang full throatedly. "La-la-laaaa."

The water gushed from all directions like a waterfall, and a feeling of satisfaction and calm suffused the Mayor's soul. "Lalaa-lala-lala-lalaaa!" he continued his little singsong, while thoroughly soaping his short hair.

He did not notice, could not have noticed, the slim tongue of water that had begun to slide under the door and soak the carpet.

Meanwhile, the Ambassador took his suitcase and headed for the first floor without a word. Judging by the greenish hue of his face, Kosta concluded that the magic of love at first sight had failed. The prospects looked ever grimmer.

Halfway up the stairs, the Ambassador stopped and listened.

"There is somebody up there." The Ambassador pointed up the stairs.

"Ah, the Mayor…" From the tone of the cook's voice one might presume that this was some sort of pet who had been in the residence for as long as anyone could remember.

The child, twisting in his hands with unexpected strength, started tearing and biting. The cook squeezed him tightly and hissed through his teeth, "You shitty little good for nothing, you're just like your mother!"

"Mayor?!" asked the Ambassador anxiously.

"The Mayor of Provadia." The cook elaborated with a hint of condolence.

"And how does he happen to be here this … man from Provadia?" asked the Ambassador queasily.

"They accommodated him. There was no space in the hotel."

The Ambassador said nothing. He stared at the carpet, which was malignantly soaking up water, as though on board the Titanic. He heard the slap of feet and swearing overhead. The Mayor of Provadia sprang out onto the upper landing, wrapped nonchalantly in a small towel beneath which his Herculean attributes bulged.

"Look at those stupid English!" he started shouting. "They forgot to make one little hole in the bathroom floor! One simple little hole! What's the big deal? A hole! A drain!"

He rolled up his fingers to make a little hole and looked though it to demonstrate the obviousness of that idiotic omission. Immediately his eyes lit upon the gloomy gentleman, who was inspecting the wet path on the carpet with a pained look on his face.

"Good morning," said the Mayor and threw a quick glance at Kosta.

"This is the new Ambassador," said the cook without too much enthusiasm.

"Brilliant!" boomed the Mayor in his loud voice. "Congratulations!"

The gentleman visibly jumped.

"I am very pleased to meet you!" shouted the big man with the Tartar face. "Excuse my appearance. It's really good we've met. It's a shame I'm going back today, otherwise I could tell you more about these hypocrites. But, I want you to remember one thing: there is no democracy in England! This is not a real democracy!"

Signs of real panic appeared on the Ambassador's face.

"There is no need for me to explain that to you, of course," continued the Mayor brusquely. "You're going to see it for yourself. And don't forget to remind them about the bathroom. They put in a carpet and forgot the pipe! You must tell them at the first official meeting! And about the W.C.: Did you know that the ancient Bulgarians invented the water closet? I didn't know myself but, recently, some archaeologists came to report to me. They found it in the dig. A whole 600 years before the Europeans! In the town of Provadia!"

Happy with the effect that his words had visibly had on the important man, the Mayor of Provadia leaned over the banister and shouted to Kosta, "Mate, is there any more of that tasty pig's-trotter jelly?"

"There is," said the cook. "Do you want me to reheat it?"

"Will you have some pig's-trotter jelly for breakfast with a nice ice-cold beer?" The Mayor turned affably to the Ambassador. "A very healthy way to start the day."

"Hardly," the man nodded his head stiffly. The corner of his mouth trembled malevolently. His last words were to Kosta, "I intend to go for a walk. Do not expect me for dinner. And clean out this pigsty!"

He turned sharply and hurried to the doorway, leaving his suitcase on the stairs. Just in front of the doorstep, he stopped, stood rigidly in the entrance and shouted in a squeaky voice, "93!"

"What's wrong with that lad…?" The Mayor of Provadia shrugged.

3

Varadin Dimitrov left the residence under the influence of a volatile cocktail of contradictory feelings – anger, ecstasy, disdain, and shame. Half in a daze, he crossed the two hundred yards that separated him from the bustle of High Street Kensington and froze in front of the rivers of cars and buses running in both directions. Opposite him, the grass of Kensington Gardens was a tender green. People were roller-blading quietly along the paths like creatures from some distant utopia. Varadin Dimitrov headed to the nearest traffic lights. Leaning on the railings, an elderly English lady was waiting to cross. Without even looking at her Varadin hissed through his teeth, "74!"

The woman looked at him speechless and then quickly looked away, pretending she had not noticed him, as if strictly following the instructions of the famous pocket guide How to avoid troublesome acquaintances. The pedestrian light went green. The traffic had stopped and Varadin Dimitrov crossed the road with long, slow strides like a pair of dividers. The old lady followed him at a careful distance.

The park was full of running dogs and small children. The day was dry, people from all parts of the world were scattered across the grass, some of them already chewing their lunchtime sandwiches. Varadin Dimitrov took the main path past Kensington Palace – home of the late Princess Diana. Here and there on the railings dangled bouquets of flowers or postcards with messages from the endless stream of the princess' fans. He walked indifferently around those touching signs of people's love and stopped for a second in front of the Queen Victoria memorial. It seemed to him that the late Queen bore an astonishing resemblance to one of his relatives who had given him many a drubbing in the past. Then he turned towards the duck pond and followed the water's edge, sown with bird droppings. He found a free bench and sat down. A goose browsing nearby stretched its neck towards his leg and screeched piercingly.

"55," he said out loud.

Varadin Dimitrov stayed on the bench for nearly half an hour, without any particular thoughts in his head, gazing at the flat surface of the pond, on which white down floated. The geese and the ducks slowly lost interest in him. Then, totally unexpectedly, he mumbled, "One."

And smiled, relieved.

The 'Numerical Therapy' of Doctor Pepolen was delivering astonishing results. As a man always exposed to nervous stress, Varadin Dimitrov could appreciate that. Doctor Pepolen's system was based on a few very simple principles. He claimed that human emotions (similar to earthquakes) could be arranged on a scale from 1 to 100, according to their intensity. Registering your emotion – taught Pepolen – is a step towards overcoming it. He conducted specialised workshops, with unstable, easily excited individuals, in which he instructed them in how to measure the level of their emotions. The method comprised the following: when the patient felt he was losing control of his nerves, he had to shout the first number to come into his head, between 1 and 100. After a certain interval, he had to say a further random number, with the proviso that it be smaller than the first. The next time, the number should decrease again. And so on and so forth until the number reached one. At that particular moment, according to Doctor Pepolen, the emotions would be completely conquered, encapsulated and neutralized and the individual would have regained his psychological balance.

Varadin Dimitrov had the pleasure of meeting Dr Pepolen during his mandate in one of the Scandinavian countries. Under the influence of concerned relatives, he enrolled in the famous workshop and for almost three years had been practicing the 'Numerical Therapy' method. It works was the only thing he could say. The proof was that he was here now, and not being fried, so to speak, in the consular section of the Embassy in Lusaka. In his line of work, healthy nerves were like ropes for a mountaineer. If the rope does not hold, you fly briefly and then the Sherpas gather up your remains with a dustpan and brush. He had witnessed many such incidents. He had no intention of being one of them. There was only one path – upwards.

Now, when the murky stream of his overflowing emotions had drained away, only pure joy remained in his soul, sparkling like a mountain spring. He had achieved his goal. That moment of surprise. The usual mob that populates embassies the world over had been thrown into turmoil. With indescribable pleasure he imagined the feverish scurrying in the residence. The hysterical phone calls. The panic in the Embassy. They surely expected him to appear at any moment. They were already postponing planned meetings. They were tidying up their desks. He had managed to mess up everybody's plans.

"Permission to report," he hissed. "The first stage of Operation Arrival of the Boss, completed with success!"

4

To be, or not to be?

The question repeated itself obsessively in the mind of Second Secretary Kishev as he gazed at the letter on his desk. He dared not open it. The envelope was distinguished by the seal of the Royal Chancellery. The letter had arrived that morning and immediately found itself in his office correspondence drawer. He had no need to open it to guess what was written inside. There were only two possibilities. The first would bury him. The second make him a hero. He was not a gambling type and already cursed himself for taking on this engagement so light-heartedly. This was definitely more than he could handle.

The man who sits quietly by will miss the miracle as it passes, as they say. But how, how could he sit quietly by when his mandate was relentlessly running out; when the days were draining away, one after the other, like the grains of sand through the hourglass? Maybe that was the reason he had grabbed at that straw in the hope of gaining some brownie points and impressing the power-players of the day. He liked life on the Island. He had spent more than two years here and it seemed a cruel injustice to have to pack his bags just now, just when this life had worked its way under his skin. And what was waiting for him back home? That, no one could say. Much water had passed under many bridges during those two years. The government had changed; people he had done favours for and who had supported him had been thrown out of the Ministry; new and hungry people had replaced them and were certain to be making their own arrangements for him. Panicked by the potential results, he had ditched his healthy bureaucratic instinct (he who does nothing makes no mistakes) and thrown himself into feverish activity. He had taken on this delicate mission, which was obviously beyond his capabilities. He had imagined that as a reward they would allow him another mandate in London. Or a year. Even six months would be something! But what could a small Second Secretary do against an Imperial Establishment, centuries old? How could he influence it? From what position? With what means? Nobody would so much as ask. Quite the opposite in fact, they were bound to make him the guilty party – the worm.

You're out-trumped, Kishev, you've out-trumped yourself, he thought to himself, staring gloomily at the envelope. But what if he hadn't? He should be thinking positively. Positive thinking lies at the heart of every success. Negative thinking is the inheritance of socialism. He carefully opened the envelope and took out the piece of paper with trembling fingers.

Dear Mr. Kishev

Her Majesty thanks you for the kind invitation to attend the cultural festivities organized by your Embassy. Unfortunately, Her Majesty's official programme is fully booked and she will be unable to attend.

Yours sincerely,

Muriel Spark
Public Relations Officer.
On behalf of The Palace.

Kishev read the letter another ten times. In both directions. The content remained the same. Then he held the sheet up against the light to examine the watermark. He sniffed it; and he caught that scent of wealth and power given off by objects originating in the world of High Society. Deep metaphysical fear froze his heart.

The bearer of bad news is killed, isn't he?

At that moment someone knocked at the door. A curly head appeared for a second and then fired the news with the precision of a professional killer.

"The new Ambassador has arrived!"

Varadin Dimitrov turned out to be a very bad psychologist. Contrary to his expectations, the news of his arrival had not hit the Embassy immediately, but had travelled by an overly long and meandering route, following human laws as opposed to nature's.

Kosta Pastricheff was a lonely and desperate soul, to whom the mere idea of solidarity and mutual aid was foreign. It did not so much as cross his mind to grab the phone and warn his colleagues of their imminent danger. In reality, a cook cannot have colleagues. There is no position in the world lonelier than his. Beneath him there is the assistant-cook. Above him there is God or, according to ones beliefs, an even more frightening Nothing. And Kosta was an atheist.

He served the Mayor a plateful of trotter jelly, opened two ice-cold beers and sat down to keep him company. There was less than two hours left before his flight, but the Mayor was not especially worried: on the contrary, he could not believe that the plane would take off without its most important passenger. They chatted indifferently in the brief pauses between some of the Mayor's mouthfuls. Kosta had no doubts that the new Ambassador had run directly to the Embassy, and the thought of that made him pull gently at the corners of his greying whiskery moustache. At 15.30 the driver, Miladin, rang the front-doorbell. The Mayor and the cook shook hands.

"If ever you find yourself unemployed," exclaimed the Mayor, "you are more than welcome in Provadia. With those trotters you'll not fail, my man!"

The driver, of course, had not the slightest suspicion regarding the dramatic turn of events. He first heard about it from his chatty interlocutor, who did not fail to congratulate him on his new boss. Miladin, who was also a less than outgoing individual of stunted social instincts, decided to keep the news to himself. There was a mobile phone in his pocket, which he deliberately switched off. After he dropped the Mayor at Heathrow, Miladin headed towards one of London's famed car-boot sales.

Left to his own devices, Kosta dropped the mask of arrogance and indifference, which he always put on in front of other people, and became as gloomy as a peasant watching thunderclouds looming above the harvest fields. He let his wife's bitching drift past his ears unheeded – she was, as per usual, railing against the social position fate had decreed for her.

"They come here, the dregs of society, stuff their faces, screw everything up, and then guess who gets to clean up after them!" she complained, carrying a stack of dishes to the kitchen. "They all became big-shots! There's no life left for common folk!"

She was a tiny, thick-set woman with big, workers hands and a bitter mouth. Through eyes that were forever screwed up, she regarded reality around her with mistrust and reproach. As the wife of an international cook, she had 'done' a fair chunk of the world, but deep-down she believed that only one patch of her homeland truly mattered – somewhere between the river Iskar and Mount Vitosha. No matter where she stayed – in Paris, Berlin or London – she arranged the family's way of life according to her pre-Columbian image of the world, slowly reclaiming from the Western jungle a small clearing for her domestic civilization.

Of late, Kosta had frequently asked himself, why the hell had he married her? Or more precisely, why, for fuck's sake, did he continue to be married to her? Out of laziness, that was the truth of the matter. He had been too lazy to search for the woman of his dreams and instead had opted for the closest one available. He had been too lazy to divorce her afterwards and here they were, already a good twenty years trundling around together. Sex not working. Quarrelling all day. She despised him. He despised her. They had managed two children with a long interval in between. They had some small savings, but too little to be divided up.

After lunch, Chavdar Tolomanov put in a call to the residence. He had been living in London for some years and presented himself sometimes as a salesman, sometimes as a man of the arts, but in reality he made his living some third way, which he avoided ever having to explain. From time to time, Kosta supplied him with cheap cigarettes from the Embassy's diplomatic quota, and they had gradually become friends. Chavdar had come up with an extremely brash scenario, even judged by the cook's low standards.

"I wanted to tell you that I've pulled a really great chick! Would you believe it? Real Latin American! Do you want her to phone you? Her name is Juliet. It's just that she doesn't speak any Bulgarian, ha-ha..."

Loud music was blasting down the earpiece and Kosta concluded that Chavdar was calling from a pub. He was tipsy and obviously having a good time.

"Listen, mate, lets arrange some business..." continued Chavdar. "Is the Mayor gone? Good. Look, I'm making out to this Juliet that I'm the Bulgarian Ambassador. Is it all right if I bring her to the residence? Just for one night, yeah?"

"No way! The new Ambassador's already arrived."

"What?!" Chavdar was surprised "How come so suddenly?"

"He dragged his sorry ass in here two hours ago," the cook replied dryly. "Anyway, I've cleaning to be getting on with..." Try making out you're the Ambassador to me! he thought and slammed down the receiver.

The news, however, had now leaked out. Chavdar Tolomanov did not have the same habits as Embassy people. Without so much as putting down his mobile phone, of which he was inordinately proud, he dialled the first number he came across. At the other end of the line a woman named Dafinka Zaks answered. Zaks lived off her late-husband's rent and had a reputation as a happy widow. She thirstily soaked up the fresh gossip and delicately declined Chavdar's proposition that she play the role of the rich, old auntie who lavishly provides space for the intimate adventures of her nephew. Dafinka Zaks shot off the news in several directions and the news spread like wildfire, along the approaches of the entirely unsuspecting Embassy, where the working day was winding towards its natural end.

At 4.30 p.m. the secretary's telephone rang and an oily voice said, "Could you put me through to the Ambassador, please?"

The secretary, Tania Vandova, flinched as though scalded. She was familiar with that voice and in no way found it congenial.

"The new Ambassador has not yet arrived," she declared in icy tones.

"Don't hide him! Don't hide him!" the voice at other end sang sweetly. "I know from a perfectly well-informed source, that he arrived this very afternoon. I only want to congratulate and welcome him."

"Your source must have misinformed you," the secretary attempted a nonchalant tone. "There is nobody here. Goodbye."

In reality, Tania Vandova was not quite so sure and decided to trust to her well-honed secretarial instincts. A short conversation with the residence followed and Kosta was forced to spit out the truth (a big black mark for the cook!). The news whipped round the offices at the speed of light. At 5.30pm the Embassy emptied as though stricken by the Plague.

5

The eyes of the diplomats were filled with melancholy. They were sat fidgeting around the long empty table in the meeting-room beneath the map of Bulgaria, with its cold pink and yellow colouring. Malicious tongues had it that the map had been put there not so much to arouse patriotic spasms in the employees, but to serve as a reminder of where they came from and where they could be returning if they were not sufficiently careful. In practice, that was the only thing that could truly make them feel anxious. The ghost of going back! This ghost was a constant, inexorable presence around them. It sniggered maliciously in every corner and poisoned their lives with the memory of the finely scented black earth of their birthplace, from the very first to the very last day of their mandates. The subject of 'going back' was taboo, shrouded in painful silence. To ask somebody when he thought he might make the return journey (a blatant euphemism) was considered an act of bad taste, base manners and even hostility. Nobody talked about going back, nobody dared to say it out loud for fear of catching the attention of the evil powers that slumbered somewhere deep in the Ministry of Foreign Affairs. Despite the fact that everyone, down to the last telephonist, knew that this was their irrevocable destiny, as inevitable as winter or death, deep in their hearts they still sheltered the hope that that dolorous hour might pass them by, that they might be missed or forgotten in the overall mass of people and that the awful notice might never reach them. But the notice invariably arrived, along with its sinister title: *Permanent Return* – the creation of a vengeful bureaucrat from the distant past, the title had remained unchanged throughout the decades. And then began the time of the great retreat, the slow ebb. The condemned soul took to the road, watered with the tears of their predecessors, back to Heathrow Terminal 2, through Gate 7 or 9, and into the gloomy vessel of the national airline 'Balkan', after which the door slammed behind their back permanently.

It was soon after 10 p.m. The presidential chair was still empty. At a reasonable distance of a few empty chairs, the diplomats were sat with open pads, pens at the ready. The technical staff had crammed themselves at the other end of the table – the driver, the accountant, the radioman, the cook and the housekeeper. Very few things bonded those people together as did mutual dislike, slowly built up, layer on layer, over the course of all those years of enforced co-existence, resigned to financial and cultural restriction. Nevertheless, it could be said that for some time they had been leading relatively bearable and even carefree lives. They had all had their little pleasures, and they had all had one big, unifying one: they had had no boss. Several months had already passed whilst Sofia dithered over the appointment of a person to this important and sought-after posting. The interests of several lobbies intertwined and hindered one another. So many favours and counter-favours had been called in, so many obstacles found, so many traps laid, that the path to the UK began to look like a cross between an assault course and a mine-field. During that time, while it enjoyed a relative lack of authority, the life of the Embassy reorganized itself independently, on the principles of reason and progress, far from the chaos of administrative orders. The tensions between the employees had eased, some vague spirit of goodwill and mutual aid had been born, which had had a beneficial influence on the actions of the whole collective. Not that the denunciations had stopped entirely, but there was nobody to read them. There was nobody to give red or black marks – Sofia was far removed. But now the bell tolled the end of that calm and natural existence. The boss had arrived. He had arrived suddenly, without prior notice, which made his hostile intentions clear. The life of the diplomats had become messy again.

Shortly, the secretary Tania Vandova came in carrying a big diary-notebook under her arm. "He's coming," she said succinctly

Unperturbed, she installed herself in the chair to the right of the presidential seat, opened her pad and also started waiting. Silence reigned supreme in the room.

As he made his way down the stairs, Varadin Dimitrov was imagining the dispirited faces of his underlings and a smile slid across his face. Let them wait, let them tremble! He found no cause to doubt what he had always known: he had in front of him a gang of good-for-nothings, parasites living on the back of the state. At first, their indifference and self-satisfaction amazed him, then made him angry. He started planning ways to poison their existence more efficiently – in order to remind them that this job was not a winning lottery ticket. He liked to observe how they returned to their habitual forms of frightened little beasties. And that was only the beginning.

"Hello to you all," Varadin greeted them dryly and took his place at the head of the table.

The pens clicked alertly, ready to take note of his immortal instructions. Reflexes die last, he thought happily to himself.

Then, suddenly, he frowned. "Where is Mr. Kishev?"

The diplomats looked at each other and shrugged. The Ambassador shook his head reproachfully.

"I'll tell you something unpleasant," he started, as though it was possible that he would announce something different. Long speeches were not to his taste. Speaking frightened him, because it betrayed the chaotic nature of his mind. His thoughts jumped to and fro like grasshoppers that have just crawled out of a closed jar. He found it difficult to gather them back together. For that reason he preferred to open his mouth as little as possible. "In Sofia they think that anarchy reigns here." Carefully, he gathered the bugs back into his head and continued, "The Embassy is not actively engaged in building Bulgaria's new image. We are lacking contacts at a high level."

Silence. Looks, overflowing with devotion.

"As you all know, the European conference opens on Monday," he continued. "The Prime Minister himself will be participating, along with various members of the Cabinet. It is expected that the EU will announce a new integration strategy. I assume that you are all up to speed on this."

The diplomats nodded energetically. For just that reason, a dozen faxes had been exchanged between the Embassy and the Ministry. The details of the program had been approved, and speeches and memoranda regarding the intentions of the Cabinet, on any subject, frenziedly translated. The program and the speeches, however, were constantly undergoing some change or other and thus needed to be approved and translated again and again. It was hell on earth, lavishly spiced with hysteria that wafted in clouds from the kitchens of power.

"I am warning you that from now on…" he raised his finger. "I will tolerate no gaffes!"

Gaffes – everyone lived with that nightmare, which often assumed reality. The diplomats were so frightened and overburdened by the system, that they dared not make any independent decisions. The tension often degenerated into apathy, bordering on catatonic stupor at its most decisive. It was at such moments that the nightmares came true.

"What is happening with Mrs. Pezantova's concert?" asked the Ambassador suddenly, once he was convinced that the previous subject had run its course.

"We are working on it," called out Counsellor Danailov with the agitated tone of an electrical engineer working on a hopelessly damaged cable. "We are doing everything that's possible at our end!"

"Then why has it already been postponed twice?" Varadin played the severe inquisitor, narrowing his eyes.

Panic appeared on the faces of the diplomats.

The technical staff observed the inquisition maliciously. Fortunately Tania Vandova was able to explain, "We still cannot ensure a representative from the Palace."

"Are you inviting them at all?"

"Naturally," Tania Vandova responded calmly.

Her mandate was coming to an end during the summer, so she did not have much to lose.

"Who is dealing with this?" he enquired coldly.

"Kishev!" they all chorused.

"Does he so much as know that we are here?" asked the Ambassador sharply.

"I don't know," shrugged Tania Vandova, "I haven't seen him since this morning."

"Go and find him!" he ordered.

This doesn't look good for Kishev, she thought and quickly left the room.

Oppressive silence reigned.

"The post office workers' union promised to buy 50 tickets," the Consul, Mavrodiev, broke in totally inappropriately and at exactly the wrong moment, though probably with the secret hope of gaining the boss's goodwill.

Big mistake. The Ambassador threw him a look full of hostility.

"As it seems, you are not entirely up to speed!" he spat bitterly, "The idea is not to gather a bunch of riff-raff. We want only the most select audience – aristocrats, world celebrities – the cream of society."

What am I doing sitting here explaining to this savage?! he said to himself angrily. He imagined Mrs. Pezantova's address: Dear Ladies and Gentlemen, in front of a crowd of postmen and drivers – unthinkable! It immediately struck him that lying beneath this seemingly well-intentioned proposal lurked a deeper plot: to discredit him in the eyes of those presently in power. From that moment onwards, in his eyes, the good-hearted, clumsy Consul was transformed into Enemy Number One, whose destruction was not to be delayed. With their delicate receptors the others immediately sensed that something bad was happening (danger, danger!) and did not utter another word.

The name of Mrs. Pezantova was a source of worry and agitation for everyone, including Varadin Dimitrov. In fact especially for him. Devorina Pezantova was the wife of an influential Bulgarian politician. She could not possibly accept the secondary role handed to her by history and hungered for her own aura as a woman of social significance. As often happens with such simple folk, lifted suddenly by some twist of fate to the very peak of the social hierarchy, her head was a murky vortex of boundless ambition and grandiose plans. Mrs. Pezantova frantically aimed to join the exclusive club of the world elite, without sparing resources – above all state resources. She dreamed of seeing herself amongst the shiny entourage of celebrities, who filled the chronicles of those fat western publications. In this unequal battle for prestige, Devorina Pezantova had stubborn and ubiquitous opponents – her own compatriots, who inhabited the hopeless space between hunger and darkness. It seemed they could not, or would not, comprehend how important it was that they look good (comme il faut!) at this decisive moment. They failed her at every step and did it energetically too, in a typical Balkan way. Ungrateful tribe! The lady did not give in easily, though. The misery of the masses at large was a good reason for the fine people from all over Europe to gather together, listen to some music, and eat some canapés. Proceeding in the light of that noble logic, she started with great élan to organize charitable events in all those European capitals which sported Bulgarian embassies. This was a heavy task for the missions concerned. The lady was rigorous and was not prepared to acknowledge the limited social effect of her humanitarian activity. She saw treachery, sabotage and conspiracy everywhere. The diplomats were not up to the job and did not take her work to heart; they wanted, more or less, to get the whole thing out of the way and withdraw once more into the swamp of their pitiful existence. Varadin Dimitrov had perspicaciously caught on to her trials and tribulations and managed to persuade her that he was not indifferent to them. For months he was constantly at her side suggesting that he was just the man to bring her dreams to fruition in this Mecca of all snobbery. She had played a more than significant role in his appointment. He owed her.

His gaze slid across the faces of the staff, but it only found downcast eyes. A good sign. He was doing well. A guilty employee was a good employee. Who had said that…?

Carried away by his triumph over those crushed souls, he permitted himself some distraction and his thoughts crawled off in different directions. Dr Pepolen did not have a cure for that ailment. Maybe the only salvation would be to put down poison in all the nooks and crannies of his brain. But there was the risk that the leading thought might die. Which one was it? They were looking frighteningly similar. Which one to choose…?

After a while he said, "The windows are not clean," with a deep sigh.

The faces of the diplomats showed some relief at the expense of those of the technical staff. Several long, sticky seconds passed. The accountant, Bianca Mashinska, struggled to come up with some sensible explanation, but could not find anything.

Tania Vandova appeared and informed them that Kishev had not come to work at all. She had spoken with his wife: he had heart problems and had been taken into hospital for tests.

Helpless fury overcame the new Ambassador's heart; he blinked quickly several times and snapped, "You may go!"

6

During that day, many of the employees tried to contact him, but he resolutely refused to see anyone. He wanted to play with their nerves; to leave them with the impression that he knew everything about them and their doings, and that he had no intention of listening to their pitiful explanations. Let them tremble in expectation of his call!

Varadin threw himself into the thorough exploration of the multitudinous drawers and cupboards in his office; the cashbox, the wardrobe and all the other little places where he supposed the spirit of his predecessor might be hiding. Not much was left. People in his profession were secretive and erased all traces behind them, where possible. In the library, the Encyclopaedia Britannica and the 'Who's Who' of 1986 feigned an air of dusty importance. In the draw of the desk lay three lonely paperclips and one used marker. In the safe he found a half-disintegrated washing-up sponge. That looked to be everything. He examined the toilet, tested it and sat behind the big boss's desk, twisted around this way and that in the armchair to get used to the feel of it. He was almost feeling at home when the red phone rang.

He stared fearfully at it and picked up the receiver.

"Hello!" said a serene female voice. "Already in your work-place, eh? Bravo! Well done!"

"Thank you!" his ingratiating response conveyed little enthusiasm.

He knew the voice well and clearly he could not tell it to go to hell.

"You haven't forgotten about me, have you?" He sensed an edge of suspicion.

"How could I forget you!" his voice filled with sincere indignation.

"Easily! Some people immediately forget everything, as soon as they land themselves a little mandate," the subtle accusation rang from the receiver.

"I am not one of them. You know me."

"We-ell, I've been let down so many times," sighed the voice. "You think you know somebody but when they go abroad – they prove to be a completely different person. Ungrateful people! They imagine they have become untouchable. But they are mistaken."

"They certainly are mistaken."

"You are not one of them though, are you?" the voice quavered hopefully. "You know how the things are. You are experienced; that's to say, you know how to prioritise."

"I've learned that well."

"I hope so," there was a pause before the decisive question: "And, how are things going?"

"I don't know yet. People here don't look to be on the straight and narrow."

"I had no doubts about that. They are a bunch of crooks. You must report to me every week."

"Agreed," Varadin nodded. "Do not worry."

"Don't be so relaxed. You don't know her yet. She is so solemn! Every time I pass through London, I invite her properly for lunch or breakfast, but she always plays dumb. She is busy. And how is she so busy, if you please? Counting her coins, I suppose. The humiliation I have to endure."

"We mustn't lose hope, the stakes are high!"

"Yes, we have to draw her in somehow!"

"Leave it to me," said Varadin authoritatively.

"If you betray me …"

"Not chance of that, of course not," he assured her.

"Oh, well in that case, goodbye."

"Goodbye."

The first number that burst into his mind was 98. For some moments he stared blankly at the phone, then quietly, but passionately, he pronounced, "73!"

7

'Borscht & Tears' was a famous Russian restaurant, situated in South Kensington. It was run by descendants of White Guardsmen. An important peculiarity, which very few people knew about and which was entirely absent from any advertising, was the fact that underneath the Russian restaurant, in the basement, was another restaurant – a Bulgarian one. This Bulgarian restaurant, carefully stored away within the belly of the big Russian doll, had been conceived fairly recently, due to the simple fact that the owners' daughter had married a Bulgarian. An enterprising patriot, he had taken the risk of investing in nostalgia, whilst lacking a decent working knowledge of the peculiarities of its native version.

Bulgarian Nostalgia differed from Russian Nostalgia which was lachrymose and dripping in mineral resources – a big vein of gold, which generations of capable salesmen of swampy mirages have mined and continue to mine. Bulgarian Nostalgia was dusty and baked like a disused threshing-floor. It was fed with cheese from Finsbury Park Turkish markets and greasy Spanish bacon from Asda; it was stuffed with beans and lentils and drowned in a glass of Rakia spirit, for free if you could get away with it. It had no ambition to rule over the soul; you could easily relegate it to some solitary corner. It was too economical to be economically significant. That was why the Bulgarian restaurant was condemned to stay forever in the womb of the Matryoshka like a nameless and illegitimate embryo, fighting to be born, struggling to get out, and straining at the umbilical leash through which it sucked vital juices.

The Russian restaurant had a well-polished, decadent interior:

plush red damask, candles in champagne bottles, some dusty balalaikas on the walls, a big decorative samovar – all this, although seeming exotic to western eyes, nevertheless to some extent lived up to expectations fed by references from the vast corpus of Russian literature. In the Russian restaurant they played Russian romances, served ice-cold vodka and steaks à la Kiev; you could cry your eyes out, quarrel with God or the Devil, fall in love or blow your brains out with a revolver, if you felt so inclined.

The Bulgarian saloon did not offer such romantic extras. You reached it via a narrow tortuous staircase, as though descending into Tartarus

On the walls hung traditional 'koukeri' masks and dried corn-cobs, as well as a shield forged from copper with something like a horseman carved on it. Here a kaval and bagpipe tune could often be heard, or the bang of a drum and as for the customers, they sat right next to each other as if they were all boiling in a common pot. Wine and Rakia spirit were poured lavishly and simple peasant dishes were served. These last could be better described as fakes than as realistic reproductions of the originals. But the emigrants were easily pleased; they had forgotten the taste of the original dish, remembering only the look of the thing. It was not difficult for them to imagine they were eating the authentic Bulgarian tomato and roast pepper delicacy, lyutenitsa, whilst what they were really consuming was an ordinary salsa with onions. That made the management of the kitchen easy, but somewhat diminished the profits. Regular clientele was missing – the local gourmands passed it by, and misguided tourists did not have the courage to venture beyond the Russian section. The restaurant filled up only for special occasions – once or twice a month. Then the owner would invite Kosta to spice up the menu with some more sophisticated specialties. The cook had nothing against that – his salary was miserable and he was constantly on the lookout for ways to make an additional pound or two on the side.

On the evening in question there was no special occasion and

'Borscht & Tears' was half-empty. Not only the Bulgarian section, but also the widely advertised Russian one. It was Wednesday – a day that marked the apogee of the business week – and Londoners were saving their energy for stunts on the stock market. Only two or three couples who looked like tourists from Australia or New Zealand were picking at their plates in the hope of finding a small grain of the great Russian soul. A glum waiter, Polish no less, was observing them cynically, as he leant against the wooden column by the stairs. Kosta's appearance caused a slight lifting of spirits, as though the long awaited fictional hero had appeared on stage at last and was preparing to do something suitably unhinged, which would instantly reveal the meaning of life to them. Kosta, though, did nothing so exciting; he headed quietly down the stairs, nodding to the waiter on his way past.

In the empty Bulgarian salon two men were seated. They had taken the table at the far end and Kosta saw them only when they waved at him. One of them combined the physique of an ex-body-builder with the droopy blond moustache of a Polish nobleman fallen on hard times. This was Chavdar Tolomanov, the man he had spoken to that afternoon. The other was a stranger.

Chavdar invited him to take a seat and made the introductions. "This is Batushka. Batushka, this is our guy."

The Batushka in question, was a tall leathery individual with an angular Asiatic face and dark skin. He was wearing a loose designer-label training top, which revealed a prodigious, hairy torso. A massive gold chain sparkled on his wrist. Kosta was seeing the man for the first time, but immediately realised that it would have been far healthier to have never met him.

Batushka had a hard, ruthless handshake.

"We're drinking vodka here," said Chavdar. "Will you have one for starters?"

Kosta did not have much choice. The vodka was icy and smooth like a snowdrop at Christmas. He munched on a piece of lardy bacon. Tasty.

"And…?" growled Batushka, his voice a bass rumble.

Kosta glanced at Chavdar.

"Relax," the latter raised his hand. "Batushka is an insider. He is the one I told you about. Everything goes through him."

That was exactly what was worrying the cook the most at that moment. He suddenly realized that he was in something, and up to his neck. He had believed Chavdar and let the waster drag him into the depths. "Don't get involved with those scoundrels!" Norka had yelled at him, but who paid attention? She might not be a lady, but she was by no means slow on the uptake.

Chavdar Tolomanov was a former film actor. In the past, in the time of darkest, deepest socialism, he had played a few roles that made him famous at a local level. And that was his misfortune: this popularity (specifically popularity, not fame!) was too little for him, compared to the dazzling summit of greatness, being reached by such stars as De Niro, Kevin Costner, Michael Douglas and even that bed-wetter, Brad Pitt. Chavdar, naturally, was not going to lose out to them; the problem was that some several thousand miles away from the place where the stars were growing, cruel destiny had dumped him in an entirely different climate in which only shapeless potatoes grew. For this reason he had decided that he must act to correct this entirely unfair situation, by moving to a more favourable place. Afterwards, having been denied an American visa for no apparent reason, he found himself in London, armed with a brilliant CV and two demo-tapes. He launched an assault on all the casting agencies in the city, as well as on all the producers. The English, being, in principle, a polite people, received him warmly, although with some slight surprise; they nodded, seemingly with some respect at his artistic CV, but then politely declined to employ him. The reason was simple – his Slav accent. He made big efforts to cure that cruel disease, and had even made some progress. Unfortunately, this progress made itself heard during the final auditions for the role of a malicious computer maniac of Russian descent, who had penetrated the allies' security system. The producers decided that his accent was not expressive enough and gave the part to someone else, who was 100% English and made it sound far more sinister. That proved a heavy setback for Chavdar. From that moment onwards his life became chaotic, a typical state of affairs for people who have lost the firm ground from beneath their feet. He tried different jobs that brought him neither money nor any other satisfaction. He was kidding himself that these were only temporary jobs – a process of adaptation to his new environment. But the currents of life were carrying him implacably away from his vocation, involving him in more and more absurd enterprises that were not always entirely on the right side of the law. His depression turned into gluttony, which, given the prevailing conditions in the abundant western market, was not difficult to satisfy. Very soon his well-trained body lost shape and became fat and ugly. He was aware of his gradual decline, but was too afraid to go back to his country, where, he guessed, only venom and spite awaited him. His compatriots, like typical Eastern Europeans, were inclined to forgive the people who were leaving the country, but not the people who were coming back, because they tarnished the image of The West – the last hope of desperate souls, who had inherited the debris that was the post-communist era.

"So, what being happening?" said Batushka in his Russian version of English, leaning his body forward like an interrogator.

"The new Ambassador arrived, that's what!" retorted the cook shortly, pouring himself more vodka and drinking it.

"So it's true then!" Chavdar exclaimed as he turned to Batushka and nodded, "He has arrived."

"That's what I'm having tell you!" Batushka nodded.

"And so?" asked the actor. "What's that to do with our business, anyway?"

"What do you mean what?" the cook exploded. "He'll immediately start digging everything up now, sniffing about the place, reorganising everything. It's impossible! It's…"

"Nonsense!" Chavdar broke in. "He hasn't found his feet yet, he needs time to sort things out. Before he figures out what's what, we'll be done, isn't that right, Batushka?"

Batushka nodded dryly.

"You can talk," Kosta nodded. "But you haven't met him. He's insane. He just appears out of the blue. Anything could come into his head."

"There, there, he has other things to do," the actor calmed him. "He'll not start his digging in the fridges."

"You never know," sighed the cook. "How can I put it? You better find yourself somewhere else."

"You can't pull out now, at the last minute!" Chavdar exploded. "We've already invested in this project! Isn't that right, Batushka?"

"Hmm!" Batushka began to frown darkly.

"Batushka's opinion is that is too late now to turn back," continued the actor. "The whole thing's already going at full tilt!"

Kosta scratched his neck sceptically, "You're going to have to think of something. There are loads of other places."

"What's he be saying?" Batushka raised his voice.

"Nothing, nothing!" Chavdar sought a hurried translation. His forehead was shining with sweat and now really agitated, he turned to the cook, "Listen, Kosta, we're going to be in deep shit! I've vouched for you and now you're losing it!"

"They'll send me back!" was Kosta's curt comment.

"What?"

"If they catch us, they're going to send me back to Bulgaria, on the first plane."

"My God!" Chavdar cried out. "We're risking our necks here, and he's worried they're going to send him back. What a fool. What do you say, Batushka? Send him back – that's his worry!"

Batushka shook back his head and showed his straight white teeth. "Ho-ho-ho!" he laughed with his bass voice.

"Listen, you Pastry!" started Chavdar. "You have two possibilities here – to behave like a pussy or like a man. If you behave like a pussy, this one here – Batushka, will make sure you regret the moment you ever set foot in London! But, if you behave like a man you're going to get your juicy part of the deal plus the advance payment and we're all laughing. So, which do you choose?"

Silence fell around the table. The bottle was sweating. A random individual came down the stairs, looked around and sat at the other end of the hall.

"Only for one week," Kosta sighed at last. "And a hundred pounds up front," he reminded them.

Batushka placed his hand on his shoulder. "Molodets! You the man."

8

A piercing howl welcomed him – in one of the corners of the office the grey belly of an enormous Hoover-monster loomed like a communist mausoleum. The hose twisting across the floor ended in the hands of some girl, her nose facing the carpet. Varadin knitted his brows: she really had picked the wrong moment to clean, the idiot! The idea of waiting outside until the noisy process was over did occur to him, but then he remembered the gang of employees shunting in at the entrance downstairs and quickly reaffirmed his intentions. He stepped in quietly and sat down in an armchair. He had heard people say that if you stare at someone for long enough, something started itching in their brain and they would turn around. This obviously did not apply to her, or maybe the howling instrument created some barrier that dispersed the fluids in question.

He continued to stare at her.

She was slender, with long legs. Her stray, ash-blond hair was falling to one side and covering her face. Below a light blue working dress, colourless tights and Nike trainers enhanced the muscles of her calves. Her movements betrayed her annoyance, although she was working very hard. She hoovered all the carpet around his desk and then turned off the ugly machine. Their eyes met.

"I'm sorry," she said, confused. "I did not notice you there."

He said nothing. In his ears the sound of the Hoover still echoed. The face of the girl seemed familiar to him and he stared at it more than decency allowed. She blushed and lowered her eyes. At the same moment a fickle smile appeared on her lips.

"You must be the new Ambassador?" she asked.

"Yes."

"Katerina, Katya for short," the girl introduced herself, while she was coiling the cable of the Hoover. "I'll be cleaning your office if you don't object."

He did not but said sternly, "I would be grateful if you don't come during my office hours."

"I'm very sorry for the inconvenience," she started. "I had a paper to write. I've been reading all night. I didn't think you'd be here. I'll come to clean in the mornings or after six."

"Agreed," he nodded and unexpectedly asked "What are you studying?" Don't go any deeper, his internal monitor pulled him up.

"Design," she said, with a tone that bordered on the sleazy, while she put the hose over her shoulder and started dragging the Hoover to the door. Then she stopped and turned around. "Do you want me to dust?"

"No, there is no need."

Katya, though, was not in a hurry to go now that her initial confusion was over. Her wide silver-grey eyes did not look very red.

"Mr. Ambassador, I have one problem," she seemed to be choosing her words carefully. "Actually this is not only my problem, but one for everyone who cleans here in the Embassy."

Varadin knitted his brows but let her speak.

"I am talking about this," she pointed at the Hoover. "Simply, the time has come for its retirement. I wouldn't take up your time with this, but some people cannot see this fact…"

"Which fact?"

"That it doesn't suck anymore! What I want to say is it only sucks feebly. It's a real chore to use…"

"It might be full," he guessed with little enthusiasm. "Do you clean it often?"

"No it is not full," she insisted brusquely. "It is old!"

"What do you want from me? A new Hoover?"

"Yes," the girl nodded. "The accountant said that it depends entirely on you."

He did not like the way she looked at him: it seemed to him she had guessed the thought, which buzzed in his head like a big, nasty, insolent fly and filled him with gloomy premonitions about future implications of a personal and official nature. His exhilaration at the advantage gained by his surprise appearance disappeared. Heavy strategic decisions were looming. He realized that the advance he had gained was insignificant and would be soon swallowed by the heavy load of duties and nuisances.

"Hum." he frowned, as though he were about to consider an important offer for fighter planes. "We'll see."

"Well then," she smiled. "Goodbye!"

The end of the grey hose crawled after her like a sinister snout.

A little later, Tania Vandova carefully knocked, listened for a second and stuck her head around the door. Varadin Dimitrov was sitting behind the desk as though turned into a waxwork, staring in front of him without blinking, his eyes fixed. The secretary, terribly frightened, jumped and hurried to close the door. She waited several seconds, gathered her courage once more and looked around the door again. There was nobody behind the desk. The door to the bathroom was wide open, the noise of running water came from there along with some strange noise similar to gargling. What now? she thought, chewing her lip. Quietly she walked with short steps to the desk, deposited a pile of letters and retreated.

"Wait!" his voice, coming from the bathroom, froze her on the doorstep.

Varadin oozed out of the bathroom with his face all wet.

"Did Kishev come back to work?"

"Not yet," she shook her head.

A short pause followed.

"Are you going to attend the banquet tonight?" asked the secretary.

"Yes," he replied mechanically, despite the fact that he was hearing of this event for the first time.

"I will call to confirm," she said quickly and left.

He stared with surprise at the pile of correspondence. Apparently the mundane institutions of the former Empire had caught scent of his arrival from a distance – maybe before the decision for his appointment had even been signed. Some invitations were lying on the top, heavy, large, gilt-edged pieces of paper that could be used for playing table tennis. He randomly picked the first one and read with pleasure his own name written at the top with steady, lop-sided handwriting. Maybe it was not particularly advisable to throw himself immediately into the whirlpool of social life, but he was eager to do a quick round of High Society. To have a sip of that foamy cocktail before diving into it forever. He had no time to lose.

9

The driver came to pick him up from the residence at 6.30 p.m.

Varadin waited for him in the entrance, slightly pale, wearing dinner-jacket and tie. His shoes squeaked neurotically. The insidious smell of cooking was seeping out of the cook's lodgings and made him feel queasy. During the entire time, as they crept though the congested arteries of the city, Varadin was restlessly sniffing the lapels of his jacket; recognising that sticky national stench which could not be washed out, it nested in the tissue like a cloth nit; it penetrated the skin – into the very marrow and stayed their forever, like the scars from a shameful disease.

'Buckingham Palace,' said Miladin, without removing his eyes from the back of the black cab in front of him.

Varadin flinched. How dare he, the idiot?! Did he really imagine he was driving some peasant from Dolno Kamartsi, who didn't have a clue about landmarks? As if he didn't know this was Buckingham Palace!…He pursed his lips, while curiosity mingled with anxiety ate away at him. The invitation was enigmatically laconic. The hosts had signed only with some whirly squiggles, which told him nothing. The dinner was to be accompanied by a lecture entitled: The new challenges facing the steady development of Europe. The rain was pouring down on the front windscreen of the car; the wiper-blades were swinging with quick, rapid movements. The car finally got through Trafalgar Square and turned into Pall Mall.

The gloomy front of the club, with its heavy cornices and small windows, placed at a distance from one another, suggested hidden voluminous spaces inside. The entrance had no sign, only a number. Compared to the size of the building, the door, sandwiched between two glowing yellow lights, looked disproportionately small, as if to enhance the exclusive character of the building.

The concierge ushered him in.

Varadin left his coat in the cloakroom, passed along the line of portraits of famous activists and entered the reception. The people present were mostly over sixty, while here and there, a few confused middle-aged individuals stuck out. There were almost no women, apart from some very old, severe, obviously wealthy ladies, perched in different corners of the hall like oracle-birds.

The Major Domo found his name on the guest-list and showed him to his place. 'Varadin Dimitrov' was written on the little piece of paper, placed near the cutlery, 'Ambassador, Bulgaria' – that gave him a pleasant tingling sensation.

To his left was an empty chair, to his right, a tiny old man was seated, with a pinkish face and tight brown suit. On the piece of paper in front of him was written: Douglas Smack, followed by a mysterious line of letters, which reminded Varadin of the notes on the labels of bottles of old brandy. Mr. Smack, half drowsing, was listening to the mumbling of a large, impressive lady, with a pearl necklace wrapped around her wrinkly neck.

Opposite them sat a monster of such over-inflated ego as to make Varadin look like a genuinely pleasant, good-hearted individual in comparison. The white hair was carefully brushed back like a mane. The posture revealed a decisive man in charge of an important economic conglomerate. Said monster was wearing an immaculate DJ and tie, and his chest glowed with diamante buttons.

What on earth am I doing here? Varadin asked himself. Down the whole length of that long table, he could not see a single familiar face, not a single familiar voice rang in his ear. He was completely alone. His spirits dropped still further when the scanty hors d'oeuvre suddenly appeared in front of him. Two ribbons of red fish, some little rose of butter and a leaf of lettuce. Because he had nothing better to do, he started rolling up the fish onto his fork, at which point a gentleman flumped his large body down in the empty seat next to his. He was fiftyish, in a chic dark blue suit with fine stripes and flashy orange tie. A strong, almost overpowering scent of eau-de-Cologne surrounded him. He had yellowish straggling hair, carefully slicked onto his reddish skull. A silver ring with a red stone decorated his fleshy little finger.

He slid his eyes to Varadin's side, read the card in front and his mouth opened into a big smile.

"Mr. Varadin Dimitrov!? Nice to meet you! Dean Carver, M.P." He offered his hand. "How long have you been in London?"

"Only a few days,"

"Fresh indeed!" grinned Carver, as if he was talking about the fish on his plate. "I know Bulgaria quite well. Magnificent place! I've been there several times, in '86 and '87, at the invitation of your agricultural Minister, what was his name...?"

"Petar Tanchev?"

"A-ha! That's the one," Mr. Carver agreed with verve. "Good old times! Your old leaders, they had some style, you know! Real barons! I'll tell something in confidence: not everything was so bad, ha-ha!"

Shocked, Varadin stared at him. The other filled his glass with red wine.

"Cheers!" Dean Carver took a large sip and winked at him, "It's not so bad, considering it's Bulgarian!"

In the meantime the VIPs had taken their places around the table. Someone tapped a glass and the hall fell silent. Some bald, wrinkly old man, decorated with a huge necklace was about to speak – a Lord Basterbridge, as it became clear later.

"Ladies and Gentlemen, welcome to the annual dinner of our modest society. I am very pleased to announce the presence here of Mr. Morel – Her Majesty's Minister for Defence."

A murmur of approval circled the hall.

Mr. Morel had the radiant looks of an educated working class man who had made a career in the Unions. He thanked the people present and bowed to the old man, who was apparently the object of deep respect for all present. After the Minister, it was the lecturer's turn. He was a Jonathan Cragg – a tall, dark man with liberal views on life. He was head of the current government's strategic international research team – a key post reporting to the Cabinet. Jonathan Cragg was an agile quack: his expressions were complicated and he built an extensive construction of scientific-like clichés to befuddle the audience. Without doubt his work was well paid. The representatives of his parasitic caste travelled relentlessly around Eastern Europe and in the guise of experts swallowed the largest slice of the funding pie, designed for the revival of this deeply problematic region. Varadin was enraptured by Cragg's speech for some five minutes, and then realised that he had lost the gist of it completely. Only separate words started to have meaning as the whole speech became akin to a verbal salad. Despite the helpless condition of his mind, he made sure the look on his face remained that of an attentive listener until the end, when he enthusiastically joined the chorus of applause.

'That does not explain the differences in the exchange rates,' mumbled the old man to his right.

He felt a bit uneasy that he had until now ignored this probably quite important person. He tried to introduce himself, but Smack V.S.O.P.C.R., was already snoozing, which was apparently his usual state.

When the official part was over, people became livelier. Dean Carver filled his glass with wine again and his memories from Bulgaria came back to him. Unforgettable days! As a young lobbyist for the left, with prospects, he had dared to pass through the iron curtain…They received him like a king! Helicopter flights, hunting parties, night feasts in the residences! And what women!

"In '93 I brought some Arab investor to Bulgaria," he continued. "He wanted to build a lift in the ski resort of Bansko, but then he backed out when he saw what was going on…I haven't visited since."

The fact that Carver was sat next to him was hardly a coincidence, thought Varadin. To arrange the guests around the table so they have something in common to talk about was an art-form – one that the English certainly possessed.

"I really want to revive my connections with your magnificent country..." Carver sighed, after a long sip from his glass. "I heard you have a new government. How's it going?"

"Very well, thank you," Varadin replied without thinking.

"Then why were the papers writing about those orphans that were dying from hunger? Was that true?"

Varadin made an involuntary grimace. Apparently Carver had seen the advertisement which was in circulation in the British press. It had a picture of a hungry, disabled child wrapped in rags. The advertisement was printed under the name of some Eastern European fund, which was gathering money for the orphans in need in Bulgaria.

"The period of transition to a market economy is not an easy one..." the Ambassador's response was edgy. He thought a little and then added, "It is a shame that people tend to speculate on other people's misfortune."

"Ah, those do-gooders..." sighed Carver. "There is nothing more damaging for the image of a country. Those humanitarian parasites are like fleas in the rags of a beggar. They feed themselves on the misery of others and have no interest whatsoever in seeing that misery removed. The only thing they care about is how to expose it sufficiently to reach sponsors. I know them quite well: the worse your condition is, the happier they are! Do you know that the charity business is the third biggest, after drugs and pornography?"

Varadin's brain was feverishly trying to process all this information and was struggling to put it into a report format. He was having difficulties with it and that made him feel uneasy: everything that could not be put into a report was either too dangerous or too insignificant. He could not grasp which of the two he was dealing with. Third options did not feature in his mind.

"But you're not drinking at all!" exclaimed Carver, fixing his full glass with a contemptuous stare. "I raise a toast to Bulgarian wines. Especially the reds!"

And he downed his brimming glass in one. Original man thought Varadin and took a more generous sip for appearance's sake.

"The solution to all your problems lies in decent PR," resumed Dean Carver with authority. "Someone to take care of your image. Do you know how much money other countries are throwing into that sort of thing?"

Varadin nodded; there were certain rumours that this latest tear-jerking campaign was being organized by the intelligence services of a neighbouring Balkan country, whose aim was to discredit his government's political efforts, at a time when the discussions about European Union enlargement were reaching their climax. "Quite recently, the government decided to invest more money in this direction," he conceded.

"And it's doing the right thing," exclaimed Carver. "You have to keep your eyes open though, London is full of identical agencies. To my regret most of them are crooks. They'll wrap you up in all sorts of 'concepts' and 'strategies', and then present you such a bill that it'll make you dizzy. But there are some genuine professionals, as well. They talk little, but perform wonders."

"And who are they?" asked Varadin timidly.

"There is one agency that I know of…" Carver lowered his voice confidentially; his breath had some bitter aftertaste. "They worked for me during the elections. As far as I know, at present, they're taking care of the image of one of your neighbours; I think it was Slovakia. They're also working for countries in the Middle East! Real professionals! They have connections at the highest levels. And a spotless reputation! It is said that even members of the Royal family have used their services from time to time …"

"Do they have connections with the palace?" Varadin's face tensed.

"Undoubtedly!" nodded Dean Carver, M.P. "After they arranged a dinner for me with Prince Charles, my ratings instantly shot up a mile! Ha-ha! I may have republican ideas, as you know, but who cares? You seem intrigued. I think I still have their card."

He started looking in his wallet.

"It must be this one…I forgot my specs, can you, please, read what it says here."

Varadin lifted the card: Famous Connections. PR Agency. "Thank you," he nodded.

"You don't have to thank me! I am friend of Bulgaria. Take my card as well… You can always count on me."

As he was saying this, Carver moved his eyes to his plate and raised his finger in approval. Where the starter had been, now lay a serious piece of meat, covered with cranberry sauce. He poured himself some more wine and started devouring it with deliberate concentration. Not wanting to be left behind Varadin also took to his cutlery, but his brain was elsewhere: the chewy undercooked meat slipped across the plate and splashed him with sauce. Bloody Hell!

"It doesn't give in easily, eh?" giggled Carver. "You have to get used to the character of the roast here."

10

When Katya popped out of the bathroom with her hair so wet that she shot off volleys of little drops, she immediately provoked the envious gaze of Doroteya Totomanova. Her eyes were like two dull brooches. The two girls were sharing a room, 9ft by 12ft and all possible love between the two had been lost. Doroteya, also known as Dotty, had a spotty face and fat ankles. Katya possessed everything else which was of any value in the eyes of the opposite sex. *Pure pornography* thought Dotty, whose eyes were devouring several particulars of her roommate's body. She had the feeling sometimes that those parts had been stolen from her, and it seemed only fair that she should at least have the right to touch them. Such a small consolation, yet even that was constantly denied her.

Katya was not very keen on the idea of being stared at in that particular fashion, and on top of everything, completely for free; but the mere thought that this was doing irreparable damage to the self-esteem of the voyeuse, left her feeling it was entirely worth it. She quickly dried her hair, dragged on a pair of old jeans, a T-shirt and a jacket and threw her bag across her shoulder.

"I'm off," she announced.

"Bye," mumbled Dotty, without moving.

You bitch thought Katya. Doroteya Totomanova did not have to work because she received an allowance from her parents, and she was not at university; so she was lying in bed with fat, inappropriate books.

"You know, you should get out more," said Katya with some superficial concern.

"Mind your own business."

"Okay, then you can at least open the windows," spat Katya.

The door slammed and Doroteya was left alone. She stuck out her tongue and showed her middle finger at the now absent Katya. Then she took out a breeze-block of a book, entitled Directions in Radical Feminism by someone called Stone John Stone and hungrily started devouring the pages. Meanwhile Katya was half way to Soho.

As usual, Samantha Brick was at the entrance in her cream-coloured basque, bare legs and stiletto-slippers, and was calling out to the johns with lascivious gestures, "Come on, darling! Pop right in!"

Katya thought that this probably repelled rather than enticed the clients, but the business had its traditions and, at the end of the day, she really didn't give a damn. The entrance, decorated in tinted mirror tiles, was surmounted by a neon sign which read Bailey's Place. There were thousands of such places, dispersed across every continent, little incubators of little sins, where men took their frozen, wilted eggs in the hope that some feeble erection might hatch out of them.

"Cheers!" Samantha touched her hand.

Katya smiled as their fingers briefly interlaced. Samantha was a kindly blonde, past her forties, with almost no tattoos. She had done her time on the pole, and now life was fairly determinedly pushing her to the periphery. There were many tales that Samantha could tell but nobody wanted to listen.

Katya ran down the stairs and popped through a side door into the dressing room. The familiar chaos swaddled her, soaked in sweat and perfumes. The half-naked girls were fussing around throwing tits and arses in all directions. Through the air various items of lingerie flew together with an assortment of words in a plethora of languages. She liked the informal atmosphere. It reminded her of the prehistoric melting-pot where life came into being. From time to time, a curly head popped out from behind the curtain. Its owner, Kemal Dalali was a Lebanese-born man in charge of the whole menagerie. Several gold chains, long enough to hang him, were swinging around his neck. He was shouting out the names of the girls whose turns were approaching, "Vera, hurry up! Hurry up!…Françoise! Hurry up!…Fen Li! Hurry up!"

Katya slipped into an absurd costume, constructed of black leather straps and high boots, sat in front of the mirror and started layering coats of make-up onto her face. The boots were cool, they could hold lots of tips. Connie Delano tried to push her some powdery stuff, but drew a blank once again. On her other side, the Slovakian Beata, a student at the prestigious LSE, was swearing in her mother tongue; her inner thighs were covered with a rash and that would reduce her takings. Katya advised her to put some foundation on them. Kemal Dalali's head popped out again, "Kate! Hurry up! Hurry up!"

To grind around the pole and discard bits of her outfit was not a big deal. It was easier than hanging around behind the counter of some shop for hours or washing dishes, and most importantly, it was more profitable. Lots of students were doing it. Katya had expenses to cover: she had to pay the huge university tuition fees and to send her parents some money from time to time. She owed it to them. They had mortgaged their apartment in Sofia to pay her first set of fees. And even with those expenses Katya could lead a reasonable life, but she wanted to save up some pounds. You never know what lies round the corner as the English say. On the other hand, she found her double life rather attractive; some strange gloating sensation kept her playing the role of a poor, hard-working student, ready to do anything to keep her little hole in the Embassy.

Every time she found herself totally naked on the dance-floor, Katya felt the urge to carry on: to pull her whole body apart and throw it, bit by bit, to the public, until she got rid of her last carnal accessory, and to leave only dust in the stage lights. This self-destructive urge arose at the end of every performance, maybe it was her body's reaction against her shameless soul, but it never lasted long. Last swing around the pole. It was good for the body. Her freshly shaven armpits were sticky with sweat. The only thing remaining now was to crawl the catwalk between the male muzzles, and to gather the tips – the most important part of the performance.

And the most pleasant one! The catwalk was warm from the lights, which were glowing underneath it in green, orange and white. She slid her body forward like a big colourful cat, lasciviously bending her back while the male hands were stuffing her boots with notes. Some jerk put some paper note in her crack – very original, indeed! She hissed as a warning. Some other paper note touched her nipple, slid down and landed in her boot. 'Oh, fuck you!' she thought. She continued to crawl forwards, gathering banknotes like flies on flypaper. At the far end of the path she noticed a glassy face. This one is going to throw the whole content of his wallet in my little boot! she decided. The carpet was warm; the pieces of paper tickled her body. The glassy face became even glassier. Come on, take out your tenner, you arse-hole! she thought nastily to herself, impatiently swinging her attributes in front of his nose. No reaction followed.

"I'll stick it up your backside!" she hissed in her native Bulgarian in his face and sharply turned her back.

She did not turn around again. The walk back seemed considerably shorter. She stood up, waved playfully at the public and disappeared behind the curtains.

The first thing she did was to count her money – £55. Not bad! She went back into the dressing room and started cleaning her face. Beata was still whingeing about her rash.

"Don't you really want to try some of this stuff?" Connie said to her whimsically "It's lethal!"

"No," Katya shook her head.

She avoided staying long in Bailey's. The dressing room was full to bursting anyway. One after the other, the girls would get on stage, do their act and then make way for the next. Every act was different. Kemal Dalali was particularly proud of this variety. In one night, more than thirty girls would turn up. If any girl wanted something on top, she could stay performing lap-dances in the twilight of the corner tables. Katya had done that as well without unnecessary scruples, but tonight she didn't feel greedy enough.

A pound coin fell out of her boot. This is not a piggy-bank! she thought angrily, but still bent down to look for it.

"Kate, darling!" the voice of Gunter Chas was echoing. "I have something for you!"

Gunter Chas was a pleasant young gay guy who was in charge of the strippers' wardrobe and also did other little orders on the side. She raised her head and narrowed her eyes. Chas gambolled, swinging his arse like a peg-top.

"Some gentleman wants you to dance exclusively for him," he waved a ten-pound note in front of her nose. "He is waiting for you in his box. Apparently, darling, you stole his heart."

This was not something new: the punters often invited the girls that they liked to do individual performances at their tables. A profitable business, despite the fact that the contact was too close. The clients seldom smelled nice at that moment.

She shook her head, "I am not in the mood. Sorry. He can choose someone else." She was not obliged to do it when all was said and done.

Chas grimaced, "He'll be really upset, you know, He wanted you especially!"

"I can't help him!"

She gathered her things and stuffed them into her bag.

"You're the loser, you know! He's not like the other wankers! He looks cool!" Chas was still nagging, still clinging to the disappearing mirage of his tip.

"Then you go and dance for him. Bye!" and she waved at him.

She was really not in the mood. Strictly speaking she was in too good a mood to let it be destroyed by rubbing her bum on the crotch of some wanker. They were all wankers!

It was close to midnight when she walked out of Bailey's. Sweet Samantha was still in front of entrance, enticing the rare passers-by with her looks of a siren on drugs. Katya looked for a taxi but had no luck. So she started to walk towards Shaftsbury Avenue. Actually, she did not mind walking now. She found London streets secure even at this time of night.

Until that moment, at least.

"Miss Kate!" She heard voice very near her shoulder. "Wait please!"

She turned around sharply. It was an unknown man. "What do you want?" she asked, imperceptibly speeding up.

"Didn't they tell you that I was waiting for you?" There was a resentful note in the question. He had a long face, framed by sharp, low cut ginger sideburns, and he was wearing a black leather jacket and a silver-striped waistcoat. His tone really annoyed her. "I've got…."

"Listen!" she interrupted "I don't do that unless I want to do it! Now, clear off!"

"No problem, I didn't come for some lap-dance," he grinned. "Although, I wouldn't say no. I just wanted to see you and that seemed the easiest way."

"I don't want to talk,"

"My name is Barry Longfellow," he ignored her brush off. "And my intentions are entirely decent. If you care to just listen…."

"I am not interested!"

"Well you ought to be, because I have an attractive proposition for you."

"Aha, I see," she nodded. "And I don't do that at all.'

"You don't understand! I know what you are thinking," he spoke quickly. "But you've got it wrong. You're thinking like some ignorant girl just arrived from the countryside."

She stopped and stared at him. His last words had offended her.

"Finally!" he exclaimed then added, "I want to offer you a part."

"A part?" she narrowed her eyes.

"That is right, a part…in a small but very promising play."

"Are you a director?"

"Mmm, something like that…Executive producer, to be exact. Doesn't matter. At the minute we are looking for the right person to take the lead. I've taken the liberty of observing you for some time. I think you're a real find!"

This business seemed very fishy to her. "What kind of a play is this?"

"We put on chamber plays. But with a good budget," he said with a special emphasis. "There are not many words."

"And what about the content?"

"There is some erotic element," he said carefully. "But that doesn't bother you, I guess?"

"Hmm, depends on the story."

"Innocent! Totally innocent!"

"Hmm." She held back any further comment.

It felt strange, having a conversation like this on the street. Finally she said, "But I am not an actress."

"We'll see, we'll see," murmured Barry.

"And I have an accent," she added.

"Accent," he waved his hand complacently. "Are you Russian?"

"No, Bulgarian."

"Doesn't matter. There aren't many words!"

What a leech! she thought.

Barry, profiting from her instant's hesitation, hurried to provide her with his card.

"Call me," he said. "But don't put it off for too long!"

Then he stepped back, turned around and disappeared down the little street.

11

The van's brake-lights glowed eerily in the darkness. Then it reversed, following Kosta's instructions, and slowly but surely disappeared down the black throat of the garage. Batushka turned off the engine and pointed a powerful torch in Kosta's face. The cook covered his eyes.

"Molodets!" the Tartar's voice echoed.

Chavdar quickly opened the back door. Both of them set to, unloading a long object, zipped in a yellow nylon bag. Kosta watched them from one side. The air in the garage stank of petrol and he felt he was going to be sick. Batushka thrust the torch into his hands.

"You lead!" said Chavdar.

They inched down the stairs and across the basement. From time to time, Kosta turned around and gave a hostile look to his accomplices. He could hear them dragging their load and the nylon rustled unpleasantly. Batushka was swearing quietly in some Altaic language.

They came out into the central corridor and found themselves directly in front of the kitchen door. Here the cook stopped and started listening nervously.

"What's wrong?" asked Chavdar anxiously.

"I thought I heard something inside," Kosta whispered and continued to listen.

"Coward! You're going to fill your pants!" This was Chavdar's idea of encouragement.

The cook curled his lip contemptuously, opened the door and turned on the light. The kitchen was empty.

He made a sign to follow him and headed towards the rear of the premises. In a niche near the fridge lurked a massive, old, padlocked freezer. A glimmering red light indicated that, in theory at least, it was still working. The cook unlocked the padlock and lifted the top. Fog poured out from its innards as the water vapour in the air started to condense and freeze.

"Go on!" he mumbled turning his head towards them.

His face froze. The bag was unzipped, and in the cavity a young woman's face could be seen. The face was white and still as though made of wax. Dead.

"Allowing me to be presenting," Batushka still spoke in his uniquely gloomy style, "Diana, Princess of Wales."

Frightened, Kosta averted his face.

"Easy, man, don't be afraid," said Chavdar. "It's only a corpse. A corpse that costs lots of money. And that money is ours for sure."

"Wait a minute!" shouted Kosta in despair. "This isn't what we agreed on!"

"What saying?" Batushka's brows began to furrow.

"What the hell you are talking about?" Chavdar burst out.

"This is a corpse!" cried the horrified Kosta. "What are you going to do with it?"

"Nothing!" shouted Chavdar "They pay, then we give it back to them."

"I'm going to be sick!" groaned the cook.

"Pull yourself together! You're a cook, aren't you?!" Chavdar chipped in at his most helpful.

"I don't cook people, you imbecile!" Kosta exploded. "Listen, we didn't agree on anything about corpses. You can't leave it here!"

Batushka angrily zipped the bag closed. "Grabbing hold!" he said firmly.

Both men seized the bag from each side and dumped it into the freezer. Batushka quickly covered it with other bags full of ingredients. Then he slammed the top and patted it with his hand. Kosta looked on, effectively a helpless bystander.

"OK." grinned Batushka, "Let's scram off."

Something rang in the brain of the cook and he tried to stop the two men bodily.

"The money? Where's the money?"

"Aaa! Sorry, forgotting it." Batushka raised his hands.

"What do you mean – forgotting?!" hissed the cook. "First you bring me a corpse and then you forget the money. I thought we agreed. 100 pounds, cash, up front."

"Tomorning, Tomorning," mumbled Batushka with some annoyance.

"Not tomorrow, now!" shouted Kosta.

"Easy, my man," Chavdar decided to intervene. "The man says tomorning that means tomorrow. We're doing business for millions here, we're hardly going to cheat you for small change. Isn't that right, Batushka?"

"Right, that's exact right."

"Why don't you both go to hell and fuck yourselves," stormed the cook and started opening the freezer. "Now, you can take her with you, come on!"

At that moment, an iron hand grabbed his neck. The other was pointing a very long, razor-sharp knife at his face. A poisonous, penetrative radiation was oozing from Batushka's eyes. Very slowly and clearly he uttered some unintelligible phrases in his native language. The meaning of those words could not have been overly complicated and revealed itself spontaneously to the cook: She leaves the freezer, you enter the freezer – no empty freezer here!

Kosta woke with a plaintive groan. The wiry fingers of Batushka still fixed around his throat. His legs, stretched out on the little table in front of the television had pins and needles. His back was aching. He had fallen asleep in the chair. The duty room bell was buzzing insistently. The screens, monitoring the streets around the entrances to the Embassy were flickering with bluish light. The figure of Chavdar Tolomanov could be seen quite clearly on one of them, he was nervously stamping his feet in front of the back entrance of the Embassy. The cook got up, puffing, from the chair, dragged his body near to the button of the automatic door-release and pressed it.

Chavdar pushed the door and entered. He found himself in a small squalid corridor, leading to a second door. The automatic lock buzzed again and he walked through. Kosta greeted him, dopey and pale.

"Hey, Pastry, why didn't you open the door?!" shouted Chavdar.

"I was asleep," muttered the cook. "And as for you, why are you late?"

"Who's late?" Chavdar practically rammed his watch into the cook's nose. "Ten minutes I've been ringing!"

Kosta scratched behind his ear. "Well, I've been dreaming…" he started and stopped uncertainly.

"About girls, again?"

"She was a princess… Diana… Her corpse, to be precise…"

"No kidding! You pervert!"

"You had stolen it," continued Kosta gloomily "and dragged it to the Embassy. Then hid it in the freezer. Just like Charlie Chaplin's story…"

"I see," the actor scratched his head. "The thought hadn't occurred to me…Well, too late now! Let's go and get the job done …because Batushka is going to lose his nerve." He concluded.

"Okay then, wait for me around the back," the cook moaned.

He came back to the room with the monitors: the street and the main entrance were clear. Only Chavdar's figure appeared in one of them as he ran quickly towards a van, parked to one side of the Embassy. Then the van reversed and disappeared from the screen. The cook switched off the light, left the door slightly open and plunged into the depths of the Embassy. He got down into the basement, walked through a maze of old corridors, stuffed with old junk and then up some narrow metal stairs, twisting in the dark. He had to put some effort into opening the rusty lock. The small, heavy metal door opened finally and he entered into a spacious compartment filled with the pervasive, heavy smell of machine oils. The light switch clicked; light crawled across the surface of a long greasy puddle. The garage was empty with the sole exception of a pile of old scrap in one corner. Carefully, so as not to stumble into the inspection pit, Kosta stepped around the puddle and reached the door. Turning the switch off again, he unlocked the padlock and lifted the latch. The two sections of the door opened with a heart-stopping squeak.

The van's brake-lights glowed eerily in the darkness. The van reversed, following Kosta's instructions and slowly but surely disappeared down the black throat of the garage.

Batushka turned off the engine and pointed a powerful torch in Kosta's face. The cook covered his eyes.

"Molodets!" the Tartar's voice echoed.

Chavdar quickly opened the back door. Both of them set to, unloading some large nylon bags. Kosta watched them from one side with the unpleasant feeling that he had witnessed the scene before. The air in the garage stank of petrol and he felt sick. Batushka looked at him discontentedly, "What you being stare at?!" He thrust the torch at him and forced him to carry one of the bags.

They inched down the stairs and across the basement, then came out into the corridor, turned left and found themselves directly in front of the kitchen door. Here the cook stopped and started listening nervously.

"What's wrong?" asked Chavdar anxiously.

"I thought I heard something inside," Kosta whispered and continued to listen.

"Coward! You're going to fill your pants!"

The cook curled his lip contemptuously, opened the door and turned on the light.

Batushka whistled in surprise. The kitchen was vast; one might assume that they were cooking for entire regiments down there.

Which incidentally was not very far from the truth, especially in the not so distant totalitarian past when the life in the Embassy had been flying high. Now, social life was dribbling, squeezed drop by drop through the needle's eye of the market economy, and stagnation had settled in the kitchen. Some of the crockery had been stolen. The basins were covered with mould. The tiles around them were yellowish and cracked. Kosta drifted like a phantom between the cold ovens and the empty fridges. He rarely had to cook now; the only things left to do were the sandwiches and various nibbles, made from convenience products. From time to time he prepared the traditional Bulgarian pastry called 'banitsa', which was received by the guests with exclamations of 'Oh, banitsa!' A mixture of grief, nostalgia and hope still hid in his heart for a more substantial order, like a saddle of lamb, for example. Alas, the era of saddles was long gone, buried beneath a mountain of gnawed bones. A piece of sausage and a slice of gherkin speared with a tooth pick was the only thing he could hope for now. Without blinking, Kosta emptied the contents of the bag onto the long metal table. Around ten well-fed ducks fell out of it. Their necks were broken, twisted without pity. He noticed, on the leg of each one of them, a small silver ring.

"Wow, where did you catch these?"

"Nearby," both men chuckled.

One of the birds flapped its wing haplessly; apparently, not completely finished off. Kosta quickly put an end to its suffering. He was now feeling more at home and that reassured him. He took out two whitish aprons and threw them to his accomplices. After a moment of hesitation, they put them on and moved closer to him like apprentices. The cook gave each one of them a big knife and pointed at the stove where a big pot of water had been simmering for some hours.

"You know what to do now?" he asked.

Both men rolled up their sleeves and started.

"You have four hours," he warned them.

He went back to the duty room and checked his watch. He had been absent for no more than twenty minutes. He sat behind the desk, took out the logbook and signed in the column 'on duty', because he expected to forget about it in the morning. In the next column- 'comments' – he wrote, 'nothing unusual'. He then closed the logbook and put it back in the drawer.

Night-watch duty was awful, and, on top of that, long. From the cook to the consul – no escape. Everyone was equal as far as that sacred duty was concerned. Every day, around six in the evening, one could see the person on duty trot to the Embassy with his toilet bag, lunch box and some bed sheets. The humiliation recurred three or four times a month, according to the rota. They had to stay in the duty room like spiders in their web until the morning: watch television, answer the phone, open the door if necessary, drink, eat, and sleep. They were guarding the state's dream. Some even shagged, but the cook was not one of them.

He flumped his body in front of the television, slipped off his shoes and opened a can of beer. Under other circumstances he would have sprawled on the bed and fallen asleep immediately, but now he had to watch. He was alert and quite often looked at the glaring blue screen, hanging on the opposite door. It seemed to him somebody was watching him although the situation was actually the opposite.

The air stank of socks.

He dragged the remote out from beneath his bottom and flicked to the pornography channel, decoded for the people's use, courtesy of an able Bulgarian student. He gaped at it a bit, but could not concentrate. He thought only of the ducks. Fat birds! Wonder, where they took them from…? If the Chinese don't buy them, as Chavdar and Batushka swore, we're going to be eating duck into the next year. For fuck's sake! Hell of a lot of birds that!

The electronic bleep of the telephone jolted him out of his dream. He picked it up and sleepily said, "Yeah."

"Bulgarian Embassy?" a distant little voice sang.

"Aha."

"Excuse me, could you tell me if I need a visa to visit Bulgaria?"

A short pause followed. The cook's heart lurched into revolt. He hardly spoke a word of English, but the word 'visa' was clear enough to pour fat on the fire.

"You cunt!" he hissed maliciously in Bulgarian "What kind of visa are you looking for at this hour in the morning, go and fuck yourself, otherwise I'll do it for you!!!"

From the other end came a burst of mocking laughter.

"Dozy Pastry! Your old mother!" Chavdar Tolomanov quickly changed his intonation "Stupid Pastry!" He was phoning on his mobile from the kitchen.

"Is that you? Are you taking the piss?" gasped the cook, after he'd calmed down a little. "Are you ready?"

"What do you think?"

"Coming," he answered shortly.

It was half-four in the morning.

The kitchen was like an abattoir. Chavdar and Batushka were furiously scrubbing under the taps – their hands were sticky with blood, which had seeped deep under their fingernails. The freezer was stuffed with birds. The feathers and the offal had been stuffed back into the bags. Kosta looked underneath the tables and frowned; he would have to mop the floor. On the table top lay a plate, full of silver rings.

"Let us scram the fucking out!" said Batushka wiping his wet hands against the wall.

Something clicked in the cook's head.

"And the money? Where's the money?"

"Aaa! Sorry I forgot," Batushka raised his hands.

"What do you mean – you forgot?!" hissed the cook. "I thought we agreed. 100 pounds, cash, up front."

"Tomorning, Zavtra," mumbled Batushka with some annoyance.

"No tomorrow, no zavtra, now!" shouted Kosta.

"Easy, my man," Chavdar decided to intervene. "Zavtra says the man, That means tomorrow. We're doing business for millions here, we're hardly going to cheat you for spare change. Isn't that right, Batushka?"

"Right, that's right," said Batushka scornfully.

The cooked goggled like a zombie. They were pulling the same number on him for the second time. He opened his mouth to speak, but felt he was going to enter the same familiar script. He waved them off and spat on the floor.

12

Varadin popped up into the Embassy just after nine. He had met Kosta in the street, coming back from his night-shift, carrying a nylon bag in one hand and with an anxious sticky look on his face. This encounter curdled the Ambassador's mood instantly; as if a bogie had unexpectedly dropped into his milk that morning. They greeted each other dryly.

Behind the reception window another low-spirited employee faced him; she was meditating over an old Bulgarian newspaper. He crossed the official entrance hall and tried to go through the door, which led to the Embassy interior. It turned out he had forgotten its security code. He tried in vain for several minutes. In the end, the Consul appeared and without any sign of noticing his troubles (although he was laughing inside!), carefully greeted him and keyed in the code. Varadin rushed to slip into the lift and pressed the button for the second floor. Leaving the lift, he looked to the right, where he had noticed a particularly dirty spot on the carpet the previous day, and noted with pleasure that it had been cleaned.

Tania Vandova was behind her desk, in the front office, feverishly sorting out the usual pile of correspondence that arrived every morning.

"Good morning," she greeted him without interrupting her work.

He mumbled something incomprehensible and slammed the door behind him.

A short conversation on the phone followed, after which the accountant galloped in, carrying an armful of folders.

"Is the list of tenants ready?" he asked.

She nodded in confirmation and gave him the list. Varadin sighed heavily, like a man set the task of moving mountains.

The Embassy was overcrowded, although recently the personnel had been drastically cut, thanks to the permanent economic crisis. The clothes of the former dinosaur state were not the same size as those of its inheritor. Nature, however, did not leave empty spaces, and the living quarters were filled up to the last attic by suspicious subjects, apparently protected under the terms of 'Balkan Common Law'. Varadin knew the delicacy of this problem, but he also knew that he had to clear them out one by one. Living space was a powerful tool in the hands of any ruler: one can manoeuvre and trade with it. This resource belonged to him by right and it was he, and only he, who should decide who was to occupy it.

"Why do all these people live here?"

"Weeell…." Bianca Mashinska drawled, while she grumbled to herself, why do you pretend you don't know anything, you asshole? "It's an inherited situation!" she spat out at last, happy to have found the exact formula.

"Mm-hmm, inherited situation!" It was disgusting. "But they cannot stay here anymore," he added sharply.

"Of course, especially those who do not pay their rent. Like the Bobevs for example…"

"And why haven't they already been evicted?!"

"Because they have filed a lawsuit. Rasho Bobev, the ex-attaché for trade and commerce, is suing the Ministry. He has filed for unlawful dismissal."

"And so what?" Varadin exploded "He can go back to Sofia and sue them as much as he wants from there!"

"He does not want to go back. He says that he is waiting for the court's decision. He hopes they are going to reinstate him."

"As if they would reinstate him!" Varadin pursed his lips. "He calculated it quite well. Those court proceedings go on for months. Throw him out!"

Bianca Mashinska said nothing.

"What is the matter? Are there no police in this country?"

"But then the whole thing will blow up in our faces and that will hit our reputation again."

"Yes, correct. That is not a good idea," he sighed, massaging the base of his nose. The sort of idiocy he was forced to deal with! A feeling of rage overcame him, "Then think of something else," he spat out with a hissing voice. "Cut his electricity. Stop his water. I want him out!"

"I'll inform the housekeeper," she nodded indifferently.

"Work on it!"

Very well, one by one he was going to take them out of the honey-pot like small, repugnant insects – with tweezers. This pretty vision made him grit his teeth with pleasure. He poured himself a glass of water and dropped one fizzy pill into it, which immediately coloured the liquid a poisonous yellow. He swallowed it and burped.

At that very instant one of the telephones on his desk started ringing furiously.

"Hellooo, is that you?" a capricious female voice sounded in his ear.

"It is me," (without a drop of enthusiasm). "I am very pleased to hear your voice."

"Don't be so pleased!" she snarled. "I thought I could rely on you!"

"Of course you can!"

"I can't, that is the problem. Why you are hiding it from me?"

"What am I hiding?" his adrenaline jumped.

"Are you kidding me? I know everything," she shouted, then added, heartbroken, "a refusal has arrived!'

"My god, is that your worry?!" he exclaimed. "Don't even think about it, the situation is under control."

"Not to worry?!! I am furious! That snail, Kishev, it took him almost half a year!" she exploded. "You have to punish him!"

"I will punish him, of course!" he hurriedly agreed. "I'll punish him good and proper."

"Yes, but it is too late now. Who knows what kind of mess he's caused," she sighed. "He probably broke with the required etiquette on purpose to annoy her; to make her reject us forever. Saboteur! And you protect him!"

"I do not protect him!" he was indignant.

"I do not want to see his sorry face next time I come around, you hear me!"

"Well, his mandate is nearly over," he cooed. "And he is not going to see a next one."

"That is exactly what he deserves," she grumbled. "And what are we going to do with this situation?"

"I was thinking of hiring a special agency for exactly this purpose."

A suspicious crackling noise appeared in the line and he suddenly wondered if they were being tapped. They were not discussing something incredibly secret, but he felt really stupid.

"What agency?"

"Public relations."

"Oooo!" a certain respect entered her voice, as though they were discussing the use of some exceedingly sophisticated domestic appliance.

"Tomorrow, I have an appointment with their director. They look kosher, but I cannot tell you more than that right now," added Varadin cautiously.

The thought of the phone tap had upset him.

"When are they going to bring her out?" Her question caught him on the hop.

"She isn't a cow!" his anger threatened all his safety valves.

"I don't care!" she shouted. "In two months time she should be on line! You owe it to me, damn it!"

"I'll do what I can," he groaned, half-suffocated by resentment.

"That would be best for all concerned!"

The connection was cut.

"94!" he shouted pathetically.

For the next several seconds he stayed motionless. The internal telephone rang several times, but Varadin did not react. Somebody knocked on the door and Tania Vandova's head appeared.

"Major Potty is waiting to be received," was her edgy explanation.

"48," he said with a stony face. "Show him in."

The lanky figure of the Major appeared behind the small body of the secretary.

"Seventy seven!" shouted Major Potty, entering into the room like a gale-force storm but with his hand stretched in front of him.

"What?" Varadin flinched.

"Nice to meet you!" the major squeezed his hand fiercely. "I've no time to lose. I have arranged 77 crates of humanitarian aid, which need to be exported to Bulgaria immediately. People there are starving!" he ended on a note of pathos.

Varadin looked at him fearfully. Major Potty was an ex-colonial officer, who radiated an inexhaustible desire to slap down any naughty aboriginal. He was a tall bony old man, well past his sixties, with a shiny bald pate and a grey, bristly moustache. He was wearing a dark blue suit without a tie and spit-shined dress shoes – as if he did not have to walk on the streets at all, but moved from one office to the next like a spirit. He was carrying the ID-card of the organization he was representing on a chain around his neck.

Throwing himself onto the sofa, he started pulling various brochures from his bag. Varadin stood warily opposite him. A little later, Tania Vandova appeared carrying the coffee-tray.

For the first ten minutes the major jabbered incoherently about his organization, and the various celebrities on the board of governors. When he had piled up enough titles and crests to stand on, he looked down at the Ambassador and asked why, in principle, Bulgarians were so unresponsive to humanitarian aid.

"What do you mean?" Varadin raised his eyebrows.

"What do I mean?" repeated the Major sarcastically. "Well, we are moving heaven and earth to gather these essentials together and apparently nobody gives a damn!"

Varadin tactfully kept quiet.

"I have received information to the effect that a large quantity of this aid so selflessly donated is aging away down in the storerooms of the Embassy. Is that correct?" the ex-soldier asked harshly.

"I have no idea," the Ambassador raised his arms. "I've only been here a week."

"They tell us, would you believe it, that we must arrange the transportation for ourselves! As if the items we are sending were not worth the cost to transport them," said Major Potty with disgust. "As far as I'm concerned, if you carry on like this, you'll upset the entire charitable community. Think of your image!"

"Our new image will be my first concern!" the Ambassador assured him, feeling the first symptoms of his migraine.

"It had better be," exclaimed the Major. "I wouldn't want my seventy seven crates to be left to rot in some godforsaken storeroom."

Varadin decided he would make a good impression if he showed some concern about the subject and asked politely, "And what do the crates contain?"

This was a serious mistake. The Major flinched as though stung by a wasp, "You ask what is in there! What is the content of my crates! Oh, My Lord!" He threw up his arms and let them drop enervated. "Oh, Jesus!" He repeated the same movement, expressing his deep despair at the insolence and audacity of this aboriginal. "Are we going to play Customs Officers here? Or do you think we are sending you any old rubbish, eh?"

"I said no such thing!" objected Varadin fearfully.

The migraine was already thrashing his brain cells.

"But your sneaky curiosity is implying just that, isn't it?" spat Major Potty. "Either way, I am not ashamed of the content of my crates! Inside, you will find only simple yet sturdy objects, which served my compatriots for a long time and will serve your impoverished denizens honestly for the same long period of time!"

"I don't doubt it!" Varadin hurried to agree.

"Prove it!" boomed the Major. "Those crates have to reach their destination as soon as possible."

"I will personally see to it that they do!"

"Excellent! Because then I will send you another hundred crates of…" the Major paused before adding solemnly "bedpans."

"What?!" the Ambassador blinked quickly.

"The Saint Barnabas Infirmary in North Hampshire closed recently," Major Potty was happy to explain. "They are auctioning everything, but they are donating the bedpans to us. And we, in turn, will donate them to you. If you deserve them, of course!" he waggled his finger jokingly at the Ambassador.

"I really do not know how to express my gratitude," mumbled Varadin.

"Gratitude and charity are two sides of the same coin," concluded the Major sagely and quickly stood up. "Unfortunately, I cannot stay a second longer. Lady Broad-Botham awaits me. We are expediting ten tons of winter clothes to Bombay, or Mumbai as they call it these days."

He shook the hand of the dazed Ambassador and walked straight out with a decisive step as though impelled by some mechanical aid.

Varadin crawled back into his chair; leaned his head on the back and closed his eyes.

He quietly pronounced the number 95.

But he felt no relief. His skull was pulsing with pain, rubbery and soft like a bladder. It was only noon. A lunch in the French Embassy awaited him and he expected it to be formal and cold because of the well-known dislike of the French for anyone who did not speak their language. In the afternoon he had to see a line of clerks in the Foreign Office. In the evening he had to attend a reception at the Carlton for some occasion his brain categorically refused to retain. It was under attack from the intrusive image of that student that cleaned his office. Obviously there was nothing stopping him from taking her to bed. The question was: what would it cost him?

13

As she drifted through the London Underground, Katya caught herself thinking about the new Ambassador. They had spoken that morning. He had informed her that he had given the necessary orders for the purchase of a new Hoover. She had thanked him, but had been left with the impression that Varadin was somewhat disappointed by her reaction. Perhaps he had found it a bit flat. Perhaps he expected more than that. Tough. At the end of the day, the Hoover was not only for her. Although it was a gesture of good-will. If nothing more…. But, Bulgarian diplomats, in principle, were of no interest to her. The truth was that one could expect more trouble than real support from them.

Green Park. An Indian family got into the train and sat down opposite her. The women wore colourful dresses and the man a high, deep-purple turban. He gave her a sidelong glance, nothing more.

Next stop – Piccadilly.

Bailey's was boiling and steaming, giving off a sharp smell of sweaty bodies. Katya looked for her costume but could not find it in its usual place. She noticed Beata, still with rash-ridden loins, attempting to squeeze her chubby ankles into the boots. Katya snatched them from her hands, "Those are mine, in case you didn't know!"

Beata blinked gormlessly and whined, "But, Mr Dalali told me to wear them."

Gunter Chas made his entrance at that moment, a guilty smile on his face and a hanger in his grasp. Some gauzy, golden garb shimmered on it.

"I've got something for you Kate darling. Something brand new!" His voice was at once chirpy and sleazy.

She grimaced. "Did you arrange that little number for me?"

"It's about time for a change dearie. That's what Mr Dalali said. Nice body, he said, but…we need to spice it up a bit."

As far as Kamal Dalali was concerned, all the working girls were bodies and nothing more.

"So it's spicing up they want…." she murmured, critically eying Chas' creation, "It looks silly. And those lacy bits will get in the way when I'm dancing."

"Put it on. Put it on!" he insisted.

There was no point in arguing. She sighed, threw Beata a nasty look, and went to change. She returned looking like the High-Priestess of some long-extinct oriental cult. The others looked at her enviously, but Katya was far from impressed. The material felt slimy, like wearing a jellyfish, and slid off her with every sharp movement. Obviously, that was the whole idea, but equally obviously, no one had given any thought to her part in the equation. If she did not want the costume to drop to the floor in the first five seconds she would have to radically change her style. Which carried its share of financial risk….

"Oooh you're so sexy." Chas soothed her, whilst giving her two clips, with little bells on them.

She gave him a questioning look. He indicated her breasts. Suddenly, she felt like laughing.

"You put them on!"

"Why, thank you…" Chas accepted graciously.

He opened the clips and carefully fixed them to her pert, pink nipples.

"Ouch!!" she screeched, pulling away sharply.

"Tinkle, tinkle-inkle." The bells chimed merrily.

"Ahh! They're beautiful!!!" the assembled girls exclaimed in chorus.

Katya, however, did not share their enthusiasm. The clips

painfully pinched those most sensitive spots like vicious predatory insects.

"Fuck!!" she gasped, as she desperately tried to take them off.

"Katiina, hurry up!" came the voice of Kamal Dalali.

"Go fuck yourself!" she blessed him in Bulgarian.

"Is something wrong darling?" asked Chas worriedly.

"You try them on for size!" she hissed, throwing the clips at him.

"Hey, cool it! I already did, if you must know," Chas said.

"Well, I'm not a masochist!" Katya shouted.

"Hurry up!" screeched Kamal Dalali once again.

"Come on, it's only for ten minutes."

"Not happening!" she snapped.

"Hurry up!!!"

"I'm not wearing them and that's final!" she insisted. "They're killing me. You'd better go invent something else!"

"Mr Dalali, we have a problem!" Chas whined loudly.

The Lebanese materialised instantly, wiping his face with a silk handkerchief. A still smouldering cigar drooped from his mouth, giving off a sickly smell. Chas brought him up to speed on the situation. He frowned, "Put the bells on!"

"Look what they did to me!" she said, holding her red nipples.

"There's nothing wrong with your fucking nipples!"

"They hurt! Look how red they are!"

"Quit whingeing!" the Lebanese fumed. "Get on stage!"

Chas gave the clips back to her, waving them playfully in front of her nose. "Tinkle, tinkle!" Katya batted his hand away. Dalali slapped her forcefully.

"Bitch!" he ground out through his teeth.

"Arsehole!" screamed Katia in his face, rubbing her cheek. "Dirty butt-fucker! Pig!"

"Get out!" roared Kamal Dalali. "Get your arse out of here and don't let me catch you round here again! Chas, see this whore out of here, d'you hear me!"

Katya stuck her tongue out at them and threw herself onto a chair. The girls busied themselves with their make-up once more, muttering discontentedly amongst themselves. Gunter Chas sidled up to her.

"Don't let it get to you darling. He'll get over it, you know how he is."

"I've had it with the lot of you!" she sighed.

"Niina! Hurry up!" called Kamal Dalali from somewhere behind the curtains.

"Fuck you!" whispered Katya.

She shrugged sharply out of the slimy garment, not so much as bothering to pick it off the floor. She grabbed her rucksack and locked herself in one of the toilets. A notice was plastered on the door: 'The smoking of weed is forbidden!' She made herself comfortable and pulled out the mobile she had bought for just twenty quid two weeks earlier. She brought up Barry Longfellow's number of and dialled. It was answered almost instantly.

"Hi, this is Kate," she said hesitantly, "from Bailey's. You offered me a part in your performance."

"A part?!" The voice sounded strangely distant. "Oh, yes, I remember. I was beginning to think that you'd never call."

"Well, I did."

"Okay. Tomorrow evening, The Athenaeum, room 165. Come at 11 pm, sharp."

"Okay."

She had wanted to ask something else, but Barry put the phone down. That is what I call a business-like approach to things, she thought. Someone tried the door-handle without success. Katya chuckled. Then she dialled another number. This time she had to wait longer for a reply.

"Daddy?" she queried, once she heard a voice at the other end.

Usually, she phoned at the weekend when it was cheaper. Today was Thursday, and close to midnight at that. Her father started to fret, "Are you all right? Why are you calling?"

"I just felt like it. I wanted to hear your voice. How's mother?"

"She's sleeping. She's well." He sounded like a man counting seconds and pennies in his head.

"What are you up to?

"Television."

"You're watching telly?" she asked, bewildered.

"Well, yes! Look you're blowing a lot of money...."

"Don't worry about it. What's on?"

"Rubbish." He fell silent.

She also fell silent. The line hissed gently. Katya realised that her parents always spoke to her in that absurd and broken manner, no matter who was paying the bill. Most frequently it was herself, but to them it made no difference. The expense of the words seemed to paralyse their ability to talk. Silence, however, was no cheaper, and she sensed her father's anxiety at the other end. She should not torture him any longer.

"It was good to hear you," she said finally. "Give my love to mother, ciao."

"Good to hear from you too, cherub." Suddenly his tongue came unstuck, 'Goodbye!'

The door-handle rattled once more.

Katya stared at the phone's screen until it switched itself off. I'm never going back alive! she thought, grinding her teeth. Even the clips were preferable to the enduring humiliation of life over there.

Leaving Bailey's Place, Katya felt a certain sadness. She had had some good times in that hole, but most importantly, she had gained her freedom. She had not only stripped clothes from her body, but also those odorous garments that wrap the virgin minds of the folk from the East. Here she had had a taste of financial independence for the first time. She had gotten to know her body and how to manage it.

She had felt mistress of her destiny.

On the way out, Samantha caught her hand tenderly – the

memory of which stayed with her as she walked away down the streets of Soho. Drizzle hung in the air. The streetlights glared brightly, reflected by the wet tarmac. Katya crossed Shaftsbury Avenue, and continued down into China Town. She dived into one of the many little restaurants where one could stuff oneself to bursting for less than ten pounds, and ordered Peking Duck, her favourite dish. Whilst watching the small Chinese waiter dismembering the fowl with a spoon, she thought to herself, Life goes on, and should be lived to the full.

14

"Your Excellency!" Robert Ziebling exclaimed, from the very threshold of the office, "I cannot begin to express how delighted I was to receive this invitation."

The Managing Director of 'Famous Connections™' seized the Ambassador's hand and proceeded to shake it fiercely. He was of average height, slightly over forty, with thick, unruly ginger hair. A pair of fashionably thin glasses, with yellow lenses, were wrapped around his face. He was wearing a severely cut, single-breasted jacket, buttoned to the neck, which gave him a military air.

"Please, have a seat," Varadin responded woodenly, nodding to the heavy leather suite that graced the forward half of his office.

He waited for Tania Vandova to serve the tea for his guest, and began warily, "I received an excellent recommendation for your agency from Dean Carver."

"Oh, yes!" Ziebling nodded energetically. "He is one of our regular clients. A very original man. Such a tireless imagination...!"

Varadin blinked bewildered. "Mr Carver let me know that your agency has connections at the highest possible levels..." He continued hesitantly, "I won't hide from you the fact that that is precisely what interests me. As you can see, my own connections are purely official, which imposes certain restrictions...you understand, of course."

"Of course...." Ziebling began to nod.

"The possibility of less formal ways of communicating has always interested me," the Ambassador added. "Sometimes such connections can turn out to be far more fruitful than official ones."

"That's usually how it happens," Ziebling agreed, and asked slyly, "And in which sphere do your interests lie exactly?"

"Excuse me?"

"Our network of connections is tremendously wide," explained Ziebling. "That's why they are grouped into different categories. For example, Show-biz stars: Spice Girls, Elton John, Boy George, Mr Bean, Benny Hill…"

"Wait a moment!" cut in Varadin. "I thought Benny Hill was dead?"

Ziebling stared at him shocked, "So what if he is?"

"Excuse me?" Varadin was confused.

"Aristocrats are, of course, in another broad category," continued Ziebling unperturbed. "As are the politicians, Lady Thatcher, Gorby. We also have some very effective contacts in the Catholic line of things."

"You have connections with Lady Thatcher?!" Varadin was awash with respect.

"All the time!" proclaimed Ziebling. "Did you know that she is an extremely sought-after lady. Such style! Such an iron hand!"

"I don't doubt it," muttered Varadin.

"She is fully booked. Naturally, one can always find a slot, but, usually she has ongoing engagements."

"I assume that is not cheap?" Varadin narrowed his eyes, amazed at his own audacity.

"Good investments are never cheap," Ziebling, shook his head sagely. "Let's be serious, these things last a lifetime!"

"That's true," Varadin nodded timidly. "All the same, how much?"

"My dear, we are not talking lettuce in the supermarket here!" Ziebling warned him playfully. "It all depends on the character of the engagement. As well as its duration: one hour, two, the whole evening. Who the client is, of course, is not without importance either. To sum up, every offer is treated individually."

"I understand," the Ambassador nodded.

"You see, we do not wish to profit from chaotic, short-term

contacts!" Ziebling was on a roll. "When we create a particular connection, we look at it in a larger perspective. For that reason, connections made with our help are usually stable and last a long time, often for years."

"Most impressive!" whispered Varadin.

"And so, Lady Thatcher…?"

"Actually, no…It concerns the Palace."

"Ahhh, the Palace," Ziebling nodded again, then continued, "Well, why not? We often work with them."

"We are organising a charity concert," Varadin began timidly, "and we would like Her Majesty to grace us with her presence."

"Her Majesty?" Ziebling raised his eyebrows.

"Exactly!"

"An interesting choice," Ziebling clasped his hands together thoughtfully. "Audacious. Of course we can arrange it. I don't see any problem with that. However, this concert concerns me a little. What exactly did you have in mind?"

"Well, a charity concert, you understand," replied the Ambassador, confused once more. "For Bulgarian orphans."

"Orphans?" Ziebling sounded worried. "Do you mean minors…?"

"Mmm, yes. At least I assume that they are under eighteen…."

"I cannot allow them to participate in the entertainment!" Ziebling's tone brooked no argument.

"Of course, they won't participate," agreed the Ambassador. "They're in Bulgaria, aren't they? You see, they are merely the reason for the event…We want to gather together the most select audience. High Society, as such."

"Uh-huh," nodded Ziebling, relieved. "Fine. We have plenty of experience with similar undertakings. It's beginning to look like a very ambitious project."

"That's exactly what it is."

"We will have to work out a preliminary scenario," continued Ziebling. "We have a specialist who deals with just that. He'll get in touch with you in the next couple of days. His name is Thomas Munroe."

That's what I call a business-like approach to things, Varadin thought. Maybe Carver would turn out to be right.

Robert Ziebling left the office in high spirits. He even shared a joke with Tania Vandova, who seemed a little worried.

Varadin decided that he should take advantage of this brief moment of partial satisfaction (the satisfaction was never complete and never lasted long), to sort out some family matters that had been left to one side in the haste of his departure. He ought to call his wife. This was something that he had been carefully avoiding ever since he set foot on British soil. There was no way to erase it from his mind, and in fact he had no intention of doing so. He looked at his watch: it must be almost 10 am in Sofia now. A good time, he decided, dialled the number and waited. Would she still be in bed? When had she gone to bed? What had she been doing until so late?

"Hello?" a confident male voice answered.

Varadin stood open mouthed in shock, but did not say anything. Nor did he put the phone down.

'Hello...?' repeated the voice, suspiciously this time.

Varadin listened carefully, straining to hear better. The man at the other end started to do the same, so the only thing to be heard for several seconds was the hiss and crackle of the line. Then both of them put the phone down almost simultaneously.

"Wrong number," Varadin told himself, less than convinced.

He dialled again. This time a sleepy female voice answered.

"Hello, Nadya, did I wake you?" he asked, relieved.

"Hello, yeah, pretty much. Are you calling from London?"

"What do you think?"

"From London, or else it would have been the doorbell ringing, I know you. Why are you calling?"

"I want you to come," his voice brooked no denial. "I need you. I hope you've thought it over."

"Yes, I've been thinking quite a bit."

There followed a short pause.

"So you'll come?"

"No, of course, I won't."

"We are talking about London, in case you happen to have forgotten."

"We are talking about the London Bulgarian Embassy," she put a special emphasis on those last two words. "There is an important difference."

"What's this load of rubbish?" he hissed.

"You heard!" snapped Nadya. "I don't like the environment and that's that; I still feel sick when I think of your last mandate. Not to mention the previous one! All those holes stink as badly as each other, no matter where they are. It was that way before and nothing has changed, nor will it because this half-arsed country hasn't changed a bit!! D'you get what I'm saying here?"

"Nadya, Nadya!"

"Ahh, so you don't get it then?! You think you've got God by the beard, but in reality he's got you. And you know where? By the balls, the nuts, the privates. And he's slowly crushing them. Squish, squeeze for fifteen years now. You're not the man I married all those years ago. Now you're like someone who's had a steam-roller go between his legs. You all get that way after you spend a few years in that mill! I, on the other hand, don't intend to be a part of all that. I'm not going to be one of those misanthropic little women, who accompany their husbands for cocktails, and spend the rest of their time at female get-togethers and organising charity events. Finita la commedia!"

"You'd rather rot over there then!"

"YOU are not telling ME where to rot!" she yelled. "I'm going to the UAE."

"Where?"

"You're the diplomat, you should know: the United Arab Emirates."

"What are you going to do there?" Varadin felt stung.

"I found myself a job in a clinic."

"You're going to work as a doctor?"

"Exactly, that is what I'm trained for. I'm leaving in two months. You'll have to send me some money."

"Forget it!"

"Then I'll just have to send your old Communist Party Membership Card to certain department chiefs...."

"My old Communist Party Membership Card? There's no such thing."

"You wish! I fished it out of the trash. I can courier it to you, if you send me five hundred pounds. I'll need them for my lawyer."

"Bitch!"

"Don't piss me off, small fry! You go calling me at some ridiculous hour of the morning, wake up my boyfriend, then wake me up as well, and to top it all you then talk shit down the phone. I told you, it's over. What more do you want?"

"Bitch!!!" Varadin repeated helplessly.

Hearty laughter gushed from the other end of the line. "You woke me up nicely; Ciao for now!"

The line went dead. Varadin shook the phone as though he wanted to shake all the negative energy out of it, then put down the receiver. First privatized Embassy was what percolated through his mind. But all he could vocalise was the number 100.

"100!-100!-100!"

Doctor Pepolen did not allow for numbers outside the framework of 1 to 100 – that was the iron rule. However, there existed no categorical statement that numbers could not be repeated, and thus Varadin often bent the rule by pouring out his spiritual turmoil in small packages of 100, fired off like a machine-gun, until he emptied the well of his anxiety. Dr Pepolen was unaware of this little innovation, otherwise he might have banned it.

15

For the opening of the European Conference, a huge heap of Bulgarian Cabinet members fell on London, headed by the Prime Minister himself. The local press was extremely sceptical about this gathering; there was even a note of cynicism, but for the transition-tormented governments from Eastern Europe, it was manna from heaven, an overwhelming prelude to their eventual membership of the club of prosperous Western cousins.

Throughout these three days that were filled with general commotion, long speeches, exultation and not very well hidden disappointment, Varadin struggled merely to survive. The reality of the situation blurred before his eyes, like the countryside outside the window of a speeding train; he saw clearly only the obstacles, hazards and pit-falls that he had to avoid. His immediate proximity to the Premier horrified him. That strict and powerful politician, who had swum out of Post-Communism's primordial soup, looked to be the sort of man who breakfasted every morning on bureaucratic destinies, cooked al dente with garlic and horseradish sauce. Varadin had cause to believe (he had half-heard it from somewhere) that this man was far from happy about his ambassadorial nomination, and so Varadin was quaking lest something happen that might confirm the Premier's suspicions. On the other hand, like all true careerists, he felt a pathological attraction to people in positions of power, and threw himself ferociously towards them, taking on all the risks that came with such dangerous proximity. For the moment, however, he had to be careful not to be dazzled by the Premier's aura, which would, without doubt, attract the hatred of the other two ministers, who could easily harm him. He also strained to keep an eye on his staff, who circled like hyenas around those currently in power, and were only waiting for the right moment to discredit him. The task was daunting.

The Conference was being held in Lancaster House – the most imposing element of the St James' Palace complex. The place was breath-taking in its lavish splendour, but contributed nothing to the spiritual comfort of the Eastern European government representatives. Beneath the heavy gilded ceilings hovered feelings of both victory and defeat. Victory, they had all tasted; whereas defeat was something no-one was suffering from, visibly at least. But if the victory was for all, then why were all of its fruits gathered on one side, leaving only the stalks on the other? This new division of the old continent was what the leaders of the new democracies strove to understand and internally complained about. Even between themselves, however, there remained too little brotherly love. The simple and obvious fact that they were so similar that they could see themselves reflected in each other, infuriated them. They preferred to see themselves reflected in their rich Western relatives with their aristocratic habits and noble manners. They were envious and suspicious of one another, inclined to take the advancement of their neighbour as their own personal failure. They scrambled desperately to get out of the communal manure, without looking where they trod. The big competition for Europe had begun. The favoured countries celebrated the fact that they had come out a whisker ahead of their former allies, but their joy was overshadowed by the knowledge that between themselves and the developed European countries there lay many miles yet. The remainder, which included Varadin's fatherland, were happy that they had so much as made it into the competition at all. They did not put much effort into drawing level with the West, because an old adage, from some unknown Balkan sage, lived on in their subconscious: Even sprinting, we aren't going to catch them. Their pride thrived on the fact that there were even worse cases, such as Moldova or Yugoslavia. These had not so much as found a seat at the negotiating table.

The western diplomats looked with reluctance at this cloudy cocktail of vodka, palinka and rakia, which they were being forced to swallow. At the end of the day, what they would like to do was to tip it under the table, without anyone noticing. But they could not – everyone's gaze was fixed on them – and any false move might bring with it unforeseen repercussions. It was unavoidable!

For Varadin, the Conference was an excuse to make official contacts at every possible level: from foreign Ambassadors and high-level employees of the Foreign Office, to Foreign Ministers and Heads of State. He did not allow himself to be carried away by the fact that he performed all this communication with ease. He stayed alert, trying to analyse the possibilities that each new contact opened for him. But he always remained disappointed with the low horizon and narrow perspective of their potential development. The infertility of those ephemeral introductions now seemed like the spark of an empty lighter. They lacked the depth and the resources to be worthwhile contacts. Their names slipped out of his mind as easily as their visiting-cards into his pocket. Conversing with these people required no more than three hundred words, and for the first time in his career, he came to realise that a well trained imbecile could quite easily carry out this function! And perhaps he was precisely that imbecile.

He lifted his anxious gaze towards the Premier. What if he had heard his thoughts? People with power usually possessed a well-developed intuition regarding their inferiors. For the time being, though, the entire attention of the Premier was focused on the President of the European Commission's speech. The little headset running the simultaneous translation was buzzing persistently in his ear, but did he hear a word of what was said? It was impossible to tell. For the last few years, Varadin had been observing the people at the head of the government closely, and had caught on to the processes they underwent internally, almost without exception. Power sucked them from the inside: like shrimps, their faces tightened onto their skulls, their eyes became round and bulged, ready to jump out of their sockets like bullets. Their senses also changed: the old ones atrophied, and in their place new ones developed, akin to those of lizards or insects. First they lost their ability to listen, as though they no longer grasped the meaning of words, and then they stopped seeing – they looked through people as though they were made of glass. They trusted only in the vibrations they gave off in all directions to gain information about the world around them.

The vibrations of power were universal and had no need of an interpreter; they warily scanned every body they met: they examined it for form and consistency, they checked its durability and colour, they searched for irregularities and cracks, and they gauged the strength of its vibrations, if it had any. Then they reported back. The bodies were either animate or inanimate. The animate ones were divided into subdued and non-subdued. The non-subdued were subdivided into hostile and neutral. The hostile were subdivided into strong and weak.

One had to be careful with the strong ones!

The President of the EC was strong, although he looked soft and well-polished – he was smooth and had no cracks; his vibrations were low and unobtrusive, yet powerful. Not so much strength of character as the strength of the institution he represented. He was not to be underestimated and the Premier was alert. Cold and immobile, his head raised (the wire of his headset hung lifeless from his ear) only the slow movement of his adam's apple gave him away. Up and down. On his other side was the Foreign Minister, who was continuously taking notes in a gilt-edged, leather-bound, luxury notebook. He also had a headset, although his was crammed into his ear, not that he needed translation, but to show solidarity with his superior. Varadin threw a glance at his own notebook and realised with horror that the only thing he had jotted down was a little stickman in the bottom corner. He was straining to catch up on what he had missed, when the President's speech, somewhat unexpectedly, ended. There was polite applause until some other leader took the podium. At that exact moment, the Premier inclined his head towards Varadin and whispered, "Is my speech ready?"

The Ambassador nodded instinctively. In reality, he was not so sure. Of course the question concerned the English translation of the speech, which would be distributed to the listeners. This creation had been tirelessly edited, until the very last minute, and only this morning the staff at the Embassy had started its feverish translation. He quietly got to his feet, and went to talk to one of the diplomats that had accompanied the delegation.

Counsellor Danailov was chatting carelessly with the mighty Minister for Industry and some other upper echelon aides in the Cabinet entourage. This picture turned the Ambassador's stomach. He drew him to one side and asked him whether the Premier's speech was ready. Danailov calmly looked at his watch and said, "It should be here already. I'll go and get it."

Varadin, relieved, watched his figure until it left the Negotiation Hall, then immediately returned to the group.

Danailov left Lancaster House at the pace of a well-fed man, crossed the courtyard full of shiny limousines, and went to the gate. The young intern Nikola Turkeiev was already waiting for him there, looking around impatiently. He did not have a pass for the Conference, his job was merely to bring the translated and printed speech from the Embassy to the gate.

"How are you, lad?" Danailov gave him a friendly thump on the shoulder.

"Did you get it?" The intern looked worried and confused.

"What should I have got?"

"Well, the speech."

"Weren't you bringing it?" asked the Counsellor in surprise.

"I gave it to someone to give to you, just a minute ago," the intern said and hurried to explain himself, "I was worried it might be late."

"Wait here, I'll go check," The Counsellor's voice was suddenly grim.

He came back a short while later, even grimmer.

"Can't find it anywhere," he scratched behind his ear. "Why the hell didn't you wait for me, Smartypants?"

"I waited," the intern quavered. "You didn't turn up and I got worried. I asked some guy to call someone out, but he offered to take it to you himself."

"What did he look like?" asked Danailov suspiciously.

"Well, I mean..." stuttered Turkeiev. "He had a raincoat and glasses; he was extremely polite."

"And you gave him the Premier's speech?" the Counsellor's eyebrows jumped. "Every copy?"

The intern nodded, devastated.

Danailov quickly questioned Security. The cops confirmed that Turkeiev had given the copies to a tall gentleman in a green raincoat. The man had been coming to the gate every hour and people had been bringing him documents that he had taken inside. Maybe he was from the Romanian Embassy, no one was sure. There was always a crowd around the entrance.

Danailov left the intern to stew in his own juices and quickly headed into the building, checking at every step for green raincoats. Varadin lay in wait for him, hidden behind a column in the foyer.

"Where is the speech?" he asked, white as a sheet.

"What? Haven't they brought it yet?" asked Danailov – his surprise was not very convincing.

"No! No! No!" repeated the Ambassador staccato.

"That Turkeiev gave it to some Romanian," said the Counsellor. "He promised to bring it to us."

"Filthy idiot!!!" Varadin punched the column with his fist.

"Well, they still might bring it."

"You wish! What if they don't?"

The Councillor stayed sensibly silent.

Powerless hatred blazed in the Ambassador's eyes. "We've got to find that man!' He cast about in panic. 'The Premier is on in ten minutes. They're going to crucify us."

They're going to crucify you, said the experienced Danailov to himself, but tried to look as though he cared. He described as best he could the supposed Romanian and they ran off in opposite directions to find him.

The numbers flew through Varadin's mind like the balls in a lottery machine. The green raincoat had either been buried or put in a closet, because nobody was wearing outdoor clothing. "Fuck! Fuck!" he added as he ran around in a trance. "I knew something like this would happen! I knew it! Those fuckwits!" The portraits of old British politicians looked down on him with veiled contempt. Suddenly he stopped as though nailed to the spot, as a sinister suspicion dawned on him. Were they lying about this mythical Romanian? Was that not actually some Bulgarian? That fox Danailov! Or the secretive Turkeiev, who always plays the idiot! Or perhaps the pair of them – a criminal duo who planned to bring him down? He returned to the Hall: he was almost certain that the Counsellor had already attached himself to the delegation and was explaining the situation to them, putting him in the worst possible light. But there was no one there. Varadin sighed briefly, then his panic started riding him again; the Premier had stopped listening to the other leaders and was carefully reviewing his notes. He was preparing to take the floor.

Varadin strove to find the Romanians. Their delegation was situated at the other end of the Hall. He left the hall, made the circuit and re-entered. Finally he came across a group of diplomats who nodded to him politely but coldly. No one was wearing a raincoat. Simultaneously, Danailov made an appearance. He quickly scanned those present, then his gaze slid to the piles of documents scattered across the tables. Their eyes met. Danailov shrugged.

"Ask them!" hissed the Ambassador.

"They'll laugh at us," the Counsellor whispered.

He was right, dammit!

They separated again and continued the search. Varadin began to look in all sorts of crazy places: behind curtains, vases, armchairs, even in the rubbish bins. He gave the impression of an agent looking for a time-bomb in the last minute before detonation. Security followed his actions with increasing concern, until a young man with an unobtrusive headset approached him decisively.

"Can I help you, sir?" he asked unceremoniously.

Varadin stared wildly at his well-shaven, pink face. Could he actually help him? At just that moment the Prime Minister's name flew from the hall with a sound like the awful beat of the gong announcing the Second Coming. His body wavered. The agent lightly took his arm.

"Your Excellency!" he exclaimed, frightened: he had obviously already managed to read his ID badge.

Varadin heroically maintained his equilibrium, and uttered what was appropriate in such complicated situations, "99"

"I beg your pardon, sir?" the agent raised his eyebrows.

"99"

"Ah!" he smiled, happy that he had understood the meaning of the foreign words purely from the other's expression. "The toilet! This way, please." And he pointed to the end of the corridor.

Varadin headed mechanically in the direction indicated.

The agent shook his head and slowly pronounced, "De-ve-de-se-di-de-vit."

Foreign languages were amazing.

What was this strange and beautiful place? Varadin asked himself curiously. How did I get here? The narrow cubicle gave him a feeling of security. The walls, the tiles, the ceiling shone with cleanliness. It was warm and smelled lovely. The water murmured gently beneath the lid. 'I'm in the closet!' the thought occurred to him. Just a second before he had said the blessed number '1' He was calm now. Suddenly, his eye was caught by a stack of paper balanced on top of the cistern. It didn't look like toilet-paper. He read the title. Adrenalin whipped his brain once more.

The Premier's speech!

The fucking translation of the fucking speech in all fifty fucking copies here in the closet!

The door of the cubicle opened wide and the frame was eclipsed by the impressive silhouette of an elderly lady. She had carefully styled hair and a beautiful, cruel face. She frowned and tightened her lips like a matron in a Victorian girls' school.

"You naughty boy!" she waggled her finger at him and slammed the door.

Wasn't that Lady Thatcher? he asked himself, his jaw on his knees.

With a few skilful jumps Varadin reached the corridor, hugging the priceless sheets to his chest, and stared at the little-shoe cartoon on the toilet door in embarrassment, it was a female shoe.

He rushed to the hall. At the entrance he ran into Danailov.

"So you found them!" he exclaimed and helpfully took the entire stack.

"I found them!" Varadin snapped.

'Just in time!'

"What?!" Varadin shook himself. "Hasn't he started speaking yet? I though I heard them announce his name."

"They announced that he was going to speak after the interval," Danailov said.

Those words seemed to caress the Ambassador's spirit like an angel's feather. It was the most beautiful thing that had happened to him in the last two days. Even the vindictive Danailov seemed benevolent in that brief moment..

"Take care of distributing the Premier's speech!" he said after the moment of sudden and undeserved bliss had passed.

He puffed out his chest and brushed off last traces of ill-humour and re-joined the delegation with the grace of a well-groomed lion.

16

The hotel Athenaeum was to be found at the lower end of Piccadilly, opposite Green Park – a modern construction wedged between Victorian mastodons. There was a pizzeria nearby, out of which drifted strains of jazz. On the other side of the street loomed the shadowy colossus of the Ritz. Katya had never been inside, just as she had never been near the Athenaeum before, but it seemed to her that were the Ritz to fall, the foundations of the world must have crumbled. There were certainly no strippers running around in the Ritz.

A few marble steps led to the entrance. The girl on reception could be seen through the glass doors, in the glow of the yellow lights pouring over her. The foyer looked deserted. In the twilit gloom, one could make out some well-tended, decorative plants. The porter shot her a suspicious look, but allowed her in, even tipping his top-hat. The girl behind the polished mahogany desk looked up and stared at her. Her hair glowed like a swiss-roll made of copper threads. On her lapel there was a name-badge: Mary-Jane. Behind her, the huge bank of pigeon-holes for the keys. Though for years now they had held only magnetic key-cards.

"Room 365," said Katya, and waited to see what would happen.

Mary-Jane had obviously been informed of her imminent arrival. She lifted the internal phone and dialled a number, without removing her gaze from Katya.

"The lady is here," she informed the other end emotionlessly.

A short command followed.

"Go straight up," the receptionist nodded towards the lifts.

Her heart started beating faster. She had reached the final

straight. She stopped briefly in front of the enormous mirror installed near the reception and stared at her reflection. Then she headed for the lifts. The numbers above the door quickly changed as the lift moved between floors. It stopped at the third, went on up to the sixth, and then set off downwards. The doors swished silently open. The lift was empty.

The thick carpet deadened the sound of her steps. Katya headed down the corridor, hypnotised by the number-plaques on the doors. At the end of the day, she was not obliged to do it. She could still turn back. But she did not turn back. 361, 363, 365. The door was no different from the rest. She stood in front of it for a few seconds, as though she was waiting for it to open of its own accord. No sign. No sound. She knocked. Nothing. She turned the knob and went in.

The room was simply yet tastefully furnished, which gave a touch of class to its regular visitors. The beige wallpaper gave a feeling of warmth. The bedside light was on.

The man was sitting in the armchair, his legs carelessly crossed, reading a newspaper. He was wearing black trousers with a sharp crease. From outside, the half-muted rumble of traffic on the street drifted in. It was exactly 11 o'clock.

"Hi," she said. "I came."

Barry put down the newspaper, "Hi." He was in no hurry to speak. He just looked at her.

"And?" she smiled awkwardly.

It suddenly struck her that this could be a trap. And she had taken the bait like a dumb carp. She was overcome by fear.

"Listen carefully, Kate," he started unexpectedly. "After one hour you must leave the hotel. There are two ways you can go about it. The first is to leave as you came – an ordinary girl. The other is to leave as a princess. Your choice."

"What is expected of me?"

"For starters, put on the clothes that are in the wardrobe."

She shrugged. Getting dressed, and undressed – a considerable part of her life had been spent on those activities. It was no big deal, but clearly paid well. Now she felt even surer of herself, because it seemed that things were taking a turn closer to her expectations. A simple black dress hung from the hanger. An unsealed pack of tights and a pair of high-heeled shoes, also black, completed the outfit. She got dressed and instantly realised that the dress cost a considerable sum. As though it had been made not just to be put on but to be worn as a demonstration of the idea of the general inequality between people. It was the first time she had ever put on such a dress. The shoes made her a few centimetres taller. She suddenly felt awkward, as though she had entered another body without permission. She moved woodenly to the centre of the room and stood before her client, as she had already come to think of him.

"Good," he nodded, and pointed to the chair in front of the mirror, 'Sit down.'

He pulled a pearl necklace from his pocket and put it around her neck, without demonstrating any feeling whatsoever. The pearls were cold.

"I'll need to make you up." Barry opened some sort of bag and took out a make-up case. "I assume you don't mind?"

She said nothing. He obviously knew what he was doing; he was business-like and precise, like a professional make-up artist. He reinforced some features, reduced others and put others into the background. He gave her complexion that golden tan that only people from the upper classes possess, and rouged her cheekbones, which had suffered from ordinary food and bad air.

"Hey, you're not some kind of designer are you?!" she could not help but ask.

"Yeah, the Head of Make-up for the RSC," he answered casually.

"Yeah, right," she threw back at him.

Barry looked at her with obvious pleasure and said, "Close your eyes."

She obeyed.

"And you're not to look," he warned her. "Otherwise you'll ruin the effect."

"I won't. Get on with it!"

Barry carefully put her hair up in a net, then put some sort of wig on her head – a feeling that she could never mistake for any other, and which she did not particularly like. He pulled it this way and that and then told her to open her eyes.

She shouted in surprise. She instinctively went to remove the wig but he caught her wrists and lightly, almost tenderly, pushed them down.

"I wonder," said Barry, "if anyone has ever told you how much you resemble the late Lady Diana Spencer?"

Katya stared dumbfounded at her new face. "No," she whispered.

"I'm telling you!"

"I feel horrible," Katya confessed. "She's dead."

"I'm not so sure any more," Barry shook his head.

From the depths of the mirror, the face of the Princess of Wales regarded them in surprise, with a hint of repulsion, as though not wanting to accept the fact of this cheap resurrection.

"Stand up!" he ordered.

Katya stood up.

"Walk!"

She started to walk from one end of the room to the other. The miracle had happened.

"Take this," Barry, gave her a small flat black handbag. "A Lady never walks with her hands empty."

Then his face suddenly soured. "Take that off!"

"Why?" she asked, looking at her nice plastic watch, with its big face.

"SHE would never wear such a thing," Barry spat. "The Princess had only the finest things."

Wow, crazy bastard, she thought to herself; she pulled her

hand through the elastic strap and let him put a slender, golden ladies wristwatch in its place. He had thought of everything!

"That's better," Barry sighed.

Were there no real British girls for that purpose? Katya wondered, as he contemplated her in speechless admiration. Now he'll pull it out and start to masturbate, she tried to guess at what was to come. That, however, did not happen and she continued to stand awkwardly in front of him, clutching the elegant handbag. Really, how come no one had ever noticed the resemblance, why had she herself not seen it? Was she blind? And how on earth had Kamal Dalali missed the opportunity to profit from that chance: to show the Princess naked?!

"Time to go," said Barry business-like, and clapped his hands. "Let's move."

"Where?" she asked, frightened.

"We'll drive around a little. Do you like to be chauffeured?"

"I can't go out like this!" she protested.

"You'll wear this." He gave her a thin black headscarf and dark glasses.

Katya obeyed unenthusiastically. "Christ! Everyone will recognise me!" she exclaimed, looking in the mirror.

"You?!" Barry raised his eyebrows. "Who on earth will recognise you?"

"I meant her." Katya was confused.

"Good to see you live your role," he chuckled. "Otherwise, everything goes to hell. Don't forget: he's expecting a princess, and not some screeching street-trash."

"Who?" she trembled.

"The boss," explained Barry, unmoved. "Look, this is only a casting session. He'll judge whether you'll do for the role or not. Do what he says. In my opinion, you've got it, but he has the final say. I just want you to know that whether or not you get the part, you'll receive £100, for your participation."

"Very kind," she said. "And my clothes?"

"I'll bring them, don't worry." Barry quickly gathered up her things into a black bag.

Katya crossed the small foyer of the Athenaeum, followed by Barry, the big black bag slung over his shoulder. Several people turned to look at her. The porter's jaw hung stupidly agape. A long, black, Lincoln limousine was waiting out front. The chauffeur, in a faceless grey uniform, was holding the door open. She slid into the twilit interior of the car. Her escort installed himself in the front seat.

Once her eyes adjusted to the half-darkness, she realised that she was not alone. At the other end of the seat there was a strange individual, with a bowler hat and long black overcoat. Beneath the brim of the hat there was a lively round face with ruddy cheeks. He turned his head towards her and chuckled playfully. "Your Royal Highness," he enunciated grandiloquently. "I am honoured to be able to offer you my hospitality. Would you care for some champagne?"

He leaned forward, took a frosted bottle from the mini-bar and gave it to Barry. Then took out two flutes and a tin of caviar. She now noticed his long, yellow little-fingernail; it looked like a coffee spoon. The cork left the bottle with a cautious sigh. A slight white wisp floated up out of the neck.

The little curtains of the limousine were fully closed. Katya had no idea where they were going. The car stopped and started frequently, which led her to believe that they were still in the centre. But she always liked to know where she was and such a situation bothered her. She was asked most-politely to remove her dress and she complied. She felt silly: totally nude, in only stockings and shoes, champagne in hand. It was not a particularly new experience for her to act in this manner, but in spite of that she still felt somewhat uncomfortable. Maybe it was the fact that she was in the middle of traffic, separated from the outside world by only a door and a thin curtain that led her to feel that way? What if they decided, of a sudden, to throw her out? They did not seem to have any such intentions, however, at least not at this stage. And what's more, the boss's interest in her seemed to have lessened as soon as she removed her clothes. Now he looked more like a bored husband, taking his wife to some society party. From time to time his gaze fell on her and he would raise his glass and encourage her to have more caviar.

"You must eat it all," he had told her at the beginning.

The tin held 150g. It seemed only a little, but with each further mouthful, she realised that that was not the case. It was lukewarm, greasy and heavy. The feeling that she was eating some kind of delicacy diminished and gradually gave way to the feeling that she was swallowing some kind of medicine designed to grease and loosen up her innards. She swallowed a healthy gulp of champagne. Some roe dropped from the spoon and fell on her breasts. He watched her: not so much lustfully as curiously. There were no napkins and no one offered her any. She scooped of the roe with her finger and licked it. Fuck it!

Warm air licked her body like a fine silk veil, blowing from the unseen heating vents. She was tipsy, or perhaps vaguely horny. They had been stationary for some time, most likely stuck in a traffic-jam. She tugged at the curtain to see where they were. She caught a view of the parapet of a bridge, the brown waves of the Thames and another bridge in the distance.

"What are you doing?" shouted the boss. "Put the curtain down immediately!"

Then he lay back on the seat and started to look at the upholstery.

"You haven't finished your caviar. Eat up!" he added softly.

Now I'll have diarrhoea for sure! she thought to herself, scraping the bottom of the tin with the silver spoon. The bottle was also empty. The man appeared to be deep in thought. They had made it off the bridge (maybe Waterloo?!) and were now on the south bank of the Thames. Here the traffic was less dense and the chauffeur made better speed. Katya had the feeling that they were driving down a wide, multi-lane road. Then they turned suddenly. The car slowed and stopped. The boss looked at her and smiled, "It was a pleasure to be driven with you, Your Highness. See you soon." He nodded ironically and got out quickly, slamming the door.

Barry followed and they exchanged a few words.

"Where should we drop you?" he asked once he had got back in.

"Chelsea," she replied shortly.

Katya flew back as the car accelerated. The seat seemed enormous to her. She spread out full-length on it, dropping the flute to the floor.

He turned around and passed the bag to her. "Come on, get dressed!"

"I failed, didn't I?" she asked hoarsely.

Barry gave her an envelope. She opened it and counted the notes, still lying down – £500. Her stomach flipped over, as though the caviar had spawned thousands of little sturgeon.

"We'll call you. Maybe at the beginning of next week." His voice was devoid of feeling.

The car dropped her close to Chelsea Bridge. It was almost one. Katya was once again in her old clothes. Her hair had been messed up by the net and looked like the nest of a marsh-bird. Her thoughts were in a similar state. He was looking at her closely, as though debating whether she was in a fit state to get home alone.

"I'm not sure there will be a next time, Barry," she said, surprisingly clearly.

"Did you find it hard, or was the money too little?" he seemed concerned.

"I don't like it," she shook her head.

"But you're already a part of the game. Whether you like it or not." He stated calmly, "You chose the role of a princess. You have to go through with it."

"What if I say no?" she persisted.

"So you've decided to go back where you came from. Because sooner or later the Embassy will find out about your double-life." He raised his eyebrows. "I don't think they'll be too ceremonious with you, Kate. That's quite a conservative environment. You'll be out on your ear."

"You know quite a lot about me, huh," she said.

"Just a preliminary investigation," he threw it at her. "Welcome aboard."

The little fish in her stomach swam about uneasily. I need the loo! she thought to herself. Barry stood looking after her over the top of the limousine.

17

Today was a big day.

The official entrance to the Embassy was wide open, and the marks of a thorough mopping were still drying on the stairs. The staff were milling about excitedly in the foyer, dressed in their Sunday-best; from time to time, one of them ran to the entrance, looked up the street and returned to the group disappointed.

"Are they coming?"

"No," he replied. "Not yet."

The carriage was scheduled to arrive at exactly eleven o'clock. There was still a long time before then, but the staff were impatient. An event of such magnitude rarely took place twice during one mandate and they wished to live it to the full – like a wedding, or a soldier's send-off. Even their relatives had turned up, armed with cameras and camcorders to record this incomparable spectacle.

The ceremony of the Presentation of the Letters of Accreditation.

The last living witness to such an event had been returned home six months previously, however, the stories he had passed down had left indelible marks in the imagination of the remainder of the staff. For some time they lived in hope of being included in the delegation for the Presentation, until it became cruelly evident that there would be no delegation, and the Ambassador intended to go to the Palace alone. That had been a great blow to the diplomats. Is he ashamed of us, or something? they asked one another acrimoniously. The technical staff gloated. But, in spite of the contradictory feelings that tortured them, they were all animated today, even pleasantly thrilled. The insult had faded into the background. Now Varadin incarnated the National Ideal. He was 'Our Man'. 'Our Man' was going to be received by the Queen with all due respect. A carriage would convey him both to and from the Palace. They would all see Our Man! That was the exciting thing.

The appearance of Varadin in tails, decorated with some shiny, obscure Order, brought sweetness to even the most sceptical soul. What a hero! How handsome! Their hearts swelled with pride. The omnipresent fear of the boss had evaporated. With hitherto unseen audacity, the staff, with their other-halves, crowded around him to have their photos taken as mementos, as if he were a tourist attraction, a wax-work in Madame Tussaud's, or a Horse-Guard at his post. Varadin felt helpless in front of such festive euphoria – he could do nothing except shift his weight from one foot to the other, a silly smile on his face, attempting to keep his spirits up.

At exactly eleven o'clock, the cortège appeared at the top of the street and made its way towards the Embassy. It consisted of two carriages, covered and uncovered, pulled by massive, thorough-bred horses. It was escorted by police outriders. The Major-Domo, Stanoicho waited on the steps, in a pleasant dark-blue blazer, light trousers and a silvery, polka-dot tie that resembled a large, dead fish. A cigarette smouldered in his hand, and he was staring blankly at the passing cars. He seemed to be debating some difficult question, something along the lines of: How did I end up here? Why am I here? Am I actually here or not? The clatter of horseshoes brought him out of his nostalgic reverie. He caught a whiff of fresh manure. One of the horses snorted loudly; Stanoicho stared at the Royal Arms on the doors of the carriages.

In the open carriage sat the Marshal of the Queen's Household, Sir Justin Glough, holding a baton, wearing a glaring white peaked cap, and full dress uniform. One of the footmen quickly jumped down and opened the door for him. The Marshal got out and looked around importantly. Very tall, built like a bear, with a round head and small playful eyes, he bore a striking resemblance to the late Benny Hill, whose former house was only a hundred yards or so from the Embassy.

Stanoicho stared at him, his eyes wide, like a Halloween pumpkin. He had no idea who Benny Hill was, in spite of the fact that he passed the memorial plaque on the side of his former home every day, but he was so overwhelmed by the appearance of the Royal Emissary that he totally forgot to announce his grandiose arrival. For his part, the Marshal stared at Stanoicho, no less impressed.

That, he told himself, must be the Bulgarian Marshal.

The cigarette burnt between Stanoicho's fingers; he flinched and threw it over the parapet. The two Marshals shook hands.

"Dobur den," said Stanoicho in pure Bulgarian, blushed to the roots of his hair, and invited the eminent guest in with a broad Slavic gesture.

Justin Glough bowed slightly. Throughout his long and loyal service, he had seen all sorts of ethnic rituals and nothing surprised him any more.

The first person to notice him was the cook's wife. She gaped in surprise and pointed at him. Varadin instantly shook himself out of his stupor and hurried towards the Queen's Emissary. The others rushed out to see the carriages. A considerable crowd had already gathered in the street outside – passers-by and tourists. The diplomats dutifully arranged themselves in a semi-circle, their faces suddenly enlivened by the sight of the second carriage. Maybe the boss had changed his mind at the last moment? Or maybe it was merely required by Royal Protocol? Who would be chosen?

This fleeting hope was nipped in the bud. The footman informed them that it was in reserve, in case it should suddenly rain. The diplomats were visibly disappointed. Bitterness returned to their hearts in all its poisonous strength. There was no longer any doubt that they had been cut out of the ceremony, like an unwanted and embarrassing appendix. Despite the fact that they were accustomed to all sorts of humiliations, this last insult seemed entirely beyond the pale. The most disappointed was the

Defence Attaché, Colonel Vladimirov. Especially for the occasion, he had put on his brand new dress uniform with piping, which, in his opinion, was just as good as the Marshal's. Could the Ambassador be ashamed of him too, an old veteran?

In the meantime, a Japanese tourist managed to climb nimbly aboard one of the carriages and take some photos of himself, before being hauled off by the cops. The diplomats exchanged bitter smiles – even that opportunity was denied them.

The Marshal and the Ambassador descended the steps with Stanoicho still in tow. Sir Justin was paying the latter an irritating and entirely inexplicable amount of attention, as far as Varadin was concerned. Dozens of cameras and other photo apparatus followed their every move. The Ambassador surveyed his scattered troops and read the bitterness stamped on their faces. Just what they deserved! Did they really think he would drag them all the way to Her Majesty, merely for the show?! He checked their shoes: they were all carefully polished, with the exception of the ragged moccasins of the damn intern. Maybe he was saving his pennies like a mad squirrel?

Sir Justin Glough slapped Stanoicho on the shoulder like an old friend and gave him his hand, "Very nice to have met, indeed!"

Stanoicho strove to think of something appropriate to say. "Dosvidanieh!" he said in Russian, the one foreign language he had any grasp of whatsoever, before Varadin shut him up with a look.

Dammit! The diplomats were chortling spitefully, with the exception of the colonel who suffered silently, eyes downcast. The Marshal looked over his uniform with interest. Then he raised his eyes to the sky, checked it was not going to rain in the next 20 minutes, and invited Varadin to get up into the open carriage.

The big wheels turned on the asphalt.

The same big wheels brought him back to the Embassy two hours later. The reception to celebrate the Presentation of the Letters of Accreditation had begun, and the housekeeper rushed down the steps once more to receive the guests. The instant he saw the

Ambassador, Stanoicho said to himself: This is no longer the same man! What exactly had happened to Varadin during those two hours was difficult to imagine, yet, his entire being glowed with the after-effect of some important and irreversible change. He passed the speechless Major-Domo without so much as looking at him, and walked up the official steps with a slow, ceremonial gait, as though balancing an enormous vase atop his head. In the grand hall, there were some twenty people gathered, chatting casually, glasses in hands – Foreign Office clerks, diplomats from former allied states, representatives of the Bulgarian community and a few strange birds who had flown in somehow or other. The reception was only just starting. Suddenly the conversation dried up and all eyes turned to the entrance where Varadin now stood, pale-faced, his temples damp and pulsing, but the aura of his new-found dignity seeping through the tails he had rented for £18. Those present rushed to congratulate him.

"Your Excellency, I would like to wish you all the best for your shining path in Diplomacy!" Dean Carver, M.P. shook his hand energetically. His face was flushed from the wine.

"Mr Carver!" exclaimed the Ambassador. "I am very pleased to see you."

"I was touched by your kindness. Old connections shouldn't be left to rust!"

"What do you mean? I'm so much in your debt," Varadin protested.

"Are you indeed?" Carver's eyebrows rose.

"The agency you recommended to me," Varadin graciously reminded him. "I think they'll do an excellent job for us."

"Oh, please, think nothing of it,' Carver murmured nobly, whilst depositing his empty glass onto the tray of a passing waitress and snagging himself a fresh one, "Cheers!"

"Mr Ziebling, we were just talking about you!" the Ambassador shouted.

Carver turned his head mechanically. His face emptied of

all character and content, as though it had been drained with a siphon.

"Gentlemen," Ziebling greeted them. "It is an honour to be here in your exquisite company."

He was wearing his usual grey jacket, reminiscent of Chairman Mao, beige trousers and a pair of shoes with shiny buckles. This time the lenses of his spectacles were blue.

"What are you doing here?" whispered Carver.

"Ha-ha, are you surprised?" Varadin was happy. "We don't waste time here, hey? We head straight to our goal! If you'll excuse me for a second! I should go and entertain some of my other guests."

"Amazingly cool-headed!" Ziebling shook his head, turning to Carver. "You'd make a superb adverting agent!"

"I don't know what you are talking about!" the other hissed.

"Come off it, you recommended us to His Excellency, that's quite something!" Ziebling said smoothly.

"I have no recollection of doing any such thing!" Carver objected.

"You even went so far as to give him my card!" continued Ziebling. "I didn't even know you still had it! How did you manage to become so close? How many had you had?"

Blood rushed to the Honourable Member's face.

"How dare you?! It was a terrible mistake!"

"No mistake, my dear!" Ziebling reassured him. "His Excellency oriented himself rather quickly. We came to an understanding in the first instant. He knows exactly what he wants, as opposed to certain people I might mention. Ambitious project! These people aim high, don't you know! They may not have style, but they have scope!"

"Oh, yes!" Carver agreed, crestfallen. "Their old leaders knew how to live. They were true Barons!"

"So, you're up to date, then?"

"Don't try to get me involved!" The Honourable Member pulled back quickly. "I don't want anything to do with it!"

"A favour is a favour," whispered Ziebling, sidling up to him again. "You'll get a 50% discount next time. Our new Britney is an absolute sweetie."

"You evil tempter!" croaked Carver. "Fine, I'll phone you later. Now, I must go, apologize to the Ambassador on my behalf. Goodbye!"

He looked around uneasily and hurried to the exit.

Ziebling briefly drifted aimlessly, then attached himself to one of the tables. He took a piece of banitsa and cautiously took a bite. He nodded in approval.

"Banitsa!" someone exclaimed enthusiastically behind him.

A tall, almost skeletal woman headed towards the table. Her bony hand shot greedily forward.

"A national pastry," she explained when she caught Ziebling's blank look.

"Ba-ni-tsa," he repeated after her, chuckled, and took another piece.

Varadin appeared next to him and said, somewhat uneasily "I hope you are not bored. Where is Mister Carver?"

"Urgent engagements…" Ziebling waved his arm dismissively and added with concern "Your Excellency, I think we should have a talk, immediately!"

"I hope you've not encountered any problems?" asked Varadin.

"Quite the opposite!" Ziebling reassured him. "You will have an unforgettable experience! That's the reason I wanted to ask you to be a little more discreet!"

"Excuse me?" the Ambassador raised his eyebrows.

"Dis-cre-tion!" insisted the other. "That is our main principle. I'd be obliged if you don't inform anyone of our little gathering, or else the event will be automatically called off!"

"Reall-lly?!…" stammered Varadin.

"Exactly! You see, whilst I respect your open style, British society is a great deal more conservative than you'd imagine," Ziebling lowered his voice. "I came especially to warn you. If the media gets wind of this…It's all over!"

"The media only ever see the bad side of things…" the Ambassador frowned. "And they ignore people's successes!"

"Exactly!" agreed Ziebling. "I am so glad we think alike. Formal and informal contacts should never be mixed. They are two parallel dimensions. In principle, we avoid such situations, but in your case we shall make an exception."

Varadin blinked blankly. A student appeared next to them with a big tray full of sandwiches. Suddenly the tray tilted dangerously to one side.

"Oops! Be careful!" exclaimed Ziebling.

Katya caught her balance, her gaze not leaving Ziebling. She would have difficulty forgetting him! It was Him!

The imbecile who stuffed me with caviar!

What was he doing here?!

"Hi!" Ziebling said easily. "Do you work here?"

"Yes," she dropped her gaze.

"Do you know each other?" asked Varadin uneasily.

Ziebling ignored the question. He picked up a sandwich, examined it critically and said, "You see, these sandwiches distance you from Europe."

Varadin gazed at Kosta's culinary creation and was forced to admit (deep within himself) that it was chunky.

"I'm not a snob," Ziebling shook his head. "Even though I come from a good family, I value the virtues of the simple life. As far as sandwiches are concerned, however, the British have some sacrosanct standards that your cook would do well to learn. The size of the sandwich is inversely proportional to the host's position in society," continued Ziebling ruthlessly. "You'll notice that the more exclusive the society you are in, the smaller the sandwich. The outside is cut away until only the kernel remains, so to speak, which is often so small as to be inedible with fingers alone, and one is forced to use a cocktail stick. There are, naturally, some places where they simply disappear, leaving only the idea of a sandwich, and in reality they only serve brut champagne in extremely fine-cut crystal glasses. Not that I would suggest such a thing to your good self," Ziebling hurried to clarify. "Let's not forget that it is the sandwich which should reflect the status in society, not vice-versa. In this context, some not very well thought out small canapés might be mistakenly interpreted as evidence of stinginess or nouveau-rich attitudes. That is why one should not rely too heavily on the good sense of one's cook! One should, therefore, collect samples from other cocktail parties, at every possible occasion – if not personally, you should give the task to some member of your staff; measure them, compare them, classify them into groups, take notes – in this way, before you know it, you will begin to grasp the logic of various sandwich formats, and thus, you will develop an idea of how your own sandwiches should look."

Ziebling swallowed the ugly sandwich in two bites, and washed it down with wine. Varadin's mouth hung stupidly agape. He felt incapable of differentiating the truth from the joke. The guests swarm around them and only few limp lettuce leaves remained on Katya's tray.

"At the beginning of this century," added Ziebling. "An Ambassador, by the name of Emilio Barbarescu, studied the English sandwich throughout two consecutive mandates. His treatise, entitled On the hierarchy of diameter, was never published, but copies continue to circulate in the diplomatic community. If one, by chance, should come to your possession, read it at all costs!"

So saying, he ceremoniously took his leave.

18

Dale Rutherford was responsible for the fauna of Richmond Park. This was a pleasant occupation, involving many walks in the great outdoors and communication with nature. Dale Rutherford loved animals and especially the small groups of ducks, which nested around the edges of the Pen-ponds. That is why he was confused when, one morning, heading for the small lakes, he didn't hear their merry quacking.

The poor little things, he said to himself touchingly, where can they have got to?

In the park there were various smaller lakes, where the fowl sometimes went to swim around for their amusement. The closest one was called Sheep's Leg, but there was not the slightest sign of his favourites there. Eaten by vague worry, Dale hurried down the bridle-path to the Isabella plantation, where, amongst the orchids, laurel bushes and other decorative flower-beds, three small ponds lay hidden. Disappointment also awaited him there, however, if one excluded one lazy swan, who was regally rearranging his plumage. Now seriously worried, Dale left the Isabella plantation and made for a very little known pond by the gloomy name of' 'The Gallows'. Three geese swimming there started to hiss in hostility as soon as they saw him. He suddenly realised that the whole environment had its hackles raised, ready to defend itself against unwanted intruders. The trees had closed in, whispering amongst themselves and the deer ran around the park as though bearing unpleasant news.

Dale pulled out his mobile and called Ray Solo, head of security.

"Ray," he said weakly. "I've cause to believe something terrible has happened..."

"What's wrong?" Ray's voice sounded stressed.

"My ducks have disappeared," sobbed Dale. "My little ducklings!"

Ray Solo had just been reaching for the packet of biscuits, he liked to dunk one in his morning coffee. The news made him temporarily forget about the biscuits and he mechanically dipped his two fingers in the boiling liquid beneath him.

"Christ!" Ray yelled in pain.

The day was starting badly.

After overcoming their initial stress, the management of the Park took some over-energetic measures. They immediately contacted the police, who immediately sent out an impressive investigation team. They mobilised every available officer, and the latter then searched the park to the last square inch. The result of these sizable operations, however, was not particularly forthcoming. A handful of feathers and tracks from chunky wellingtons were found on the right bank of the Pen-ponds. The only fact confirmed with certainty was that the entire population of ducks had disappeared. By evening the grim tidings had made the rounds of the whole of Richmond, had been through Twickenham and Kingston-upon-Thames, and even made it as far as Teddington.

The ducks of Richmond Park had disappeared!

People's strong reaction forced the management to call an urgent press conference. The hall of the cafeteria, where this event took place, was filled to overflowing: journalists, members of the Board of Directors, local councillors, representatives of Green organisations, as well as some ordinary members of the public, all wanting to know, immediately, the fate of the birds. There was also an entire class from the local school, who had become the birds' sponsors the previous year. And, of course, Dale Rutherford. He looked as though he hadn't slept a wink. He sat in the front row next to Ray Solo, drawn and pale, though his eyes blazed, thirsty for revenge.

The President of the Board, Jeremiah Kaas, opened the conference mournfully, "Citizens of Richmond, honoured guests! The reason for this conference is already known to us all – unfortunately, bad news travels fast. For now, I am only able to confirm what we all already know: the ducks of Richmond Park have disappeared, whereabouts unknown. I assume that you have many questions. Here with us is Dale Rutherford, in charge of the Park's fauna, Ray Solo, the head of Security, as well as Detective Nat Coleway, from Scotland Yard, who is heading the investigation. I'm sure that these gentlemen will be able to satisfy your curiosity better than I can. If you please, gentlemen."

Jeremiah Kaas stepped back discreetly and, once the three men had taken their places, quietly mingled with the crowd.

The old fox knows when its time to go, Ray muttered to himself, looking the most dispirited of them all.

"Mr Rutherford!" A small man in a green suit immediately jumped up. "Kenneth Bowl, Twickenham Star. Rumour has it that the ducks were killed by feed that was past its sell-by date. The Twickenham Star has reason to believe that the bodies of the ducks were buried somewhere nearby to cover up the gaffe."

The hatred of the people of Twickenham for their richer neighbours from Richmond was well known, but this time it had gone beyond all reasonable limits.

"I categorically deny any such insinuations!" Dale's voice trembled in indignation. "I personally oversee the feeding of the birds and can assure you that we never give them anything that is beyond its sell-by date. I have the documentation to prove it!"

"Susan Tipper, Richmond Press." A short-haired, ash-blonde woman, in a stylish beige jacket, stood up. "Mr Rutherford, is it possible that the ducks may have suddenly migrated owing to worsening ecological conditions?"

"I strongly doubt it," replied Dale coldly. "I believe that I know the character of these ducks better than anyone. And I can assure you that they felt entirely at home in their habitat."

"Detective Coleway, what is the police's take on the incident?" the new question came in a flash.

Nat Coleway's thick brows furrowed, and he said tiredly, "I think we're dealing with a robbery."

He did not like long speeches, and the attention surrounding the incident was also annoying him. He did not feel remotely as though he had found the winning lottery ticket.

"How many ducks are missing?"

The detective blinked helplessly. Dale rushed to his aid, "Forty-five."

The hall filled with a judgemental and hushed muttering, that sounded like breaking ice. Then an enraged voice was raised, "How is it possible for so many ducks to be stolen at once without Security so much as noticing?!"

Glares focused on Ray Solo, who had stayed wisely silent up until this point. His wide face blushed deeply. He smiled awkwardly and spread his hands. At that moment Nat Coleway intervened, "As far as we can tell, the ducks were drugged beforehand. That probably took place after the Park's closure. The hit-men stayed hidden in the bushes of the Botanical Gardens near to the Pen-ponds. Then they gathered up the birds and made off under the cover of darkness."

This new revelation dropped like a bomb. The journalists hurried to take notes. Nat looked over the auditorium with the bitter realisation that he'd lost control. He had drawn his conclusions from the fact that they had discovered some ears of wheat that had been dipped in Lidocaine, near to the ponds. He had to save those spicy details, however, in the interest of the investigation.

"What, in your opinion, might be the motive for such an abominable act?" cried an old lady, whose hat looked suspiciously duck-shaped.

Nat Coleway coughed into his fist, and said without feeling, "To eat them."

"To eat them?!!" Her mouth dropped open in horror before she could cover it with her hand.

The assembly stared, sickened, as though the mere thought of such a thing was an outrageous attack on society's mores. The figure of the Inspector suddenly darkened; it was no longer reliable, but guilty of the crudeness of spirit and secretive malevolence of the lower classes. If he can think of such a thing, he could do such a thing. This frightful thought afflicted the most delicate amongst them. Then a youthful voice tore through the grey veil of despair like the carillon of church bells, "Do you think, sir, that these monsters will be caught quickly?"

The voice belonged to the young scout, Todd Robins. The presence of his youthful French teacher, with an arse like a horse, intoxicated him and made him want to shine with courage and nobility.

"Yes," replied the Inspector laconically.

He felt that the public wanted more, but suddenly felt totally empty himself. As though he had spent the last penny from his purse. He had no more.

Ray Solo sat silently, his head bowed.

"They won't get away with this so easily," called out Dale Rutherford unexpectedly. "We've a small surprise in store for them too, which they won't like at all."

Nat Coleway reacted instantly: he grabbed Dale by the elbow and hissed in his ear, "Are you trying to ruin everything?!"

"What do you mean Mr Rutherford?" Kenneth Bowl of the Twickenham Star instantly jumped in.

Dale pulled himself together by force of will alone, and said, "All in good time."

19

The cook had had a bad day. When he had finished his culinary duties, he was effectively free and could mess about as much as he liked. Which obviously annoyed the Ambassador. Varadin ordered him to paint the bathroom and the toilet at the residence. The cook was deeply displeased by this unusual task, but had little say in the matter. From time to time he found some excuse to go to the Embassy to check on the freezer. The battered old chest rumbled deeply in the depths of the kitchen, its lone red eye flickering. Having verified that all was well, the cook would then lock up the kitchen and return to his brush. He tried to phone Chavdar in the evening, but got no answer. And his mobile was switched off. *The evil bastard's hiding!* He knew that when things slow down, they often head for disaster. The whole business with those ducks had looked dodgy to him from the very start, which was why he had wanted his share up front. They had duped him. Now he had a load of ducks but not a single penny in his pocket. His salary had run out two days previously. They were living off the remains of the last reception and the small savings that Norka managed to squirrel away.

Chavdar Tolomanov called the following day, in the afternoon. It was evident from his voice that he was not doing so of his own volition, but because some extreme circumstance forced him to. He was against the wall. He sounded frightened. "We have to meet up straight away!" he said quickly.

"What's up?" asked Kosta, all his awful premonitions crowding round.

"I'll explain, come over! I'm in the bar of the Consort, you know where it is, right?"

He knew. The Consort hotel was directly opposite the Embassy. It was owned by a Serb, for whom Chavdar had worked for ages, until they had eventually become friends. The hotel looked no different from the other well-maintained facades on that side of the street. It was equally unremarkable on the inside, although well kept; it was patronised by middle-of-the-road tourists, and Balkan citizens who found themselves in London for a variety of reasons. It was reputed to be a nest of spies, and the diplomats avoided it as a rule. But that was not the case for the staff. In the Consort one could find work on the sly, trade in various small items, and on the whole it was a priceless source of supplementary income.

"Your health, Simich!" Kosta waved to the barman, who was mixing some cocktail behind the enormous bar.

"Good day," Simich nodded.

He was a strong, blue-eyed, horse-faced Serb. He was wearing a short-sleeved shirt, with a black bowtie and played with his cocktail-shaker as though it were a hand-grenade. It was rumoured that Simich was wanted for crimes he had committed in Bosnia, but that did not stop the cook from providing him with cheap cigarettes from the Embassy. Simich always paid cash. Chavdar was sat at a small table near the window. The bar was half-empty. The cook approached like a black thundercloud. His hands were spotted with paint.

"Have you got the cash?" he asked.

"Sit down," Chavdar nodded.

The cook sat down unwillingly, the question still in his eyes. The actor looked worried and pale. He looked around and said in a low voice, "They nailed Batushka!"

"What?!" the cook's eyes popped out of their sockets.

"They nailed him," Chavdar repeated.

"How do you know?"

"Here, look at this!" Chavdar pulled out a paper and opened it before the cook's eyes.

"Hmmm," he mumbled; the headlines meant nothing to him. Chavdar pointed to a picture in the top right-hand corner, and read the following text, 'Crime Wave strikes the West after Fall of Berlin Wall. Yesterday, at 6.30 pm, whilst leaving the Vodka restaurant, Azis Nikolayevich Asadurov, a citizen of the former USSR, was shot. Asadurov owed money to the Russian mafia, and had been hiding in the UK, according to police sources.'

The face in the picture bore a striking resemblance to their mutual acquaintance. But Kosta was not convinced, "Are you sure it's him?"

"Hundred percent!" the actor was agitated. "I haven't been able to contact him for the last two days. He's disappeared off the face of the Earth. I knew there was something about him. He was so secretive."

That was the actual truth of the matter. The personal life of Batushka was hidden in murky fog. Chavdar had no idea where he lived, nor even what his real name was. They had met in the Russian restaurant. Mobiles had been the only link between them.

As they were hiding in the Botanical Gardens, he had regarded his accomplice's angular face and asked himself why he was getting involved in such chicken-feed deals when he was obviously destined for much greater ones. But then, as they gathered the drugged ducks from the ground and stuffed them into the bags, he realised that Batushka saw no difference between the robbing of the Bank of England, the hijacking of the Trans-Siberian Express, and poaching in the public park. He had known the wasteland outside the law, and nothing else interested him.

"What are we going to do now?!" cried the cook.

Chavdar rustled the paper and showed him another headline, "It's on about us here!"

"What does it say?" asked the cook worriedly.

"BARBARIC ATTACK IN RICHMOND PARK"

"Shhh..."

"Don't worry! It says here, 'the investigation is bogged down.'"

"Well, I'm not so sure," Kosta was gloomy. "We're done for. Did you bring the money?"

"What money?!" exploded Chavdar. "Batushka promised to get a deposit from the Chinese. But what we planned and what actually happened..."

"Get it yourself!"

"I don't know them. They were his people."

The cook clenched his fists instinctively. He wanted to smash Chavdar's face in. "And what the fuck are we supposed to do with these ducks now?! And your mother!!" he hissed maliciously. "You got us into this mess!"

"How come I'm to blame?" retorted the actor indignantly. "They're in no danger of going off, are they?"

"They can't stay there forever!" Kosta shouted.

"We'll shift them, mate!" Chavdar reassured him. "Bit by bit, here and there."

"Won't the Serb buy them?"

"I'll talk to him," said Chavdar, nodding. "You ask at our restaurant."

"Well, at least we're not going to starve," moaned Kosta, his voice laced with a hidden threat.

Chavdar threw him a frightened glance. "Hey, pal, we're still partners aren't we?!"

The cook said nothing. He suddenly felt a surge of power. He was in control of the situation. He had both the ducks and the knife. Fucking actors!

20

"Do come in, Mister Mavrodiev," said the Ambassador in a mock-flattering voice.

The big man walked heavily towards his desk. The Consul had just finished his night-shift: he was unshaven and his tie hung loosely. Scum! thought Varadin.

"I assume that you are aware of this publication?" he disgustedly raised the page of the Evening Standard which lay on his desk. In the upper corner of the page, a not overly large article had been outlined in yellow highlighter, accompanied by a photograph of epic significance. The picture showed a destitute family of four, wrapped in sleeping bags, candles in their hands. The photograph was reminiscent of the suffering of the Bosnian refugees, except that it was set in an apartment in central London.

The headline needed no commentary, Bulgarian Diplomat Stuck in the Stone Age. The article detailed the struggle of the Bobevs to survive for the last two weeks without electricity. 'This barbaric measure was taken by the new Ambassador, Dimitrov, in an attempt to push the Diplomat onto the streets, after he had been sacked for political reasons.' The newspaper went on to comment, 'No one has the right to stop the supply of electricity without the authorisation of the London Electricity Board.'

The material had been published the day before. Varadin sensed the secret delight of his inferiors, and was tortured by the suspicion that they had allowed him to be exposed on purpose.

"What should we do?" asked the worried Consul.

"Why are you asking me? This comes under your remit."

"We'll not get out of this one easily," Mavrodiev shook his head.

"Shall we cut off his water too, then, hey?!" the Ambassador hissed.

"If you say so...." agreed the Consul unconvincingly.

"You're obviously trying to tar my image," Varadin said with sinister calm.

Mavrodiev blushed to his neck under the accusation.

"That is what you all want, I know!" The Ambassador's outburst took his listener by surprise. "Why did you tell the journalists that he doesn't want to go back to his homeland, why?"

"But isn't that the whole reason for this circus – about staying here?" said the Consul in confusion.

"The fact that he wants to stay here does not specifically mean that he doesn't want to go back!" Varadin spelled this out angrily.

"Why would he not want to go back if he doesn't want to stay?"

"Because he wants to stay!" the Ambassador stamped his foot. "And not: he wants to stay because he doesn't want to go back, as you made out."

"So he wants to stay because he wants to stay."

"Exactly! He wants to stay because he likes it here. But when you say, he doesn't want to return! People start to ask, why? Why on earth would someone not want to go back to their homeland? Well, simply: because he'll be thrown out on the street immediately and then be unable to find work. And even if he does find some, he'll still starve!"

"I didn't say that," Mavrodiev sighed heavily.

"Yes, but it's obvious in context."

"And? We all know that!" The big man could not restrain himself.

"You have no right to think that way!" shouted the Ambassador. "We are all Europeans here!"

"So shall we put his electricity back on?" the Consul clutched at an unexpected straw.

"What the hell for? He's already put us in it, hasn't he? Let him struggle if he's so obstinate." Something clicked in his brain, and he suddenly asked, "Why have you always got your hands in your pockets?!"

'Well, I mean, I'm....' stumbled the Consul.

'Not just now, but during the reception as well,' continued Varadin impatiently, 'I saw you, don't deny it! That is not European behaviour!'

'I'm sorry, if...' started the other.

'I want you to throw him out without any more scandal!' Varadin cut him off, tapping the paper with a finger, 'Otherwise I'll throw you out instead! You may go.'

He carefully folded the page and returned it to his drawer. He did not particularly want the article to end up in the press review, but he was certain that some helpful hand had already faxed it to Sofia. And? So what? Varadin massaged his temples. Rubbish! Rubbish everywhere!' His gaze fell on some small scraps near the foot of the desk, he picked them up and threw them in the bin. The room had not been cleaned for several days.

Fuck it! That little slut – he should have sacked her. His brain told him this. But his brain was helpless in this instance. And all for one very simple reason: he had not had any sex for several months, and whenever he thought of Katya, he had an instant hard on. In a better world, the problem would have been quickly solved by a short trip to the bathroom. But, he was the product of a cruel system: despite the political changes of the last few years, the idea that someone was constantly watching him had driven itself deep into his subconscious and no one would ever get it out now.

His hands were tied.

All that was left for him was to hope that something might actually happen in the real world. That seemed less punishable to him, as well as far less compromising. He was prepared to take that risk, but, for that end, Katya needed to be kept around. Until then every other comfort was forbidden.

He raised his gaze from the bin and noticed the stupid face of

Turkeiev, peering around the door. He had not heard him knock.

"What is it?" he asked. "Come in then!"

"There's a fax for you..." started the intern, giving him the sheet.

Varadin read it angrily.

Sent. 34500456
Town Council, Provadia.

Dear Mr. Ambassador,

From 24/05 to 24/06, on the invitation of the British Museum, the unique exhibition: 'Hygiene in Bulgarian Lands' will arrive in London; on which platform the first Water Closet in Human History will be unveiled. The latter was discovered in recent archaeological digs in the territories of the town of Provadia, and dates from 923. The authenticity of the object has been confirmed by such internationally renowned scientists as Professor Van Meis, from Holland, and Professor Charlie Reeds, from Oxford. We believe that the public recognition of this achievement of the ancient Bulgarians will greatly support the new image of our dear Homeland. The exhibition will be opened by the Mayor of Provadia, Mister Firstomaiev. We would be obliged if the Embassy could arrange accommodation for him and involve itself actively in the preparations for the event in question.

"Whaaaaaaat?! To involve ourselves with some toilet?!" Varadin raised his eyes from the fax and stared at the intern with loathing. "This falls on exactly the same day as Mrs Pezantova's concert! Do you realise what that means?"

"Is there no way to combine the two?" the intern proposed simply.

"Concert with Closet, eh?!" spat Varadin sarcastically, "Well, you can try..."

"After all, such a discovery!"

"Look, I'll tell you what," the Ambassador cut him off brusquely. "We have priorities! And Mister Firstomaiev's WC is not amongst them."

"What should I tell them?"

"Nothing for the time being," he spat. "Why are your hands in your pockets?!"

"What?" the intern threw up his hands in surprise.

"Not now!" explained the Ambassador nervously. "Before, and during the reception, I saw you wandering around with your hands in your pockets like some kind of Director. You and that other one, the Consul. That is not European behaviour!"

For fuck's sake! the intern swore internally. His contract ran out in two months and he did not see it being extended. "But the English go around with their hands in their pockets."

"Are you an Englishman, all of a sudden?!" shouted the Ambassador. "When you are an Englishman, then you can talk!"

The intern headed for the door without a word. Varadin stared at the fax once more. That was all he needed, that cretin from Provadia! Pezantova would have a fit. Concert and Closet. Absurd!

"Wait!" he shouted before the intern was out of the door. "Check whether it has the approval of the Ministry of Culture. And of our Ministry too!"

He had a sharp pain at the nape of his neck. It seemed to him monstrously unfair, that, whilst he was flying freely amongst the highest levels of society and creating Foreign Policy, those spiders were still trying, tirelessly and unpunished, to weave together the cobwebs of their domestic idiocies. It was impossible to be rid of them, one could only keep them at a distance, in the corners and holes where they belonged. Ah, but he was very good at that!

"88" he said grimly.

21

The radioman, Racho, was staring at the steeple of St George's and chain-smoking. The metal shutters were wide open and a refreshing breeze blew in from the outside. The radioman was thinking that if they put an antenna on the steeple then their connection to Central would be vastly improved. The session had finished only ten minutes before. There had been some atmospheric interference and the transmission had taken longer than usual. The signal swung drunkenly on the oscilloscope screen, and the information flowed at the speed of glue through the eye of a needle. In spite of that, he had managed to process the material arriving from Sofia, as well as sending it to the Press Review, along with two short telegrams. He had finished for the day, unless some urgent cryptogram came through. But the likelihood of that was slim. There were still three cigarettes in the pack of Marlboro. There were another seven packs in the box on the table.

Racho left the communication's room, leaving the door ajar and trundled down the stark white corridor, lit by neon lamps. He was a tall, flabby individual, with a face that said I don't give a damn, behind which sheltered a crafty and calculating mind. He made a quick detour via the kitchenette, put the coffee machine on, and continued down the corridor. The other end of the Secret Sector looked onto the street. The radioman opened a window a little, stared blankly at the passing cars, and then returned, pouring himself a coffee on the way.

The Secret Sector had been constructed during the Cold War: several isolated compartments, insulated against listening devices and all sorts of unwanted intrusions. The windows were fitted with metal covers, and the outside walls were reinforced. This is where the communications hub of the Embassy, as well as the safes containing confidential information, were to be found. According to instructions, in case of enemy attack, the secret service personnel were to lock themselves in and destroy all traces of their activities. To this end, a vast metal furnace had been installed in the central compartment, for burning documents. At various points in the past the furnace had blazed merrily as it burnt tons of potentially explosive information. Now it lay dead. The only inhabitant was Racho the radioman. He burnt various bits of rubbish there, from time to time, to warm himself. Recently, the volume of operational work had dropped sharply, and Racho had very few other duties. That was why he could devote himself entirely to the fat catalogues of duty-free goods available through the Embassy, which he received regularly. Because he lived, for the most part, in the Secret Section, Racho disposed of considerable sums, which the diplomats could only dream of. Here there were no big city temptations and their consequent expenses. Life was simple and healthy, almost as cloistered as a monastery. All capitals are different, but all Secret Sections are alike.

The radioman took a gulp of hot coffee and turned to a small device that he had found in some dusty old trunk containing 'special equipment', which he had inherited from his predecessor. The apparatus, of Soviet manufacture, served to detect listening devices by detecting their transmissions, but hadn't been working for some ten years or more. Racho had a weak spot for electronics, on top of which, he intended to sell the thing in a car-boot sale if he got the chance. In any case, no one took any notice of him. That morning he had plugged it into the charger, to check how reliable the battery was. The needle had showed that it was charging. That was not enough, however. He unplugged it from the charger, put on the headphones and listened. At first, the gadget made a whole heap of chaotic noises, as though cleaning itself from the many years of silence. The radioman regulated the sound-level and adjusted the antenna. Slowly, the noises cleared up, and only one signal remained, chirping like a grasshopper in the distance.

'Well, what have we here, then?' he exclaimed.

Memories from the days of the Cold War, filled with tension and hard work, arose in his mind. His overwhelming nostalgia, however, soon turned to worry. The sound in his headphones reminded him of an active Secret Intelligence Device. Just in case, he turned off all the equipment in the comms. room that might be generating the signal. But the signal did not fade and if anything, became clearer still. Could the Embassy be 'bugged'?

He checked the Secret Sector, with the device over his shoulder, but found no change in the parameters of the signal. The bug was obviously not there. That led him to sigh, because the heaviest responsibility no longer sat on his shoulders. From there on, he was eaten only by his own curiosity. Where the hell are you, you old bitch?!

He went down to the floor below, where the signal became perceptibly stronger. Most of the offices were here, including the Ambassador's, and access was far easier. All sorts of riff-raff came in and out: from Xerox technicians to journalists and dodgy business-men. He would not have been at all surprised if the bug was somewhere hereabouts. He criss-crossed the corridors but found nothing more concrete. The only person about was Turkeiev, who stared at him with fear and respect. He was not obliged to explain himself, but he decided to test the other's ignorance, by informing him that he was measuring 'the electromagnetic background count owing to atmospheric interference'. Turkeiev nodded under-standingly, flattered by this demonstration of trust.

The further down he went, the stronger the signal became in his headphones. Racho checked the reception room, as well as its service rooms, but found nothing. In the foyer, he came across Mr Kishev, to whom he gave the same old story about 'electromagnetic background'. Kishev accepted it without thinking. He had something else on his mind.

Kosta was fussing nervously around the cooker, when the door of the kitchen opened and the radioman entered, headphones covering his ears and some strange device over his shoulder. The cook was neither expecting him nor happy to see him.

"What do you want?" he asked nervously.

The radioman put a finger to his lips and stepped forward. Kosta stepped in front of him, but Racho pushed him aside with a decisive gesture. The cook's knees went weak. With the unerring sensitivity of a compass, the radioman aligned himself with the freezer.

"What's in there?" he asked.

"Nothing," said Kosta, pulling together the last shreds of firmness into his voice.

"Open it!" ordered the radioman.

The cook walked in circles near the freezer, patting his pockets. "Oops, I seem to have forgotten the keys!" he mumbled.

"Listen Pastry," cut in Racho. "I don't know what you're hiding, but I don't believe you want the entire Embassy to know about it? Come on, open the freezer!"

"There's nothing in there, mate! Why're you bugging me?"

"So I should report to the Ambassador then, eh?"

"What are you going to report?" the cook visibly cringed.

"See this little beauty?" Racho said threateningly, "She'll report, not me!"

22

The air in the electronics-stuffed van was stale and Nat Coleway went to smoke in the fresh air. He felt totally useless at this stage of the operation, which otherwise rarely happened to him. Dale Rutherford stayed in the van, thirstily watching the radar, along with two men from the special unit for electronic surveillance that had been created in the last 24 hours. The van was parked in front of the gates of Richmond Park, ready to move out the instant Intelsat-2 received a transmission from the birds.

Ray Solo approached the policeman and cautiously asked him, "How is it going?"

"We are waiting," replied Nat shortly.

Solo had been temporarily relieved of his duties, pending the results of the investigation. The police were working on a theory that someone from Security may have been involved in the robbery.

"Wait until we catch them the filthy bastards!" Ray said darkly.

"How do you know they were more than one?" the detective reacted instinctively.

"I don't," he mumbled.

The door of the van opened and Dale stuck his head out of the van. His eyes burned feverishly. "Coleway!" he shouted excitedly. "We've got a signal!"

Operation 'Duck's Leg' had been launched two years ago at the instigation of Dale himself after a similar incident in which two ducks had disappeared. All traces of them had also disappeared, despite the fact that they had been tagged in the traditional manner with metal rings that showed exactly where they came from. They had never been found. Dale had taken it badly, but he threw all of his energy into convincing the Park authorities to invest a considerable sum in a new high quality system for tracking the birds. He read a great deal about into the latest developments in the field. The result had been a joint project between Dale's department and a leading Oxford biotechnology laboratory. Dale's pets underwent delicate surgical intervention. A microchip was implanted in the ducks' bodies, which would be activated by any dramatic change or cessation of life. The implant transmitted a signal for several days that could be picked up by satellite. In turn the satellite relayed the signal to a mobile radar station that could locate the exact position of the birds. Unfortunately, the project quickly reached its spending limit and the cutting edge microchip was implanted into only ten birds. One of them had been discovered the previous year in the river Thames, tangled in some spirogyra and although Dale was naturally sad, he had a reason to be proud of himself. The system worked. He had another nine high-technology ducks.

"Where are they?" asked Coleway immediately after the door slammed behind his back.

"Here they are!" Dale pointed at the screen.

The detective sceptically gazed at the faint pulsing point of light.

"Shouldn't there be more of them?" he asked.

"They are probably piled together. Poor souls!" whispered Dale.

He twiddled a knob and heart-stopping din roared from the speakers.

"Can we pinpoint their location?" asked Nat business like.

"Unfortunately, the signal is quite weak," one of the men said. "But I'll try."

His fingers blurred over the keyboard. A greenish grid appeared on the screen.

"They are in London," he concluded after a while.

"I knew it!" exclaimed Dale.

"London is fairly big!" Nat cooled his ardour.

"West End," specified the operator. "That's all for the moment!"

"Let's move!" ordered Coleway. "To Fulham!"

He radioed the cars that were waiting in other areas of the capital and told them to regroup in the West End. Nat Coleway was thrilled at the result. He had expected, somewhere in his sub-conscious, that the birds would be found in some far-flung section of the city, packed with immigrants and other lower-class types, who did not know (or rather did not respect) the cultural norms of civilised society. The fact that the ducks were calling from the prestigious West End gave him cause to smile shrewdly. He had grown up in the East End, not far from Whitechapel, in the back-alley where Jack the Ripper had committed his second murder (the victim had been some great-great-aunt). Despite the fact that he had broken with his roots, Nat had maintained his social awareness, which helped him to deal with the underworld in general. That was why he now felt slightly confused. It seemed to him that the only logical explanation was that the ducks were in the kitchen of some Chinese restaurant or other. The Chinese would go to any lengths to drop their prices and aromatic, crispy Peking duck was the cornerstone of their menu. Elementary, Watson!

The bus made slow progress through Fulham. The spinning antenna on its roof drew the attention of passers-by.

"Kensington," announced Dale suddenly. "We're really close! Hold on my ducklings!"

The van turned left in the direction of the Cromwell Road. Nat Coleway radioed his colleagues once more. He remembered a small Chinese restaurant on High St. Ken, with a suspiciously cheap menu and he felt a pang of regret because he himself often dropped by there when he was on duty, to stuff himself to bursting before a long shift. But he couldn't let up now. The net was drawing tighter.

23

"Wow! Loads of chickens!" Racho said once the freezing cloud under the freezer's lid had dissipated.

"They're not chickens," Kosta gloomily corrected him. "They're ducks."

The radioman scratched his head. The noise in his headphones continued its persistent pulsation. "Take them out," he ordered.

"What for?" asked the cook, failing to understand.

"Because you're in the shit."

The cook began to take out the ducks one by one. The radioman listened to each one carefully, looking like a doctor. His actions were a mystery to Kosta, and it terrified him. The frozen ducks were slippery. His fingers were soon numb from handling their frozen carcasses. He got clumsy. One bird slipped from his grasp and escaped under the tables. He crawled after it on all fours, swearing himself blue.

Racho continued to listen, unaffected. Most of his patients were quiet, but from time to time one of them gave itself away with a little squawk, dinning in the headphones and ringing in his skull like a huge wasp. The radioman put the song-birds to one side. That way there were soon two piles, one large, and the other small. There were eight birds in the smaller pile.

"Now what?" asked Kosta stupidly.

"You tell me," the radioman took a bird from the small pile and looked at it from every angle. It was cold and hard as a rock. He looked at the hole between its legs, shook it – nothing. "Give me a knife," he said, turning to the cook.

Kosta gave him the big cleaver. Racho chopped off the greasy yellow parson's nose, and, using the sharp corner of the cleaver, extracted a shiny silver disc that looked like a watch battery.

"What the hell is that?!" asked the frightened cook.

"Looks like some kind of transmitter..." replied the radioman thoughtfully. "Where did you get these ducks from?"

"From the market, where else...!" mumbled the cook unconvincingly.

"Don't lie, Pastry!" Racho cut him off. 'No one down the market puts transmitters up their birds' arses!"

"Errrrrr...Well, you s-see..." stuttered the other.

"You nicked them, eh? Thieving bastard! Where the hell from?"

"It wasn't me!" shouted the poor cook.

"Who was it then?" Racho shouted back.

The cook ended up explaining the whole story. Once he knew where the ducks were from, the radioman grew suddenly nervous. There was no more time to listen. He snatched up the cleaver and extracted the rest of the transmitters.

"I'm amazed they haven't found them yet," he said thoughtfully, as he tossed the bugs in his palm. "Or maybe they have..."

"Shall we destroy them?" the cook suggested bravely. "I've got a mortar and pestle here..."

"No," the radioman shook his head; he had been brought up to love and respect all things technical, and such an unintelligent method of disposing of the bugs disgusted him. "But we have to get them out of here immediately," he added, then asked unexpectedly, "Do you have any bread?"

"Bread?!" Kosta gawped in surprise. "What for?!"

"Get on with it!" urged Racho.

Ten minutes later, the two men casually entered Kensington Gardens by the Gloucester Road entrance. They took the wide path to the oval lake and once there, started to feed breadcrumbs to the ducks and swans near the shore. The birds threw themselves hungrily at the big chunks of bread. Some insolent geese also tried to get in on the action but came too late. Then the clamour died down and the birds dispersed. Cunning satisfaction was written all over the men's faces.

Just then, a van came down the main alley, which they just had taken, a flat spinning antenna on its roof. Then the tall helmets of ten police officers appeared through the trees on the other side of the lake.

"Do you see that?" asked the radioman. "You've escaped that by the skin of your teeth, dumb-arse."

"I don't know how to thank you!" Kosta sighed.

"I'll tell you exactly how..." Racho said, thumping him on the shoulder, and added, "Now let's get out of here!"

Dale Rutherford leapt from the van and raced up to the lake. "My ducklings! My little Ducklings!" he screamed.

Nat Coleway followed him, totally thrilled.

Soon the entire search team assembled on the shore. They tracked down the transmitters, and were soon hunting down the birds with big nets. Dale could not believe his luck. He flapped excitedly, getting under everyone's feet. A large crowd began to gather.

"What d'you think you're doing! Stop at once!" shouted an angry voice.

Dale turned quickly. Behind him, arms akimbo, stood a tall, well-built man in the uniform of the Parks Police. His face was as red as a tomato. "Sir, are you the instigator of this travesty?" he frowned menacingly.

"What travesty?" gasped Dale. 'These are the ducks from Richmond Park that disappeared three days ago."

'Oh really?" The other smiled mockingly. "And I suppose they turn into swans all the time then?" He pointed to a huge white bird that was entangled in a net.

"Hey, you lot, can't you tell a swan from a duck?" shouted Dale to the embattled police who were attempting to deal with the bird.

"There's an implant inside it, sir," an officer said.

"Whaaaaaat?!" Dale's face suddenly fell.

Meanwhile, further Parks Police turned up, and not long after that, the Head Butler of Kensington Palace himself. The two groups faced off. Nat Coleway, seeing the scandal develop before his very eyes, felt the sudden urge to see every duck on the planet hanging upside-down in the windows of a Chinese restaurant. "Listen!" he started, trying to broker some kind of peaceful agreement. "Why don't you just check their leg-rings."

It was done immediately. Dale Rutherford received the news stony-faced. The police checked the birds that had somehow come by the Richmond transmitters. Three swans, four ducks and a goose. The ninth microchip was nowhere to be found.

"So what's the result?" asked someone. "Have the Hyde Park ducks eaten the Richmond ones?!"

Those words were printed all over the press almost instantly.

Hyde Park Ducks Eat Richmond's

Extreme Demonstration of Duck Cannibalism

Ducks and Duck-eaters

Beaked Monsters in Central London

Who Ate The Ugly Duckling?

Beaks – New Subject for Hitchcock

The cook and the radioman did not read the British Press, or watch the BBC. For that reason they had no idea of the after-effects of their covert operation. But they were not vain. It was enough for them that that evening was unusually quiet at home, and that their constantly nagging wives were happily working around their ovens, in which two juicy ducks were tenderly turning golden.

In his lonely quarters, Chavdar Tolomanov opened a tin of cat-food and swallowed it with the last shreds of his pride. Last month's rent had sucked out his last financial juices and his future looked grim. There was no more Batushka, and nothing was working right now. The Serb did not want to hear about any ducks without health certificates. Kosta was acting strangely, and the newspapers were publishing cock-and-bull stories. The cat-food was surprisingly tasty.

Dale Rutherford was left unmoved by the saddle of lamb, served in his favourite dish. His wife Eloise looked at the cooling meal, sad and worried, but did not want to encourage him to eat. If even his favourite dish, had no effect on him – that meant that things were serious! The kids, two in number, had eaten quickly, and sensibly gone to hide in their rooms. A dark, mourning cloud hung over the modest, yet cosy Richmond home. Eloise busied herself to clear the table. Dale stared at the dish as though seeing it for the first time. One niggling thought had been bugging him all this time. Only eight microchips had been found in Hyde Park. Where on earth was the ninth?

24

"I hope you have some good news for me!" sang a capricious female voice in the earpiece.

"Especially good," he agreed. "I was just telling myself that I should phone you. The invitation has been accepted."

"Then the Queen will come!" she shouted ecstatically.

"But we have to be very discreet," he hurried to calm her. "Those are the conditions. The information must not be let out beforehand; otherwise the whole deal is off."

"But I've already said that she'll be there," a note of worry crept into her voice. "Not officially, but, you know, amongst other things..."

"You shouldn't have! Afterwards yes, beforehand no."

"I don't understand, why all the secrecy?" she asked crossly.

"It's an informal engagement."

"What is informal supposed to mean?" a suspicious tremor entered her voice. "It doesn't sound very serious."

"I meant to say personal," he corrected himself quickly, and added in a Zieblingesque tone, "Personal engagements are more important than formal ones."

"Really?!"

"Oh yes, far more important."

"We'll have to explain that to the journalists somehow..." she said worriedly.

"Let's not put the cart before the horse!"

"Everything was okay wasn't it?" Then she remembered and added, "Then again let's not count our chickens..."

"I said let's not put the cart..."

"Look," she interrupted. "I'm fed up! I'm coming in two weeks time and if everything isn't perfect, you'll be sorry."

"Of course everything will be perfect," he assured her.

The line buzzed in his ear for a minute. Then the internal phone rang. It was the radioman.

A coded announcement had arrived from Sofia.

Cryptograms were not allowed outside the Secret Sector, and he had to go up there to read them. These moments particularly annoyed him because every time he went there he saw the hidden triumph of the radioman – that was his moment of power.

Varadin went up to the top floor, entered the code into the electronic lock, waited for it to click and pushed open the metal door. He was struck by the sharp antiseptic smell. Secrecy went with hygiene.

The radioman met him in the corridor and handed him the decoded cryptogram, printed unevenly and in block capitals. Varadin went into a small cubicle set aside specifically for reading and writing confidential information. In this innermost region of the Sector there were no windows and the laboratory smell of antiseptics was even stronger. The long fluorescent bulbs on the ceiling hummed monotonously, like a big overfed bee. In the cubicle a powerful hundred-watt bulb shone, heating it like an incubator. He began to read:

TOP SECRET!!!

WITH REGARD TO THE FORTHCOMING EXHIBITION 'HYGIENE IN BULGARIAN LANDS' WE INFORM YOU THAT IT HAS BEEN APPROVED NEITHER BY THE CUL-TURAL DEPARTMENT OF OUR BRANCH NOR BY THE MINISTRY OF CULTURE. IT HAS BEEN CREATED AT THE INITIATIVE OF THE LOCAL COUNCIL OF THE TOWN OF PROVADIA. THE OFFICIAL EUROPEAN STANCE AS REGARDS THIS QUESTION IS STATED IN THE ENCYCLOPEDIA BRITTANICA, WHERE IT IS WRITTEN THAT THE FIRST

WATER CLOSET WAS INVENTED IN 1596, BY SIR JOHN HARRINGTON DURING THE REIGN OF QUEEN ELIZABETH I. A SURVEY OF ATTITUDES IN DIPLOMATIC CIRCLES, CON-DUCTED RECENTLY, INDICATED THAT THE DISCOVERY IN QUESTION IS REGARDED AS AN INTEGRAL PART OF BRITISH CULTURAL IDENTITY, AND (IN A WIDER SENSE) OF EUROPEAN CULTURAL IDENTITY ALSO. THE QUESTIONING OF SUCH A KEYSTONE OF CIVILISATION, FIRMLY ROOTED IN THE SUBCONSCIOUS OF GENERATIONS OF EUROPEANS, WILL NOT CONTRIBUTE POSITIVELY TO OUR COUNTRY'S INTEGRATION PROGRESS WITH EUROPE, AND MOST LIKELY WILL ATTRACT A STRONG NEGATIVE RESPONSE. WE RECOMMEND THAT THE EMBASSY DISTANCE ITSELF AS FAR AS POSSIBLE FROM THE EVENT AND KEEP ALL CONTACT AT AN INFORMAL LEVEL.

MISTER G DIREKOV

HEAD OF MANAGEMENT COORDINATION AND ANALYSIS.

He rubbed his neck thoughtfully. So there were still brains at work in the Ministry who kept their National Interest in mind. Here was some crafty and cunning clerk, scrabbling to get out. That sensation was well known to him. He himself had scrabbled like mad to get out of his disconsolate office in the Ministry and knew that the result was worth the effort, and the very last drop of humiliation. He had known that sweet stupor of victory, when the posting sleeps snugly in a pocket next to the passport and plane ticket. Then you stop caring all of a sudden, you relax and only move things from one side to another for an entire three years. You earned it, for fuck's sake! Until you land back in your dusty office in Sofia, stuck with your miserable salary again. The holiday is over! And it all starts again: you switch on again, you mobilise all the energy you stored up during your posting and start to run between floors once more; you revive your old connections,

140

you look for new and more powerful patrons, you hang around in front of their offices for hours, you weep, you crawl, you listen constantly, with only one purpose – so they get so fed up of you that they kick you overseas again. The further the better!

After reading the cryptogram at least three times, out of habit, so as to grasp every nuance, Varadin adjoined a short resolution to its upper corner: to be circulated to all diplomatic staff! He signed it and left.

Almost immediately thereafter Mr Kishev ran upstairs: he took in the secret information in one fell swoop and quickly composed a cryptogram of his own. After the fiasco with the Queen he was in a hurry to prove his usefulness, sending secret information to Sofia as much as humanly possible. Usually these missives consisted of things he had read in the local press and presented as priceless gems that he had gleaned from conversations with bureaucratic Mandarins. Sofia, however, was not asleep either; the clerk in charge of information on Great Britain, a sneaky brown-nosed bureaucrat, who dreamed of taking Kishev's place once his posting was over, quickly secreted these missives and sent them back reworked as 'Analyses'. This unusual task fell on the shoulders of the radioman. In revenge, he often removed Kishev's name from his telegrams, prepared with such effort, and sent them with the impersonal: Embassy, London. However, he was actually doing him a priceless favour, because in rare moments of lucidity Sofia would ask itself: which idiot had doubled the Press Review all over again?

***

Katya was in a hurry. She was hoping not to be seen in the office. Working with the new hoover gave her an almost physical pleasure. The clean vibrations from the powerful motor and the hot air flow smelling of engine oil charged the atmosphere with euphoria. 'Red Devil' was written in fiery letters on its shiny bullet-shaped carapace. And it really sucked like a devil! The other students were equally ecstatic about the unexpected acquisition, and no one doubted that it was all thanks to Katya. What had she done to him?! They asked each other slyly.

What could she say? She did not know why the Ambassador had (with no small pleasure!) liquidated the funds that the staff had been gathering for the children's New Year's Party.

The noise of the new machine sounded far more lively than had the roar of the old beast, though no less loud. Which was why Katya did not hear the door open and then discreetly close. Varadin leaned against the wall, staring at the girl's healthy calves. All other thoughts left his mind, as though she had hoovered them up to the last speck of dust. His trousers started to bulge alarmingly; his member was outlined beneath the fine material, thin and pointy like a hound's.

She turned to unplug the hoover. His smile struck her like a lost boomerang.

"I'm terribly sorry," she started to excuse herself, "I've been very busy at the University these last few days. I thought that..."

"Does it suck well?" he interrupted unceremoniously.

"Oh yes, and then some!" she nodded, after overcoming her initial surprise. "We are very grateful indeed!"

He approached her, his gaze not leaving her for an instant, and asked her questioningly, "Red Devil, eh?!"

"Exactly, a real devil!" she agreed, her voice betraying some worry.

Her breasts stretched her t-shirt. She was not wearing a bra. Her breath smelled of fresh mint. Varadin reached out and touched the black hose of the hoover that hung across her shoulder. "I'd like you to clean the residence with that hoover," he said in a seductive tone. "Any objections?"

"Of course not." She smiled, although the idea seemed far from tempting to her, "You'll just have to tell me when, exactly."

"I'll tell you," he said cryptically, "Soon...."

25

THE VETERAN & THE PRINCESS
Scenario by Thomas Munroe
(Famous Connections)

Dramatis Personae:

Diana, Princess of Wales.
Sir Marston, Veteran of the Bosnia Peacekeeping Forces.

> *Military Field Hospital. Interior of a tent. Simple furnishings: canvas bed, battered metal locker, folding chair. Sir Marston is lying in bed, covered with a military blanket. His head is bandaged. There are some crutches leaning near the bed.* **Enter Lady Di,** *dressed in a short white uniform, basket in hand.*

LADY DI: How are we today, my hero?
SIR M: Better, your Highness, thanks to your tender ministrations.

> *Lady Di sits on the chair and opens the basket.*

LADY DI *(serious)***:** They have reported to me that you refused to eat your desert. That surprised me a great deal.
SIR M: But they always give me the same thing here!
LADY DI: Yoghurt is good for your health.

*She takes six small pots (100g) of Danone out of the
basket, each one a different flavour, and arranges them
on top of the locker.*

SIR M *(childish)*: I don't want any yoghurt!

LADY DI *(strictly)*: Come on, stop whingeing! Remember how
you rescued those poor Bosnians from the surrounding
partisans. You're a hero!

*She opens a pot of yoghurt, takes a full teaspoonful and
puts it to his lips. Sir M pulls the blanket up to his nose.*

SIR M: I beg you!

LADY DI: Eat!

SIR M *(hiding beneath the blanket)*: Nnnnnnnnnnoo!

LADY DI *(persuasively)*: Do you want to play a little game with
me? *(Pause. Sir M pokes his head out)* For every little pot you
eat, I'll undo one button of my uniform.

*She puts the spoon to his lips again. He bites it hungrily.
The metal rattles against his teeth. He eats the entire
pot.*

LADY DI: Well done, my hero! *(she undoes the top button of her
uniform)* Shall we continue?

*He nods. She opens the next pot. Sir M swallows the lot
without complaint. She undoes another button.*

LADY DI: Two!

*She is wearing a black bra with transparent cups. Sir
M gapes hungrily. The remaining buttons are equal in
number to the remaining pots.*

"Hey!" shouted Dotty from her bed, "Do you play Diana?"

"What?!" Katya frowned.

Dotty waved the scenario at her. "Yoghurt's good for your health. Do you want to play a little game?" she giggled.

"You've been going through my stuff again!" Katya got angry and snatched the pages out of Dotty's hands.

"No I haven't!" Dottie was emphatic. "They were on the table. Recently you've been really absent-minded!"

"Look, it's an amateur production for the department," Katya lied without thinking. "They offered me a part in this scene and I accepted. Now I'm learning my lines. Okay?"

Malicious sparks appeared in her roommate's eyes. Recently she had become even more apathetic and depressed. She washed rarely and spent all day in bed wearing thick woollen socks. Not that she didn't have an excuse. Her father, a dodgy businessman, had been arrested in Pazardzhik two weeks previously, and all his accounts had been blocked. Her allowance had suddenly been cut off. She already owed Katya fifty pounds, which did nothing other than to make her more embittered than ever.

"It's so easy for you!" shouted Dotty.

Katya got undressed without paying her any attention, and went into the bathroom. Whilst the water drummed against her nose, she wondered whether it might not well be time to clear out of here altogether. Actually, that decision had been taken a long time ago. From the moment she had met Ziebling in the Embassy and realised that her double-life had been uncovered. She had no idea what kind of game they were playing; but she was sure of one thing: she wanted no part of it. Apparently, Ziebling was of the same opinion, "I don't want any scandals!" he had told her. Katya was quick on the uptake.

Dotty was weeping in her corner. The fat tomes piled around her bed had not been touched for several days. A half-empty bottle of cheap Bulgarian wine completed the picture; three fruit flies flew around the bottle's neck.

"What's going to happen to me?" she said mostly to herself.

"You'll have to find yourself some sort of work," said Katya as she vigorously towelled her hair. She had cut her hair very short because of the wigs she had to wear and she liked her new self. The shorter haircut made her breasts stand out more.

"What kind of job?" wept Dotty.

"You can always clean at the Embassy. That way you save the rent on your room."

"Really?" Dotty livened up a bit.

"Uh-huh, and you know what? You can take my place," continued Katya with unexpected enthusiasm. "I need some time off. You'll have to clean the Ambassador's office. What d'you say?"

"Well, yeah, great!" nodded her roommate, unconvinced.

Katya could not suppress her smile. The whole idea seemed devilishly piquant. She threw on some baggy khaki combats, with vast pockets, and a clingy halter-top, which left her tanned midriff on display. She felt Dotty's gaze roaming over her body, but didn't give a damn! She would rent a small studio in the Portobello Road or thereabouts. As far as possible from this shit-hole.

She put the script in her bag and threw a glance at her roommate. "Head up!" she said and left.

The scenarios were written by some guy called Thomas Munroe. A tall, skinny wanker with lank greasy hair, and glasses like bottle-ends. They had met at the very start. He had come, so he claimed, to take the measure of her. His undertaker's mannerisms included such phrases as, "We must make the orgasm more stylish, like the French petit-mort." He resembled a coffin-maker.

The problem was that the agency's clients – predominantly business busy-bodies – lacked any imagination. They had only the vaguest idea of their fantasies, or the direction in which their desires lay, and were incapable of giving them a concrete or complete form. They could not build a situation nor handle dialogue, nor did they have time for those things.

Take Rube Sparks for example. He was a jeweller, whose shop

was situated near one end of Regent's Street. Rube knew everything about rocks, but next to nothing about his own soul. For him, the soul differed but little from the 'bow-tie effect', which could be found only at the heart of some extremely rare, and equally extremely expensive, diamonds. He could admire it for hours but had no concept of how to reach it. The play of light in this king of gems made him feel its vibrations. It spoke to him. It whispered thoughts and secret desires that made him blush. And aroused him. But nothing more. It required someone, such as Thomas Munroe, to appear on the scene, to polish up these uncut urges and remove the slag. Munroe, who knew everything about desire, had tunnelled for a long time into Rube's soul to bring its treasures out into the open. And then he had worked on them with all the precision and persistence of a true gem-smith to give them the form and lustre they deserved. Now Rube Sparks knew exactly what he wanted and how to get it.

Katya enjoyed that scenario: 'The Decoration of the Christmas Tree' as she had jokingly dubbed it. Rube would unlock the safe behind his desk and take out the treasures, one by one. The diamond necklace of Hera. The Onyx Eye. The Blue Moon. The necklace of Isabella of Castile. The strings of pearls of Cassandra. The Bracelet of Fire and Ice. The Medallion of the Ethiopian Princess. The Sapphire of the Dragon. The Chain of Diamond Tears. The stones radiated a cold, which reached all the way to her clean-shaven pubis. She felt their weight – to the last carat. Those priceless items rarely even made it as far as the window display. Normally they were made to order for a small circle of select clients who preferred to invest their money in things of permanent value. Bankers, film stars, producers of goods for mass consumption, and recently (horrors!) even Russians. Deep within his soul, Rube was convinced that these people were unworthy of his jewels. His dream was to work for the Palace. He believed that noble gems only shone correctly when seen against Noble skin. Skin unhampered by the annoying shadow of clothes, glowing in its natural nakedness. And here she was, standing in front of him

– Princess Diana herself, glistening as though she were a freshly polished pearl. From the tiara encrusted with gems, to the anklets with diamond hearts, her body was bathed in blinding sparkles. Rube contemplated her in silence. His heart climbed slowly into his throat and his adam's-apple began to pulsate like an iguana's. Katya could also feel that she was losing her self-control. Her body-heat had unlocked the energy of the gems; their glow cut through her skin, pouring streams of light into her veins. She felt dizzy, softened, and fluffy like an egg-white beaten into the form of an opening rose. At that moment, it would have been enough for Rube to raise his hand and dip his fingers into the sweet cream of her body, but he never did. Instead he would take his camera and take careful pictures of her from every possible angle. After which, all the treasures disappeared into his cold safe.

As she took the tube to Camden Town, Katya took out her copy of The Veteran & the Princess and reread it. The part was far from difficult, but on the whole the play struck her as a bit repulsive. Maybe it was the yoghurt. She asked herself whether that was one client's requirements, or whether it had been the artistic addition of Mr Munroe? Recently her relationship with the scriptwriter had cooled considerably. Katerina had dared to edit one of his scripts and he had created a huge ruckus as a result. She realised that if Thomas Munroe so desired, her parts would become even more repulsive, therefore she sensibly stopped poking her nose into his business. He obviously held grudges.

The agency was based in a run-down three-floor building crammed into some back-alley near Camden Market. The surroundings consisted of old industrial workshops and warehouses. At the end of the alley there was an 'alternative' bar, whence often chilling noises emanated. From the outside the building looked unoccupied, but the few neighbours there were had noticed a long time ago that the place was the centre of an intense, though secretive, social scene. Various people went in and out of the run-down entrance who were vaguely reminiscent of famous personalities. There were often taxis out front, and every so often a luxurious limousine. But there were no adverts or other signs at the entrance to shed light on the purpose of these visits. After some time, visitors usually noticed a grimy plastic plaque stuck above the doorbell. 'Famous Connections' was engraved in it.

Katya pushed the buzzer, but heard nothing. In spite of this, after just a short pause, a tall man opened the door dressed as a porter with the face of one whose trousers were stuck deep between his arse cheeks.

"Hi Cole!"

"Hi-i-i!" he replied slowly and shut the door behind her.

She ran up the stairs. The first and third floors were full of junk and practically unused. The second consisted of a spacious hall, divided by thin partitions walls into small make-up rooms. The furnishings were simple and businesslike. The floors were carpeted in ubiquitous faceless grey tiles. No particular investment: it was one of those companies that set up or moved out overnight. Every time Katya came here she had the awful premonition that she would find it empty.

Today, however, all the little cubicles were full and the actors buzzed around like bees. Barry Longfellow's office could be found at the far end. The blinds were open and one could see him talking on the phone. He waved to her cheerfully. Barry was Ziebling's number two in the agency. He was the Casting Manager, Executive Producer and Executive Director all at the same time. Ziebling himself rarely showed his face in the 'Factory', as he liked to call the Camden building. He had a far more prestigious office, somewhere in Pimlico, from which he pulled the strings. Katya had never been there. After she had passed the 'caviar test', Barry had offered her a sixty-performance deal, got her to sign a confidentiality agreement, and only then showed her the Factory.

She was now a part of the troupe.

The cubicles had no doors, so Katya caught glimpses of her colleagues as they carefully prepared themselves for their own little shows. She caught sight of Baroness Thatcher, Gorbachev, Liam Gallagher, Sir Elton John, Ulrika Johnson, President Clinton, and a stack of other celebs from all walks of life, all the way down to the Nobel Laureate, Professor Hawking. There were even some zombies, such as Benny Hill, John Lennon, and, of course, her good self: Diana, Princess of Wales. She sometimes felt their envy. No one else had a hope of reaching her level. She was the best: sixty performances in two months! Now that was impressive!

'Hi Hawking,' she said, taking a few steps back and looking curiously into his cubicle, 'What's up?'

'I'm training, can't you see?' he mumbled.

'Hawking', better known as Samuel Fogg, was sitting in that well-known pose in a wheelchair, manipulating some new gadget, concentrating deeply. It looked like a cybernetic arm, although it was almost two yards long, and was capped by an impressive artificial penis. The mechanism was tied into the small joystick-gadget on the arm of the chair. Sam was training himself to be able to slip the uber-vibrator into the centre of a loo-roll, which had been fixed to the opposite wall. Without much success as yet.

'Shit!' he roared.

The demand for 'Hawking' was far smaller than that for Lady Di. He had been hired twice a month by three wealthy, and strict, lesbians to explain Black-Hole Theory, which they regarded both as an ideological pillar of feminism and a powerful aphrodisiac. As a result of those academic requirements, Mr Fogg, an uneducated and ordinary youth, had to commit to memory the works of that great physicist, and later to recite them word for word, – no easy task with the speech machine in a darkened auditorium – over and over, until the three rug-munchers reached climax amidst crying and moaning reminiscent of a jackals' feast. In reality, Fogg had no objections to sinking his instrument into any one of them, and if possible all three of them one after the other, for which reason he had begged Munroe to make some changes to his part. The great dramaturge was unreceptive at first, 'Are you trying to screw to whole thing up?!!' he had yelled, 'They're paying for Hawking, not lice-ridden, horny Sam! Or maybe you disagree?!' That was Mister Fogg's only role and he needed it, to the extent that he would go to any lengths to keep it. He continued to cram physics and recite Black-Hole Theory, reaching the stage whereby he actually began to understand it. Meanwhile, Munroe decided that Sam's idea was not so bad after all and after a brief consultation with the clients, he came up with a new variation on the scenario, in accordance with the fundaments of the character. Which was why Sam was now struggling, without success, to master the newly approved gadget.

'Good luck, Hawking!' Katya tossed over her shoulder, as she dived into her own make-up box.

She sat in front of the mirror, staring at the picture of Diana that was stuck in the bottom-left corner of the frame. She had dreamt that the Princess was still alive. Usually, she forgot her dreams very quickly, but this one had been haunting her all week. It was not nice. In the dream, Katya was wandering the streets of an unknown oriental city, when she met a veiled woman. The veil covered her entire face, but the voice was Diana's; though she had never actually heard the Princess' voice, Katya knew it was her. The woman said only, "Now I am happy." Then she slipped into a dark side-alley, leaving her alone in the bazaar. A muezzin's call came from above her head and she woke.

The grey figure of Thomas Munroe appeared behind her. "Your Highness," he said teasingly, "I would like to present you with your new chauffeur."

She turned around. Munroe had a fat folder under his arm, full of scripts. He moved aside and another man appeared, framed by the doorway. He was thin, stripped to the waist, dark-skinned. The wide buckle of his belt shone darkly. His torso was hairless and his three-day beard carefully trimmed.

"Desmond was a big star till recently," Munroe said, thumping the man on the shoulder. He left.

The pair examined one another closely for a minute or so.

"What did you play till now?" she asked, realising she'd seen him around the Factory before.

"O.J." he replied seriously.

Her eyebrows rose, "Not in fashion any more, eh?"

"There's always hope."

"What hope?"

"O.J. is just reaching the peak of his abilities. He still has a lot to give society."

Katya got the joke and chuckled. Desmond looked like a decent bloke, but a little too self-assured. "O.J.'s going to be quiet for the next century or so," she said, shaking her head. "You'd best stop wasting your time."

Alice, her make-up artist, turned up, a new ring in her nose, today's lipstick thick and black. Without any fuss, she started to tart Katya up. Desmond hung around the doorframe sullenly, but was quickly shooed off with a high-pitched squawk, not unlike that of a peeved hen.

26

The cook sat in front of the office for a few minutes, then he stood up, paced a little and stopped next to the window. He was nervous. He had no idea as to why the Ambassador wanted to see him, but from long experience could guess that it would not be nice. The office door opened and the Consul came out, mopping his sweating brow. The secretary's intercom buzzed.

She picked up the receiver and nodded to Kosta. "You can go in."

The Ambassador sat behind his desk, fresh and cheerful. He had just sucked the vital juices from the Consul and had found them tasty. He made a gesture, as though luring some small animal forward. "Come in, come in, don't be shy!"

The cook advanced unwillingly. He was more than merely shy.

He looks like his speciality is hair soup thought Varadin. He was unsure that the risk would pay off. Perhaps he should order out to some top-class restaurant for the dinner. But it was bound to be too expensive, and would devour his already slim budget. Ziebling's expenses were fairly salty, but he could justify them. Recently it had become all the rage to hire foreign PR companies to represent government interests. At least, that's what people were saying. However, a dinner for thirty, laid on by a fancy restaurant, given that they had a chef on the payroll? He had thought of the look on the Audit Commissioner's face and dropped the idea.

"Well, Pastricheff," began the Ambassador, "I'm sure you already know that I'm arranging a large charity event. An important part of said event will be the official dinner. I don't wish to scare you, however, persons of the highest rank will be attending, including Her Majesty the Queen of England."

The chef remained intently silent. He was outwardly unmoved. What a dimwit! thought Varadin, I bet, if it was left to him, he'd serve Her Majesty bean and pepper stew. But it was not left to him, thank God.

"I think," he continued, "that it's about time for us to decide on the menu."

"No problem," shrugged the cook.

"This time we had better offer something more exquisite to our honoured guests."

"What did you have in mind?"

"You're the professional in this field, I'd hoped to hear your suggestions first."

The cook thought it over. From the depths of his mind came random notes. His brain arranged them instinctively, and eventually a pleasant melody formed. "Duck!" he said daringly. "Duck à la Chasseur!"

The Ambassador's brows rose in surprise. "Doesn't sound all that bad. Will you be able to cope on your own?"

"That is my speciality," Kosta exclaimed. "Unfortunately, I rarely have the chance to make it. Ducks, as you know, are expensive."

"Don't worry about the cost," the Ambassador waved a hand dismissively, "What do you propose for Hors D'oeuvre?"

"Liver in a white wine sauce. The French Recipe!" shot the cook.

"Well, look at that!" the Ambassador nodded in approval. "Won't it be a little heavy?"

"What are you talking about, heavy?" protested the chef energetically. "The combination is ideal. Especially with a fresh radish salad." He added without thinking.

Varadin had rarely seen him so enthused. "Why have you been hiding these priceless talents until now?" he asked suspiciously.

"Budget," sighed the cook.

"This time you needn't worry about that," cut in the

Ambassador. "Just don't screw up! I take it you've seen The Road to Sofia?"

It was obvious that he'd lived through this nightmare many times. The two of them quickly sorted the remaining details of the menu and the cook left, happy to have the chance to demonstrate his professional skills once more. Or so thought Varadin.

He leant back and closed his eyes for a few minutes. In one hour he had an appointment at the Foreign Office. The neighbouring dictator had muddied the waters in the Balkans again, and John Edge, the Foreign Secretary, was gathering all the Ambassadors from the surrounding countries together for a mass consultation. Late last night, he had received a cryptogram detailing the government's position – nothing it had contained had surprised him. Obviously, things had been carefully coordinated with the member-countries, whose Ambassadors would have been equally well-instructed by their respective governments. One and the same thought did the rounds amongst the group. The only uncertainty lay in the question of whether they would serve those little triangular sandwiches with the crab and avocado filling, like they had last time. Until that time they had only ever been fed with scones that resembled Stone Age artefacts, without the good grace to be rock buns. It was rumoured that this change had come about after Mr Edge had taken on a new, young secretary. An innocent young girl of the people, she had dared to break with the soulless Tory traditions that had been handed down conservatively by successive Conservatives. The sandwiches had been so exquisite that he had actually come close to following Ziebling's advice about taking one back to the Embassy to show Kosta. But he had not dared. However he did take note of their parameters, under the guise of taking notes. Then he gave his sketches to the cook, but the results had been far from the same. Alas!

Just then his mobile rang from somewhere under the pile of paperwork on the desk. He dug it out and put it to his ear. "Yes?" he said casually.

"It's me," a familiar voice slapped him awake.

"Nice to hear from you," he lied instinctively.

"Did the exhibition arrive?" she asked without ceremony.

"It's at the airport, I've sent someone to clear it through customs."

"I want it set up immediately!" the voice brooked no contradiction. "I don't want it left till the last minute!"

He blinked and pressed the point between his eyes with one finger. The exhibition was included in Mrs Pezantova's program as an accompaniment to her gathering. It seemed the ultimate in chic as far as she was concerned. For that purpose she had acquired a whole stack of pictures from a government gallery and was taking them to the four corners of the earth with her, accompanied by an 'artistic director' who was half-dead from fear because he was responsible for their material well-being.

"Don't worry," the Ambassador assured her. "Preparations are well under way."

"They're all asking me constantly whether She will be there," she sighed. "I don't know what to tell them."

"Be careful! Nothing definite for now!"

There was a brief pause.

"They've already written it," she said, "in a fashion magazine."

"You told them?!"

"No! They came up with it themselves!" she protested energetically.

"Okay! Let's just hope that people don't read Bulgarian fashion magazines over here."

"You'll fax me the guest-list, yes?"

"Uh-huh, it's already completed."

"And I'll need some notes on the more important ones: titles, occupations, you know what I mean." she added capriciously. "And one more thing! I almost forgot. A man will call you. He's called Spass Nemirov. He draws with fire. I want him worked into the program. He's very attractive."

"Fire!?" Varadin jumped.

"I have to go. I'll see you in London."

He shook the receiver in disgust, as though to tip out the remains of her voice. His gaze fell on the dustbin: it was overflowing, the carpet around it covered in bits of paper. It had not been emptied for some time. That excited and annoyed all at the same time. What does that panty-wetter think she's playing at!? He grabbed the phone. "Why is no one cleaning my office?!" shouted Varadin. "Find that Katya and get her here at once!"

Bianca Leithereva tried to tell him something but he slammed down the receiver.

Tanya Vandova put her head around the door without knocking, "The driver's waiting."

He looked at her, frozen.

Ten minutes later, the green Rover was taking him to Whitehall.

27

A complex mixture of guilt, fear and audacity crawled over the cook's face. He had brought a box of cigarettes, with the strange name of *Murati*, and timidly pushed them towards Chavdar. It was just past eleven, but the bar of the Consort was half-empty. Simich was polishing glasses cheerfully; his country had just started a new offensive against the Albanian separatists in the southern provinces, which guaranteed high-emotions for the next few months. Recently, life in Europe had become too monotonous.

"I can't pay you now," said the actor as he put the cigarettes away. "But you can collect it with your share of the proceeds from the ducks. I think we'll be able to shift them in the next couple of weeks. I've spoken to a few restaurants already. It's on."

Kosta said nothing.

"What's up?"

"Write them off," he said shortly.

"How come?!" Chavdar jumped.

"I wanted to tell you, but there was no answer on your mobile."

"The bastards cut me off!" roared the actor. "I hadn't paid. What happened?"

"The freezer died on me.

"What?!"

"A few days ago," added the chef. "I only noticed when it started to smell. Horrendous mess, no way I could do anything with it."

"And where did you move them?"

"I didn't," Kosta sadly shook his head. "I had to throw them out. That's why I was trying to get in touch with you. I had to sort it out myself."

"You threw out all the ducks?!"

"Uh-huh," the cook nodded. "They'd all gone green."

"Shit!!" gasped the actor, head in his hands.

Kosta looked at him apologetically, but in their depths his eyes shone coldly. He had decided firmly not to share the proceeds with the actor. The radioman was enough.

"I've got to go," he said and stood up.

"Wait!" shouted Chavdar. "I don't like this. You're putting one over on me!"

"Give me a break!" said Kosta, getting angry. "What the hell are you on about?"

"You've gone and sold them to that lot in the Embassy," continued the actor, indignantly. "I know. Your whole gang there in the Embassy are stuffing their faces with ducks."

"And why don't you go and stuff yourself?!" the chef spat between gritted teeth. "It wasn't enough that you pushed those web-foot devils on to me. so I had to get stressed about them; it wasn't enough that I had to clear up your bloody mess, now I'm the guilty one!! Did I tell you to find somewhere else? I think so! And weren't you going to shift them within one week? And what happened? Shit happened! Everything you do is like that!"

The actor had not been expecting such a righteous and irate outburst. Kosta made good use of his dumb-struck amazement to make a quick exit. He had been extremely surprised at himself, but preferred not to show it.

The Embassy van appeared at the back end of the road, u-turned and stopped in front of the official entrance. Turkeiev and Stanoicho jumped out. The interns voice caught him, just as he was about to turn the corner.

"Hey, Pastricheff! Come and help!"

They'd cornered him. He walked over to the van unwillingly. The seats had been taken out; two enormous grey trunks lay on the floor. The view did nothing for him. "And what exactly is that?" he asked grimly.

"The exhibition," replied Turkeiev, bursting with pride.

The cook made an energetic, anti-social gesture and spat to one side.

"Here, get the other end of this," Stanoicho coaxed.

The men's faces twisted. Their joints popped under the weight of the trunk.

"You exhibiting lead or something heavier?" complained Kosta bitterly.

"Carry on!" growled the intern.

Chavdar Tolomanov observed their labours malevolently from the windows of the Consort. He imagined their guts being squashed into their pants and his heart felt lighter. Then he turned around and slid the box of cigarettes onto the bar. "Do you barter?"

Simich picked up the box, sniffed it and then nodded, "All right then."

"Double-scotch, heavy on the ice!"

"Oo-hah!" the barman rubbed his hands together as he went to get the bottle.

The men man-handled the second trunk into the foyer and then collapsed on top of it like castaways. Kosta examined his hands: the metal handles had left deep red lines in his palms. "Fuck me! Heavy bastard!" puffed the chef angrily.

Stanoicho lit a cigarette and turned his pain into smoke.

Only Turkeiev shone happily. As they headed out to Heathrow that morning he had felt a crushing weight in his chest, as though he were doomed, a weight like the tar from countless cigarette ends stubbed out inside. He had felt doomed to fail. He had never before released items from Customs and he felt the task to be beyond him. Not one of his more experienced comrades had gone with him, and yet he had survived! He had found his way through the labyrinth of the cargo terminal, successfully conquered the Customs administration, and brought the priceless load home on time. In spite of them all! He awaited praise.

Tanya Vandova came down the stairs and looked down on them. "The Ambassador says to set up the exhibition immediately."

"Shouldn't we wait for the artistic director?" asked Turkeiev.

She shrugged. "He said to start..."

Kosta realised no one was paying attention to him and made his escape.

Stanoicho and Turkeiev opened the trunks.

"What the hell is that?!" exclaimed the intern.

28

The Ambassadors' conference had gone on too long. To everyone's dismay, the rock-buns were back on the menu. The old secretary had filed a suit against her (supposedly) unlawful dismissal, and the Commission for Internal Ethics had restored her to her previous post. The Foreign Secretary looked despondent. It was not clear what depressed him the most: the Balkan situation or Miss Crohne's return. His bad mood affected the others and found on outlet in the indifferent document issued by the Press Centre, with the title: 'Ambassadors share the Foreign Office's Reservations concerning the Current Balkan Crisis.' After the conference, Ambassador Martinescu had invited Varadin for an improvised lunch in a nearby restaurant. Varadin could easily have refused, but did not want to. He had to write a huge report and wanted to postpone it for the time being. The car had returned him to the Embassy around half past four.

He quickly passed through the duty-room, and stopped, rooted to the spot in the foyer. Bang in the middle of the floor some bizarre device was under construction. There were bits all over the place: bricks, rocks, planks and tiles. Stanoicho and Turkeiev were arguing over some plans that had been spread out on top of one of the trunks. The Major-domo had a thick clay pipe in his hands, which was covered in greenish gunge.

"G-8!" yelled the intern. "Why're you giving me E-7? I want G-8 for fuck's sake!"

"But it's not here," the Major-domo shrugged helplessly.

"What is going on here?" asked the Ambassador in icy tones.

"We're assembling the installation, Mister Ambassador,"

explained Turkeiev. "They've sent us some sort of avant-garde sculpture. We're following the plans but we think it'd be a better idea to wait for the artistic director."

The young man was very much into Modern Art, which was why he had been placed in charge of the Cultural aspects of the Mission.

A nasty feeling spread through Varadin's stomach. He circum-navigated the whole installation with care, and cast an eye over its accompanying documentation. The list of parts covered several pages. They also included an instruction diagram, which looked more like a jigsaw as opposed to any form of useful instructions.

"It doesn't say what it is," sighed Stanoicho.

"But the idea is clear," added the intern. "It's supposed to look like something old."

Varadin stared at the bottom corner of the list. There was a small label with tiny script: WC-983-BC.

"What the hell have you collected, you idiots?!" he hissed, throwing the list at them and approaching the so-called installation threateningly.

"Mister Ambassador!" the voice of Tanya Vandova flew from the other end of the hall, "Someone wishes to see you, at all costs!"

"What someone?" he jumped.

"Someone called Bennett, from the British Museum." she explained. "He is waiting in the reception room."

He frowned. "I don't remember having scheduled an appointment with him."

"He says that it is urgent. He's very stressed!"

Varadin shot an evil glance at the two mortified members of staff, then headed for the reception room.

The man was pacing the room like a jackal. He was short, with a square head that suggested obstinacy. He was wearing a brown tweed suit with a red scarf instead of a tie. He turned at the sound of the door opening.

"Good afternoon, I'm Clark Bennett of the British Museum,"

he introduced himself immediately, shaking Varadin's hand. "They tell me that you have it."

"What exactly?" queried the Ambassador.

"The ancient WC!"

"Pardon?" his eyebrows rose.

"I don't know quite how it happened," Mr Bennett started quickly. "The two loads must have been sent at the same time. This morning your people went to the airport and picked up a couple of trunks, which were actually destined for ourselves. In the other trunks, there are various pictures, which are yours."

"But how could this happen?!" shouted Varadin. "Aren't the loads addressed to different people?!"

"Of course they are!" exclaimed Mr Bennett. "I've no idea why they released our trunks. Maybe they look alike? But because it was a Diplomatic cargo, no one thought to check."

"Follow me," said Varadin grimly.

The pair of them headed for the foyer.

"Where is B-5? You had it a minute ago." The voice of the intern echoed

"But we want E-5 here," muttered Stanoicho.

"Ah, your granny's E-5, give me B-5."

"Oh, gosh! What have you done for Christ's sake!" a woeful cry reached them. "Stop! Please stop at once!"

Stanoicho jumped and dropped his brick on the floor. It broke in half.

"Aaaargh!" groaned Mr Bennett, as though it had been dropped on his foot. "Don't touch anything! Stop! Stop!!"

A greenish-blue flash crossed the Ambassador's face. Stanoicho and Turkeiev went pale and stepped back. Clark Bennett pulled out a mobile and dialled some number with trembling hands.

"I found it! I found it!" he shouted. "Come quickly before they destroy it. 67 Queens Gate! Hurry!"

Then he turned to the Ambassador. "Your Excellency? This antique is insured for £760,000. I cannot afford anything to happen to it! Get those two out of here. My people will be here soon to gather up the pieces. Don't worry about your pictures. We'll get them to you first thing tomorrow. What a day! What a day, indeed!!!"

There was a strange noise, like someone stepping on a frog: a squelch! The Ambassador put a hand over his mouth and motioned Stanoicho and Turkeiev to disappear. Clark Bennett watched him, startled. Varadin sneaked into the internal part of the Embassy. He went up in the lift and stopped it between floors. Then he started rattling, in his best machine-gun fashion, "100!-100!-100!"

29

The wine sparkled with a soft rusty nuance in the bottom of her glass. Katya downed it. A wave of warmth rolled through her body. Desmond stretched across and refilled the glass. It was her third.

"How's your arse?" he asked.

"Don't ask," she laughed bitterly and took another gulp.

It burned, and badly at that. She had thought at first that she would not be able to sit down for at least a week, but the pain gradually faded leaving only the heat. The whip had left fiery marks on her buttocks. She felt like she was sat on a grill, while frozen ants crawled over the rest of her body.

'The Taming of the Shrew by William Shakespeare. Adapted for private theatre by Thomas Munroe. Copyright, Famous Connections. All rights reserved!'

'La Valeta' was a small, exclusive restaurant in the upper part of Kensington. After a good thrashing, Desmond assumed that a good foie gras would not go amiss. And he was damn right. They decided not to return to the agency and Katya was still looking like Diana. That was a serious breach of the regulations. Rule number one was that they should not be seen in public places in full make-up, but she didn't care right at that moment. Especially right then. She was even enjoying the amazed looks of the staff and the few mummified clients. She sensed their burning curiosity and unease (burning like the marks on her rear!) and her subconscious felt somehow avenged. As though this small fragment of the overall social mosaic represented the whole world in which her clients lived. It was balm for her soul. Desmond Cook had perhaps sensed that soothing side-effect, which was why he had taken her there in that condition and that outfit.

"That was not in the script," she started hesitantly. "Maybe that guy got a little more excited than he was supposed to. He lost control. That had never happened to me before. Thanks for getting involved."

"You're always welcome." He shrugged.

"It's nice to have a chauffeur like you," she said squeezing his hand. He had skinned his knuckles. "You know, I like what you did to that pig."

"Well, I had something in mind."

"Oh yeah?" she said startled. "So you've got more scenarios I don't know about?"

"The answer is no," he squeezed her fingers gently. "Calm down!"

But she felt anything but calm. "You knew what would happen?"

"Look, I've been in this business for four years. And any time handcuffs are involved I'm on my guard."

He took a small piece of wire from his pocket, which looked a little like an opened paperclip, and held it up to her face. "Ordinary precaution," he said, then added, "I'd advise you to learn how to use it if you're intending to stay in this business. You don't think you're the only Diana, do you?"

"Hmm, I'd not thought about that particular question. I assume there were others before me."

"There were," Desmond nodded.

"And what happened to them?"

"Good thing you thought to ask," he smiled. "Cynthia played the Princess whilst she was still alive. She was practically her twin. She was brilliant. Though that worked against her in the end. She was so into her part that after the accident she started imagining things and then..."

"What kind of things?"

"She started to believe that she was Diana and that her double was the one who died in the crash."

"Totally barking!" exclaimed Katya.

"Absolutely!" agreed Desmond, "She was spending time in a clinic just outside London and I haven't heard anything since then."

There was a meaningful pause.

"Do I look so involved, to you?" Katya was fishing.

"You couldn't be," he shook his head. "You're foreign."

"Who was the last one?" she asked.

"Brigitte," said Desmond dreamily. "An Eastern German. She was great."

"She was?" Katya raised her brows.

"Car crash," he explained quickly, then added meaningfully, "Some Japanese apparently wanted to be in Dodi's place, and I doubt that she was given that scenario to read."

"You think it was set up?" she asked hesitantly.

"I doubted it, but when the Lithuanian went the same way, there was no more doubt."

"Car crash?"

"Yep. Only, a long way from here, in Prague. The agency has a wide network of international contacts. They could send you to Paris or Buenos Aires, Cairo, Kuala Lumpur, even the Bahamas. As long as the client is paying. And they do, believe me. You'll certainly be asked to travel soon, Kate."

"That sounds like a threat."

"I don't want to frighten you," Desmond shook his head. "You just need to know how things stand in the business with Diana. Your role attracts accidents like a magnet."

"I don't understand how someone could arrange their own death to order," she said, cold shivers running down her spine. "Even if it was with the object of his dreams. I mean, that's a real death and the Princess in the equation is a hired tart."

He looked at her steadily. "Are all Bulgarians that clever?"

She said nothing. She thought there was a hint of sarcasm in his tone.

"Do your clients achieve orgasm?"

"Why the hell else do they get involved?!" she retorted spontaneously. "Where's the link?"

"Don't you get it?!" he exclaimed. "You may not be The One, but they're enjoying themselves just as much. The fact is that no one, or almost no one, ever knew the real Diana, and they weren't interested in her. That was her biggest problem. The public gulped down what the media gave them, or Andrew Morton, and that was plenty for them, more than enough to forge an idol and worship it. In real terms Lady Diana never existed; she was a papier-mâché figure, made of newspaper articles, pictures and photographic plates."

"Then she shouldn't have died," observed Katya reasonably.

"But what else can you do, when you don't want to play your part anymore?" asked Desmond.

"You just stop playing."

"But you can't," he whispered sinisterly. "Because during all those years you were playing it, your role has destroyed your former SELF, and when, one fine day, you decide that you want out of the role, you realise that you've nothing else any more. The role IS you, and your old self is so destroyed that you can't even play at it. You can't play; you can't not play."

"That sucks. And the final result is that we were actually colleagues, huh?"

"Up to a point," he agreed. "But you're unique compared to her. Only a very few people can play with you, whereas everyone could play with her. She was put into mass usage, like a Barbie doll. And when Barbie gets broken, all the kiddies cry."

"For one cheap Barbie?"

"Is there anything sadder?"

"If I get broken, no one's going to cry."

"No one cries about Luxury toys," he added, nodding.

"You're telling me that I should make a break, before they break me?" she dared to ask.

"Thematic dolls go with their story," he observed. "Snow White has to eat the poisoned apple, Sleeping Beauty to prick herself on the spindle. That's why they're sold in a package with either an apple or a spindle. The same goes for figures like Batman or Luke Skywalker. The Diana figure is no exception. You'll always find someone who wants to play the fairy-tale to the end."

"That's practically living Voodoo!"

"Call it what you will."

"And what did you feel when you played OJ?"

"The two roles have nothing in common!" he objected angrily. "OJ is in the active position: he shoots, beats, kicks. The Princess is the exact opposite, in the eyes of most people she will always be the eternal victim. Have you ever been required to play the role as a dominatrix, whip in hand, while some unfortunate polishes your boots with his tongue?"

"No." she admitted, without having to think about it.

"But you have been driven around, haven't you? They rev their fast cars and flex their muscles, while you tremble, tied to the gear-stick with a leash, yeah?"

"How do you know?"

He stared at her questioningly. "So they're still playing that one then? Look at that sly old bastard Munroe! He created that scenario for Brigitte!"

"He's not my type," she hissed.

"You're not the only one," he nodded thoughtfully, then asked off-hand, "That one with the jeweller, is that still going on?"

"The Christmas Decorations," she smiled, "I did it just the other week, why?"

"Hide!!" he said quickly.

There was a flash. The skeletal figure of a man appeared momentarily, armed with a huge lens like a bazooka. Katya instinctively covered herself with the big starched napkin.

"Paparazzi!" hissed Desmond. "To hell with 'em! They're on every fucking corner! We can't let you be snapped!"

He rushed over to the manager and they exchanged a few words. The photographer lost no time in heading for the door, but two waiters brutally threw him out. He prowled in front of the restaurant like a jackal.

"Looks like we'll be leaving out the back door," sighed Desmond.

"Christ!" exclaimed Katya. "Even when you're dead!"

30

The hassles with the British Museum had sapped his strength and now this stench...it would be the coup de grace! He could not understand how, in such a small area as the Embassy, there could be concentrated so much idiocy! Was there no critical mass? Or was it well past that? The stink hit his nose almost instantly on the way to the airport. The driver was listening to music on the radio; pretending nothing was the matter. In spite of that, he had his window wide open and there happened to be a brand new air freshener hanging from the rear-view mirror.

"What's that smell?" asked Varadin menacingly.

"Stale air," said the chauffeur edgily.

Varadin took a deep breath and felt on the verge of puking. They were trying it on again!

"What bloody air?! It smells like something died in here, and it bloody well shouldn't!!" exploded the Ambassador.

Miladin was left without choice. "Well, you see, there was a little accident..." he admitted awkwardly. (Ha! They always started like that!)

The 'accident' had occurred the morning of the day before. Before turning up for work, he had gone to the fish market, where he had bought a huge salmon. On the way back, however, he got stuck in traffic and didn't have time to take the fish home. It had only stayed in the boot for a few hours, but it looked like something had leaked out of the fish and into the upholstery.

"I don't know how it could have happened," spluttered the chauffeur. "It was really well wrapped."

There remained less than an hour before the plane landed.

"Why didn't you say something sooner?" asked the Ambassador in icy tones.

Numerals boiled up in his brain, looking for a way out.

"I thought it would fade over time," replied Miladin simply. "I washed the whole boot only this morning. I'm really sorry, Mister Ambassador; it won't happen again."

It did not need to happen again – it could hardly have come at a worse time! But, for the moment, he had to save his strength, it was already too late to do anything about anything. Varadin laid his head back and opened his window fully. I'll give you something to remember that fish by, blockhead!!

He had to start counting down the numbers!

At Heathrow a cold wind was blowing. The diplomats were milling around on the tarmac of Gate 7, where the Balkan hearses usually pulled up. Nearby three cars were parked, of different national brands, a green Rover at the head. Two policemen in bright, fluorescent yellow jackets observed the official to-ing and fro-ing with interest. A noticeable distance from his underlings, hands behind his back, Varadin Dimitrov stood importantly.

'There it is!' shouted Mr Kishev, convulsed in artificial joy, pointing to the snout of the aircraft that was just appearing around the corner of the terminal building.

Varadin also saw the aeroplane, turned around and gave the diplomats a severe look. Aimless conversations instantly dried up and they all hurried to arrange themselves behind him in order of rank. The little group waited in ceremonious silence.

The tail of the aircraft was covered in soot, as though it had over-flown a war-zone. It made a wide turn and trundled to its parking space. As with all TU-155's this plane did not link to the automatic corridors of large airports and soon a mobile staircase could be seen making its way to the front door of the aeroplane. Meanwhile the roar of the turbines slowly faded. The diplomats fixed their gazes on the door, but it remained closed for another few minutes.

At last the door disappeared inwards with a flash of a uniform, then a head appeared. Although all that was actually visible was not a head but hair, or more precisely a mass of hair, tightly plaited into tiny dreads that fell higgledy-piggledy. Through the hair a fleshy black nose could be seen. It took a deep breath of the muggy London air and snorted happily. The black man pushed back his mane and stared at the welcoming party in amazement. He was an athlete, wearing a pink jacket and a long white robe with a shiny medallion at his neck. He was carrying a stereo under one arm. The diplomats stared back at him; they had been expecting Mrs Pezantova to be the first off the plane with her entourage. The big athlete grinned widely, then pushed one of the buttons on the stereo, releasing reggae rhythms. Swinging gracefully down the stairs he passed the file of officials and threw them a casual, "Hi!"

A company representative dashed over post-haste and pointed him in the direction of the terminal. "The Nigerian team," he shouted to the Ambassador. "They came transit through Sofia."

Another ten or so Africans made their way out of the aircraft. They were followed by a variety of glum individuals carrying impressive quantities of hand luggage. They threw spiteful looks at the welcome party and dashed towards the terminal, there to make their way to their visa Golgotha. Last came a Buddhist monk, in sarong and sandals, carrying a little black suitcase.

Varadin watched him slip past the ranks stony-faced. Then he stared once more at the door of the aircraft. For almost a minute there were no signs of life other than the stewardess. It struck him that perhaps he should send someone to find out what was happening. However, as he debated the possible consequences of such an action, a shadowy figure emerged from the plane's interior to stand at the top of the stairs. It was Mrs Pezantova.

"Here she is!" exclaimed Kishev.

From the top of the stairs the world seemed small and insignificant. She took a deep breath and forgot to breathe out most of it. She adored moments like these! Looks filled with trembling awe, faces full of devotion! The feeling gave her enough adrenalin to last a week. She smiled regally, delaying a touch longer on the uppermost step, indulging herself in the effect her appearance was causing. Then she slowly descended, turning her head this way and that, as though a teeming and enthusiastic multitude awaited her. Varadin hurried to meet her.

"At last! How long we've been waiting for you! Welcome! Welcome!" he pronounced ceremoniously, then asked courteously, "And how was your trip?"

'Fine,' she replied.

She was of average height, with a haughty face and a complicated hairstyle, atop which was affixed a still more complicated hat. A fluffy red cape hugged her shoulders like a mutant manta ray. She was accessorised with a small handbag made from the skin of some rare animal. Varadin was forced to admit to himself that she did have a certain elegance.

After the grand exit/entrance of the Prima Donna, came the rest of the troupe. First her two ladies-in-waiting rolled out, both wives of lesser-calibre politicians, who had also simultaneously embraced charitable causes, and free air-travel. Behind them came the actual concert performers: two folk singers, a piper, a fiddle player, a promising soprano, and a strange individual who would be performing some sort of ritual for summoning rain. Last of all trundled the artistic director, heavy sack across his shoulder. He was a sculptor and was carrying in his bag a little bronze statuette of a sausage-dog which he was hoping to sell during his short stay in London.

Devorina Pezantova coldly shook hands with the diplomats, decisively ignoring Kishev's attempt to engage her in conversation. She called her two companions and together with Varadin they headed to the Rover. There was a brief moment of confusion whilst the rest of the group arranged itself into the other cars. A police car escorted the column to the VIP terminal.

"Do you mind closing your window, it is very windy?" said Pezantova to Varadin.

He frowned, but half-closed it.

"Close it fully, if you please!" she insisted. "I have a cold. You close yours too!" she said to the driver.

He threw a quick glance at his boss, but the other only pressed the window-button. The driver did the same.

"But what is that smell in here?" whinged one of her companions.

"Yes, really? What is that smell?" whinged the other in her turn.

Devorina sniffed and spat, "Nothing!"

Varadin sighed with relief.

At the Chiswick Roundabout they hit a traffic jam. The vehicles crawled along at a snail's pace. On the right hand side of the road, British Airways was plastered all over the billboards. There were always traffic jams here and he suspected that the adverts were put there on purpose to get even deeper in the brains of the people waiting. That is what you call strategy!

"She will definitely come?" Devorina's voice called from the back seat.

"We have confirmation," replied Varadin.

The stench was eating his brain; he wanted to grab the driver and strangle him with his bare hands.

"Christ! Kututcheva and Moustacheva will be so full of envy, they'll explode!" she exclaimed. "That's what they deserve for not lending me the private jet! Rattling my bones in that hell-hole of a plane!"

"They will definitely explode," he nodded.

There was a worrying trend: with the number of downtrodden boiling ever upwards, the number of philanthropists was also rising. The competition between those good people was becoming ruthless, and the lack of rules – ever more obvious. Kututcheva and Moustacheva were also involved in feverish philanthropy, leaning on their husbands' enormous shoulders and on the funds controlled by them. Recently, Pezantova had got it into her head that those two had united against her. They deserved a good lesson!

"What's wrong with you, Mitche?!" called a frightened voice.

The back door opened. Miladin stepped on the brakes. A tragic wail followed, together with the expulsion of a huge volume of liquid.

"My God!!!" shouted Pezantova, covering her face in horror.

From the neighbouring cars surprised faces emerged. The door slammed and Mitche (there was no way of forgetting her name now!) slumped back into her seat, wiping her chin with a handkerchief. Her not particularly intelligent plump face trembled in horror.

"I feel awful." she spluttered from the back of her throat.

Devorina Pezantova's lips compressed into a thin line. Varadin opened the window a little. The rest of the journey passed in heavy silence.

31

"Is that the artist?" asked Turkeiev, peering through the window of the duty-room.

The receptionist nodded. Turkeiev sighed. He had been punished by being left behind at the Embassy whilst the others went to the airport to meet Mrs Pezantova. After the cock-up with the WC, the Ambassador had taken a final decision to keep the intern as far away as possible from all official events. In fact, Turkeiev was not all that upset; the incident had taught him that the less attention he drew to himself the less he risked his hide.

The fire-dancer sat carelessly in the foyer of the Embassy, looking like an Indian warrior waiting for a sign from the spirits of fate. He had shoulder-length, thick, straight hair. His face was swarthy and angular, with thick, bushy brows. He was wearing a black leather jacket and thigh-length, red cowboy boots. On the table nearby lay his wallet, tucked into a big leather album.

He was used to waiting. They would not scare him by making him wait. In the years he had been in London, he had crossed the threshold of many offices, both big and small. His backside had become as hard as the soles of a Dobrudjan peasant. Usually they listened to him, politely took his card and never called. But there were exceptions, which made it worth continuing. His art needed sponsors and social gatherings. He believed that one fine day his project would be approved and then he would wow the world. He dreamed of being Christo. Just like all the rest.

It was not clear how exactly Mrs Pezantova had come by his coordinates – who had recommended him, and why. Only the man himself did not wonder about this – as far as he was concerned, it was entirely natural that people would know about him.

"You're Spass Nemirov, right?" said Turkeiev politely, and introduced himself.

The artist looked sceptically at his freshly shaven, welcoming face. "I have an appointment with Mr Varadin Dimitrov," he murmured.

"He's at the airport," said Turkeiev. "But I am at your disposal, should you need anything. I understand that you will be a part of Mrs Pezantova's concert."

"Yes, I've been invited," the artist nodded self-importantly.

"What will you be exhibiting?" asked the intern.

"Well, an installation." There was a noticeable softness in Spass's way of speaking.

"An installation?!" Turkeiev twitched; he had become somewhat wary of such things of late.

"Yep. Shall I show you some of my work?" he said, quickly opening the album.

Strange faces, people, animals and occult symbols stared out from the pages of the album, somehow reminiscent of Nascar drawings. Their contours were outlined in fire. To achieve that effect, Maestro Spass used a variety of flammable and inflammable materials: from the simplest candles and ropes soaked in petrol, to high-tech products such as napalm, thermite, sulphur-carbon derivatives or white phosphorus. Turkeiev knew nothing about chemistry and was deeply impressed. In spite of this, his basic instinct told him that these things were not without danger.

"I haven't had a single accident so far!" protested the artist energetically.

"And you're certain that the area is big enough?" asked the intern carefully. "Your works are quite sizeable."

"That's right," agreed the other happily, "especially this one!" He quickly leafed through the pictures and stopped, his finger pointing to a picture of a large blaze on a beach.

"What's that?" jumped Turkeiev.

"It's called the Night of Neptune. Napalm on sand. Can you see the trident?"

The intern nodded in silence.

"I created it last summer when I was in Bulgaria, on the Arapia beach," added the artist proudly. "It burned all night. They wrote about it in all the papers. I wanted to make a copy here in Brighton, but they wouldn't allow it. Various eco-groups protested against it, as usual! And napalm is expensive! Over here I mainly use candles." Spass suddenly became more talkative, "They're more economical and they don't leave such a mess. This is one I did last month in Covent Garden. With the Local Council's permission. See – it was even in the Times!"

He extracted a sheet of paper, with a photocopy of the newspaper on it. It consisted of a picture and text: 'Fire-dancer – The Bulgarian artist Spass Nemirov offers tourists an unusual attraction.'

"Wonderful!" Turkeiev nodded in approval.

"Sooner or later recognition comes."

"And what are you thinking of putting on here?" asked the intern politely.

"I know that space is limited," said the fire-dancer. "That's why I've prepared something a little more delicate for you."

He put his battered cardboard suitcase on the table and opened its lid as though it was Pandora's Box itself.

"Well?" he raised his eyebrows as he gave Turkeiev a piece of card.

"But that's Princess Diana!" exclaimed the intern as he stared at the rough sketch.

"In pink flames," said Spass dreamily. "Just think of it..."

"Mmmmmm," mooed Turkeiev, scratching his ear.

"I'm thinking of using a new technique." The artist was inspired. "Magnesium oxide. They have it in Chinese shops but it's a bit expensive. You'll need to give me quite a bit of money."

Just then the door opened and Varadin himself appeared in the foyer. He threw a vague glance in the direction of the two men sat around the table and continued to drift further into the Embassy.

"Mr Ambassador!" He was stopped by the hated voice of Turkeiev.

He had difficulties understanding what exactly what was going on at first. Who was this accursed artist and where in hell had he come from? Obviously the heavy smell of fish had damaged various important brain-centres. Slowly, along with the fresh air, his senses returned. He snatched the album, looked over the sketch of the Princess and nodded. "Interesting."

The aesthetic side of the whole thing was of little interest to him. If Mrs Pezantova said it was interesting, that was good enough for him. The sum in question caused a small tic in his right temple, but he tamed it easily. It was not going to break the bank. He ordered the intern to fill out the necessary invoices and take it out of the Petty Cash.

This business-like approach to things made the artist whistle in amazement. "I think I'll probably need transport as well..." he said slyly.

"Mr Turkeiev will be entirely at your disposal," Varadin vengefully ground the sentence out through his teeth. "You must tell me personally if you are unhappy with his services. It was very nice to meet you."

As he said the latter he hurried to disappear into the depths of the building.

The artist looked Turkeiev up and down regretfully. "Don't worry about it mate! Everything will be fine!"

Fuck you all!! The intern sighed.

32

Varadin snuck up the stairs as silently as a panther. He had escaped the guests under the pretence that he had to write an important report. As a matter of fact, he did actually have such a report to write, but that was the last thing on his mind. Pezantova had immediately begun to fire off orders in the residence, causing absolute chaos. He had the premonition that that would continue for a long time – until he waved goodbye to her at the steps of the aircraft. He wanted to steal a moment of peace and quiet to gather his thoughts.

Tania Vandova was fussing around the photocopier in the offices and didn't notice him. The door of his office was ajar. From within came the roar of the Hoover.

"You're within my grasp now, little slut!" he said, grinding his teeth.

The girl was working with her back to him. Varadin slammed the door on purpose, with the idea of making her turn around. Her eyes would pop out in horror. He was just thinking of something cutting to say, but stopped himself all of a sudden. The Hoover was still screaming. Almost half a minute passed, before she thought to turn it off.

"Who are you?" he asked in a pain-filled voice.

"Doroteya," said the girl stiffly. Her wide face was a mass of red spots.

"What are you doing here?"

"Well, they sent me to clean," she replied. "I'm the replacement."

"Is that so? And what happened to Katya?" asked Varadin pretending disinterest.

"Katya won't be cleaning anymore." The girl almost spat at him.

His stomach flipped over. "But who will pay her rent?" he asked angrily.

"She has hardly got problems with her finances...What with her new profession!"

He thought he could detect a trace of spite in her tone. Why was she telling him all this? To what end? It struck him that perhaps continuing to question her would not be a good idea; but he could not stop himself, "What profession?"

"Well, she's playing Princess Diana."

"Princess Diana?" echoed Varadin, eyes wide.

The girl nodded, "Uh-huh, she is working for Famous Connections."

"Famous Connections?"

"Have you heard of them?" she asked innocently.

A black cloud passed across his face. There was no going back now. He shook his head, "No, never. How do you know that?"

"We were roommates," explained Dotty with a smirk. "Recently, she was going around the place with various scenarios like some kind of starlet. But if you ask me, I'm sure it's all soft porn."

"Porn?" he gasped. "Are you sure?"

"Judge for yourself!" She rummaged in the pocket of her overalls and proffered some folded sheets of paper. "I photocopied them, just in case."

He jumped back as though scalded.

"Maybe I've said more than I should," mumbled Dotty, leaving the pages on his desk.

"Does anyone else know what she's doing?" he asked quickly, then thought to himself, in answer, of course they know! I'm always the last to be told!

"No, no one at all!" the girl protested. "I only said because..."

"I have to talk to her. Immediately!"

"She doesn't live here any more," said Dotty shaking her head.

"She left?" he gaped stupidly. "When?"

"The other day."

"And where is she now?"

"She rented herself some sort of studio, maybe in the Portobello Road."

"A studio in the Portobello Road?"

"Something like that. She didn't leave an address or phone number. Just upped and left. Maybe she found herself a guy. I don't know, I just don't know!" She wrung her hands helplessly.

He walked up to her, looked her in the eye and hissed, "Did she rub you up the wrong way?"

"I thought you ought to know," replied Dotty gloomily.

Nasty, sticky business, he thought to himself. He was in it up to his ears.

"Excuse me," she said, and started to wind the cable of the Hoover up, clumsily.

He sat down behind his desk and waited for her to leave in silence.

'DRIVING LADY DI', scenario by Thomas Munroe. Famous Connections. All rights reserved!' Varadin frowned. His eyes scanned the lines distractedly. What filth! Which, of course, did not stop it from arousing him. 'PAINTING NUDES!' and 'THE LAST WEDDING!' were the following titles. "A cursed little whore!" he spat malevolently.

Nothing was the same as it had been anymore! Naturally, it was only to be expected when things are going so well, that there will always be some cause for doubt. Like a burning ember, covered in ash. That is how fires were started.

There was a knocking at the door. Tania Vandova came in. "The copies for Mrs Pezantova," she said.

"What?" he gaped.

"The program for the concert and the guest list," explained the secretary, leaving a thin folder on the desk. "The photocopier jammed, but it sorted itself out, thank God," she added.

He wasn't listening to her. The secretary left hurriedly.

'THE CONCERT, scenario by Thomas Munroe. Famous Connections. All rights reserved!'

"Bastard!" exploded Varadin as he remembered the script-writer. He had only met him once, but the memory of his filthy presence radiated from the folder with unusual strength. He asked questions such as, "In what role do you see Her Majesty, as a ruler or as a mother?" and then took notes. Varadin had not paid too much attention to him at the time. Maybe he should have.

The scenario had been thought out down to the very finest detail. The reception and departure ceremonies, the seating plan – even the topics of conversation had been noted beforehand. The guest list was also an agency product. Ziebling had managed to be even more demanding than the good Mrs Pezantova as far as that had been concerned; the company had not seemed exclusive enough for his liking. In the end he had involved himself personally in the quest to find guests of a high enough calibre, and as a result the first draft of the guest list had been almost entirely changed. "Take it as a bonus," he had said nobly.

The famous personages responded warmly to the invitations, and their cheques did not delay in flying in. Evan though tickets cost £100 a head, that did not discourage them and all forty places were soon filled. As compared to the agency's fees as well as all the other expenses surrounding the affair, the total seemed a drop in the ocean. However, Varadin attempted to think in terms of the state, as opposed to anything else. Otherwise, he started to have malevolent thoughts along the lines of: If all this money was poured over the heads of those orphans then maybe there wouldn't be any need for these concerts. But then, what would good people like Mrs Pezantova do with themselves all day? A difficult question. A dangerous question. When he was ceremonial mode, such thoughts did not occur to him and he felt a great deal calmer. In this case, unfortunately, ceremonial thinking was to no avail. The hard facts, both the lesser and the larger, had become the rock and the hard place that were slowly closing in on him.

Famous Connections.

Close contact with people of high society, informal contacts. Discretion and security.

Varadin dialled the number carefully. He was phoning on his own for the first time, without telling his secretary to put him through. He felt awkward, as though sneaking into someone else's office.

"Welcome to Famous Connections," sang a tender voice, "Experience the magic of informal meetings. Your idols await you. If you are interested in our services or wish to become our client, say one. If you are already our client and are experiencing problems, say two. If you wish to speak with our administrators, say three."

The words hung emptily in the cables like frozen starlings. The voice recited them once again. Varadin persisted in his silence. He imagined how the cables disappeared into the darkness: one led to Ziebling's office, the others lost themselves in the maze of the agency. He knew which road he should take but did not dare. Not yet.

A minute later he dialled the agency's number once more and the same greeting message answered. This time he did not put the phone down. He made sure to change his voice slightly, although there was no danger of his being recognised. "One," he announced clearly.

For a while he was subjected to some crackly muzak, then a recorded voice answered, "Welcome to Famous Connections! You will shortly be put through to one of our staff. At this stage we require no details concerning your identity. For your own comfort, we suggest that you use a pseudonym. If you do not have one ready, take a few seconds to think of one. Thank you for your attention."

"Hello, thank you for calling, my name is Hal," a friendly male voice said. "I'll be helping you become acquainted with the rules of the game. You're about to realise your most treasured dream. Don't stop now! Everyone has the right to touch their idol, to feel their aura, to play with them a little. The stars would be nothing without us ordinary people. We make them what they are, which means that some part of them is ours. We just have to ask for it! Isn't that so, Mr...?"

"Victor," said Varadin without thinking. He had always wanted to be called that.

"Great, Victor!" enthused the voice. "Let me just tell you how it all works. We don't want to sell you anything so don't worry on that front. Famous Connections just helps you to get what is yours by right. D'you understand, we are merely the go-betweens, everything else is up to you!"

"Not quite," mumbled Varadin.

"Doesn't matter! You just need to know one more thing," Continued Hal, "We're not thieves, so we can't deliver anything that doesn't belong to you. Don't expect miracles. If you're entitled to only one percent, then there is no way you can get one hundred percent without stealing from others, and we, as I just said, don't do that. Still there?"

"Yes," said Varadin. "I'm listening carefully."

"That was the bad news," said Hal. "But there's good news too, which is far more important: the fact that this seemingly insignificant percentage, to which you are entitled, will give you one hundred percent satisfaction. Don't believe it, eh? Experience demonstrates that that is entirely possible. Because, believe me, that little percentage is all that you need. It's got the necessary essence for you to change your vague, dreamy image into hard fantasy. Do you understand what I'm getting at?"

There was a brief pause.

"I'm not certain," replied Varadin.

"I'm talking about the grain of sand in the oyster, Victor," said Hal, like a Baptist preacher. "The grain of sand that turns into a pearl. We'll give you the grain, and you'll stay with it in the oyster. Do you agree?"

"Yes," Varadin mumbled, understanding exactly nothing. What exactly were they offering? Ziebling had never put things that way.

"If it isn't totally clear, it soon will be," concluded Hal philosophically. "Now let's get to the heart of the matter. Tell me who you're after, which member of high society you dream of touching."

"Lady Di," he replied, after summoning all his courage.

"Excellent, there'll be no problem!" exclaimed Hal.

"But she's dead!"

"Dreams never die, my friend."

"So you'll arrange a meeting for me, with her?"

"Of course!"

"But it won't really be her, right? It's not possible what with her being dead." He raised his voice unintentionally, "You'll send me some sort of actress! A copy! A double!'

"We're giving you the grain of sand," said Hal without blinking, "and whether it'll turn into a pearl relies entirely on you. Do you have a scenario?"

He typed something on his keyboard.

"Pardon?"

"Do you have an idea of what you want to do with her?"

"Well..."

"I'm sure that deep down you know perfectly well what you really want," Hal cut in. "Maybe you're a bit ashamed of talking about it right now, but there's no rush. Besides, her program is fully booked at the moment. We won't be able to fit you in before next month, unless someone cancels. But I don't think they will. People are crazy about her, especially the Near-Easterners."

"Hal, I've already got an idea," said Varadin unexpectedly; his tone had gone dead. "I just thought of it."

"Brilliant! That will make things easier," said Hal cautiously.

It cost him a great deal of effort to put his idea into English. "I'm going to shred her whoring arse!" hissed Varadin quietly.

"What?" Hal jumped.

"I'm going to shred her whoring arse!" repeated Varadin, in a voice that was breaking up, "and yours too, you bastard!"

He squeezed his mobile furiously and threw it onto his desk, as if he wanted to ram it into Hal's invisible ear, deep into his chicken-shit brain.

"!!100!!" he shouted so loudly that the windows of the glass cabinet shook, "100!!200!!300!!400!!1000!!!FuckyouPepolen!!! You'llnotstopmenow!!!2000!!!3000!!!4000!!!10000!!!!12000!!!! 100000!!!!1000000!!!!!" All the numbers he had ever stored in his head came pouring out like a stream of wasps, forming a vast swarm of ever-larger numbers that buzzed lightning-fast.

Eventually he reached numbers that were too long to pronounce before its successor appeared and he sat silently, his lips moving spasmodically, as number after number buzzed by. It was beautiful and frightening all at the same time.

33

To The Minister's Office
To The Office of The Spokesman of MFA
To The Department of ENA
To The Department of Information

British Press Review:

The British Press is paying considerable attention to the exhibition "Hygiene in Bulgarian Lands", which opens today at the prestigious British Museum. There is an article in every Cultural Section of the major National papers.

"Bulgarian WC Challenge" by Matt Goswell, *The Tribune*:

The widely accepted fact that the first Water Closet was built in Elizabethan times will undergo correction today with the first unveiling of its Bulgarian Predecessor. The apparatus, found in Bulgaria, dates from between 980AD and 982AD and consists of a functional model of a Water Closet, an idea that only cropped up in Western Europe some thousand years later. There are still arguments relating to its origin: Thracian, Bulgar or Byzantine? Or possibly Celtic?

Until now, such things have not been found in either Thracian burial sites, or Roman/Byzantine archaeological sites in the territory of Bulgaria. That is the reason for which Peter Panchev, an expert from the Bulgarian Historical Society in London, holds that this is part of an ancient tradition of hygiene, form the Ancient Greater Bulgaria, spreading through the territories of the Ukraine and Southern Russia. The Bulgarians claim to be one of the oldest peoples on earth, stemming from settlements in the fertile Ferganska Valley, in the foothills of Pamir.

There still remains the question of why the use of this device was not more widespread during the medieval Kingdom of Bulgaria. According to Mr Panchev, one explanation might be the invasion of the Turkish tribes at the end of the fourteenth century, who then set about demolishing all such cultural devices as a symbolic gesture of their victory. He does not exclude the possibility of more such artefacts being found within the territory of Bulgaria.

Elena Papadopoulos, an archaeologist from Oxford University, holds an entirely different opinion. According to her theories, the WC is of Byzantine origin. The lack of other such artefacts is explained in her thesis as being the result of their systematic destruction during the seventh century, at the hands of the invading Bulgars, who thought them to be Christian sacred sites. Her thesis lacks an explanation of the lack of any such artefacts in any other part of the former Byzantine/Roman Empire.

An original opinion comes from Professor Michael Callaghan, of the University of Glasgow. He is of the opinion that this ancient WC is a leftover from the time when the Celtic tribes populated those lands. Obviously that Celtic tradition was far separated from the traditions of the Western Celts, especially those occupying the British Isles.

The origins of the Provadian Water Closet remain shrouded in mystery for the moment. The exhibition is expected to be visited in person by Her Majesty Queen, Elizabeth II.

The Guardian mentions that the dig and the conservation of the unique artefact were carried out thanks to the enthusiasm of the local people, though sponsored by a Dutch Foundation. The Bulgarian Minister for Culture had denied funds to the project under the budget cutbacks.

Editorial of the *European Post*: "Was it actually being used?"

The Ancient Installation stands out, tragically alone, from the prevailing darkness of Balkan history. Attempts to classify it under any one cultural tradition have so far been of no avail. It seems that the first ever WC was the creation of some former-day Leonardo da Vinci, which unfortunately remained an oddity in the eyes of his contemporaries. The hypothesis is supported by archaeologists' suspicions that the device has never been used. If that proves to be the case we will be witness to a cultural paradox that could well explain the Balkans as we see them today. And even if we accept that Sir John Harrington was not the first to create a Water Closet, we are left secure in the knowledge that he was the first to put one to use.

Photos and technical diagrams, accompanied by short explanatory notes were published in *Liberation* and *The Endeavour*, the latter including a picture of the Mayor of Provadia alongside the title: "The Herald of Progress".

The Sun carries the story under the headline VULGAR BULGARS WOULD RATHER SQUAT THAN SIT ON THE POT. The fusty world of archaeologists is going potty over the ancient Bulgarian khazi currently on show at the British museum. They can't make out why the world's first flush loo was never used.

SO WHAT DID THE BULGARS USE THEIR TOILET FOR? *THE SUN* OFFERS A WEEK IN SUNNY BEACH FOR THE READER WHO COMES UP WITH THE BEST ANSWER!

The other major headlines involve the continuing Balkan Crisis

****

"And what's that all about?" spat Devorina Pezantova in peeved tones, throwing the print-out onto the table amidst the remains of her breakfast. "How come no one is writing about me?"

Varadin looked at her with deep sorrow. A 'good night's sleep' had left deep, dark circles under his eyes. He looked like a man returned from purgatory, carrying with him the secret of the end of the world.

"Why are you looking at me like that? What did I say?" she asked irritably.

"There was that small condition, if you remember..." he replied quietly. "This is an informal event and they do not want publicity."

"How could you accept such a stupid condition!" she burst out. "What use is this meeting if no one knows about it?"

Varadin said nothing. He had not actually had a good night. The ladies had occupied all the bedrooms in the residence and he had been left to sleep on the sofa in the hall. But the aches and pains of his body were nothing compared to those in his head. The empty streets of his subconscious were filled with roaming questions, as frightening as gangs of street-dogs during a harsh winter. They attacked him on the corners, barked wildly at his presence, howled at the sky. But he had nothing to feed them with, no answers at all, not even the skeleton of a plan for them to gnaw its bones. And his particular winter was getting harsher still.

The window was slightly open and a fresh breeze blew in, the thick curtain waved slightly as a result.

"So, She's going to go and see that bloody toilet, and that's all over the damn press," started Pezantova, with renewed fury. "And the fact that She's coming to my concert? Oh, no, not allowed!! And what's the upshot? That some stupid toilet is more important than I am!! How could you accept such idiocies!?"

"The exhibition is nothing to do with us," Varadin muttered.

"So who is it to do with, then?" she screeched.

"It's nothing to do with anybody in particular," he replied.

"The initiative came purely from the British Museum and the Local Council of Provadia."

"But that's stupid!" complained the now famous Mitche. "Can't we invite the BBC to do a documentary? It might not be too late? You do have contacts with the BBC, yes?" she asked turning to the Ambassador.

"What?" he frowned.

"The B-B-C," she repeated. "To call out a team for this evening."

Varadin smiled contemptuously. "This isn't Sofia in case you hadn't realised. Apart from that, allowing anyone to attend who is not on the guest list means that the whole engagement will be cancelled."

"What, even at the last moment?" Mitche's eyes opened wide.

"Are you willing to accept that responsibility?" he was almost daring her.

There followed an icy silence.

"Wouldn't it be easier," started the second lady-in-waiting, "if Mrs Pezantova went to open the famous WC herself? They could hardly object to that. Then she would be all over the press as well."

"How could you say that Veronika!?!" Mitche raised her voice spitefully. "Mrs Pezantova only associates with eternal spiritual values! She could never be linked to something so V...Bulgar."

Veronika Dishlieva, a lady of no small repute amongst the Sofia High Society, turned to look at her patroness, Just look how she's always whingeing said her look. She was on the point of voicing her thoughts on the matter, but realised in time that she would find no sympathy where she was looking. Pezantova looked very serious, almost as though she was thinking of something important.

"Listen," she said suddenly. "No one can stop us from sending an article to the press as soon as the concert is over. We won't be taking any risks. Let them be peeved as much as they like, what's done is done. Do you think it's a good idea?" she turned to Varadin for an answer.

A sunbeam danced triumphantly on her tip of her toffee-nose.

He looked through her and nodded, "Absolutely."

There were less than ten hours until the official proceedings began.

The seconds counted down, scrolling on a huge screen in the back of his skull.

Pezantova looked at him worriedly. What was wrong with the man? Yesterday he had been perfectly all right, and today he looked like a three-day corpse. He probably had various things to worry about, but that was none of her affair. As long as he does not cock everything up at the last moment, that is, she thought with her usual ruthlessness.

"I'll go and see how the preparations are going," he mumbled, then stood up and left.

34

"Sir and Lady Brandon Croft!" announced Barry Longfellow ceremoniously.

Down the improvised red carpet came two middle-aged figures, looking grandiose. A thick band of pearls was wrapped around Her Ladyship's neck; she smiled dazzlingly and arched her spine gracefully. Applause echoed to the rafters of the Factory.

'Lady Croft', known to the majority of the population as Susan Lamour, usually played Brigitte Bardot. Recently, her fame had been steadily dwindling, and she had gladly accepted the role of an extra in the new extravaganza. The role of Brandon Croft was played by a well-built, womaniser, who usually played a popular, kick-ass football player. The family of Sir Brandon, according to Debrett's Peerage was traceable back to 1234. Its heredity consisted of some land in Lancashire and a small castle in Wales.

"The Reverend Adam Sacks, Bishop of Neverbury, director of the Celestine Charitable Trust," Barry shouted once more.

A tubby gentleman appeared on the walkway, wearing a purple cassock, his eyes were playful. It did not take much to guess whose double he was. His real name was Pat Moremead, but in every other detail he was Benny Hill: voice, face, walk, mannerisms; as though the great comic had left them to him in his will.

The Reverend Adam Sacks sidled up to Lady Croft, raised his eyes to Heaven, and pinched her bottom. Everyone burst out laughing fit to cry.

"Cut!" cried Ziebling professionally. He was standing at Barry's shoulder watching the 'Parade of Benefactors', as he had dubbed it. "You are not to do that, got it? You are not Benny Hill for the time being!"

"Oops, sorry!" exclaimed Pat to more laughter.

Barry wagged a finger at him and shouted, "Baroness Remoulade!"

Remoulade had been a sauce for chips, bangers or mash, but it sounded eminently aristocratic to the ears of one Thomas Munroe, the author of the honours list. At a certain point he was bored to death with Debrett's and its dry articles and, reaching for his pint, had noticed the packet of sauce on the table and decided to indulge himself in the luxury of create-your-own aristocrat. He had listed Remoulade as an ancient Danish family, Lords of the Keep of the Baltic Island of Faarhoeighen. From the start of the fifties their descendants had moved to London.

Baroness Remoulade was a washed-out blonde, with the face of a drowned victim staring at the sky through a thick layer of arctic ice, and all the grace of a walking robot. She was wearing a light-pink checked suit, white gloves and big glitzy hoop earrings. Her Star had risen eighteen months previously, when the housewife Lorena Bobbit had cold-bloodedly cut her cheating husband's penis off, written a book about the whole thing, and achieved fame on both sides of the Atlantic. From that moment her personality had stoked the fires of passion in many of the populace, and it was pure business-sense for the Factory to respond to the new demands. The unpleasant Elaine Carter, who was also a middle-class housewife and thus very suited to the part, played the role. She did not have the courage of Mrs Bobbit, but needed money to repay the loan she had taken out for her breast enlargement. Bobbitt's star had burned itself out quickly, but her loan repayments were still a fact.

"Lord De Fazaposte, and his sister Lady De Viyent!" announced Barry.

A wheelchair appeared on the carpet, pushed by a severe-looking, eagle-nosed woman, dressed as a widow. The good Samuel

Fogg, also known as 'Hawking', occupied the wheelchair, dressed like a Chelsea Veteran. The able make-up crew of the Factory had managed to make him look respectable. But that did not stop the assembled cast from laughing, to which he responded with a maliciously vacant smile.

"Lady Marx, the Duchess Van Der Brayne, Sir De Vilajidioff!" Barry continued like a true medieval Herald. "Hugh Munroe, esquire, President of The Monarchist League, Sir Jay."

Those announced walked forward with grandeur, chests puffed out, and professional smiles in place. Once the glamorous parade was over, Barry turned to his boss. Ziebling applauded appreciatively and gestured to them all to gather round.

"Ladies and Gentlemen," he began. "We find ourselves on the eve of a unique Super-Production. Until now we have never done such a thing: every one of you had your own little show, quite separate from the rest. This evening, however, you will be called upon to be a part of a grand-scale scenario, which requires an unusually high level of realism. Despite the fact that most of you are playing minor roles, there will be many guests present and you most be in-role at all times. They want realism, so we're going to provide it!"

He looked around at the silent actors and continued, "People around the world get their kicks in different ways. Prestige, High Society, Fame, these things have always been the most powerful aphrodisiacs, and always will be. Those who are attracted to these things, however, rarely admit, even to themselves, that what they truly desire from them is actually selfish sexual gratification. Sometimes they even go so far as to disguise this behind various abstracted and ill-defined goals. But they cannot fool their own subconscious. The nature of orgasm is both mysterious and capricious. Millions never achieve its heights in their entire life, whilst others get there every day. Some spend a fortune to avail themselves of one, to others it falls like a golden shower. Blessed are those who are content with little. Our clients, though, are not amongst these blessed souls. They want it all! If that helps them climax, all the better."

Ziebling paused, before making a sweeping gesture with one arm, "Ladies and Gentlemen," he announced poignantly. "Her Majesty, Queen Elizabeth II."

Everyone turned to look at the start of the carpet. An elderly woman stood there in a light-green hat and white shoes. Behind her, in the role of the bodyguard, stood Desmond, wire in ear, wearing the obligatory strict black suit. The lady raised one hand and waved regally. She seemed almost too real, and the others stared in respectful silence.

"Who is she?" hissed Baroness Remoulade in Sir Brandon Croft's ear.

"No idea," said the Manchester player. "First time I've set eyes on her."

"Well lookie here!" exclaimed Pat, who had been with the agency longer than most. "The Return of Mrs Cunningham! Hip, hip, Hurrah!"

The queen stopped and gave him an unimpressed look, "Off with his head!"

Ziebling burst out laughing. He went over to the elderly lady and hugged her warmly. "Auntie Helen! As unique as ever! I'm extremely pleased to see you amongst us once again."

"Well I'm not so pleased," she replied harshly. "But I need a new fridge. And with that teacher's pension..." Mrs Cunningham shook her head angrily.

"Well, you might even make it two fridges!" said Ziebling, nudging her elbow, "What do you think of our little scenario?"

"Dull as life itself," she spat. "But I'll manage, it's not like this is the first time."

"Now that's what you call a professional," said Ziebling, turning to the others. "Are you all ready?"

The group nodded.

"Good," he said. "Enough rehearsals then. I think we all know what we're doing here. The scenario isn't complicated but you need to be on your guard. Don't get drunk, don't get chatty, remain grand and reserved, and it'll all be fine. I'm off to see that the stage has been properly set. Barry will look after you all. I'll see you this evening."

Katya had followed the rehearsal, idly leaning against one wall of the make-up room. She was not involved in the scenario for obvious reasons but did not feel any pangs of regret. The fact that that grotesque spectacle would be taking place within the bounds of the Bulgarian Embassy, threw her into confusion. Why, who needed it?? And who was footing the bill? She felt personally degraded. Then she simply stopped caring. She was happier than ever that she had left the place far behind.

She stood in front of the mirror to try on a new wig, a light-pink one. They had brought it in to her that afternoon. It was an important part of a new scenario that had been written to order for some wealthy old punk rocker.

"So you're my new daughter-in-law," an ironic voice broke in behind her.

She moved slightly and looked at the reflection of Mrs Cunningham in the mirror. She liked the old lady; she had a bold voice.

"How old are you?"

"24," answered Katya.

"Do you like the role?"

"My timetable's fairly busy," mumbled the girl.

"Then they need another Princess," spat Mrs Cunningham. "This show will go on for a long time. You won't find yourself on the street, believe me!"

"I've nothing against that," said Katya. "But I don't intend to stay in this business forever."

"Are you Russian?"

"Bulgarian." Katya said, shaking her head.

Mrs Cunningham narrowed her eyes, as though trying to

remember something important. "Ah, you're the girl who used to work there, aren't you?" she asked in lively tones.

Everyone knows! So much for confidentiality!' Then Katya said aloud, "Work is putting it a bit strongly. I cleaned every so often in exchange for lodgings. It was a real chance at first because I had no money. But things are a little different now, so I moved out."

"Well, well, what is the world coming to!" sighed the old lady disapprovingly. "Masturbation at such a level. It's going a bit far, don't you think?"

"High-level, low-level, it's all the same," Katya shrugged.

"I still don't approve," said Mrs Cunningham, shaking her head. "Think what you will, but personally I don't approve. Onanism stops people from developing. That's what I was taught when I was young. Now I finally understand what they actually meant."

She reached into her handbag and pulled out a cigarillo. She lit it. Her head almost disappeared in a cloud of sweet smoke.

"Everybody knows how to jerk-off in the dark," she continued, puffing away. "You don't have to be handsome, intelligent, wealthy – nothing! You can even have 'bad personal hygiene' as I've heard it called. People are becoming sloppy. Why bother making an effort to look good, improve the mind and so on, when you can sort yourself out? And that's that. Once you start, nothing can stop you. You return to being an animal."

The queen casually blew some smoke-rings. "When someone jerks themselves off, that's their business. But when the whole country is jerked off, it gets a bit much," she concluded philosophically.

"Brilliant! Why don't you profit from the occasion to tell them that?" proposed Katya.

The queen considered for a moment, then shook her head, "It's not in the script. And it's none of my business. But don't you worry, one day they'll find someone to explain it to them. There's always one to explain."

The elderly lady headed off to her make-up room, muttering under her breath, "Who the hell came up with that damn dull concert? Probably that half-wit Munroe! That man is a complete idiot!"

35

"You've played me for a fool," snorted Varadin. "You Bastard!"

His voice spewed from his oral cavity like a thick black, pestilential stream.

"Your Excellency," replied Ziebling coldly. "I've no idea what you are talking about. You wanted the Queen, you have Her! What more do you need!"

"The real Queen, you bastard!" The Ambassador groaned and then almost choked. "100!"

"Pardon?" Ziebling raised his eyebrows.

"75!" said Varadin and repeated himself furiously, "The Real Queen!"

"The real Queen?" Ziebling seemed genuinely surprised. "Are you mad?"

"No, I'm not!" spat the Ambassador, "300!"

Pepolen's system was coming apart at the seams. Obviously it was not designed for such heavy use. The emotional valve could not hold the pressure; there were too many numbers and with no other escape-valve, the whole system was blocking up. At any moment it might blow, and bury him in the debris. He had to save his brain.

Ziebling stared at him, as though trying to guess what was going through his client's mind.

"Why don't you bring Lady Diana along as well," the Ambassador continued cuttingly. "Just for the look of the thing."

The Famous Connector blinked rapidly, "But you didn't ask for her!"

"Enough!" shouted Varadin, stopping both Ziebling and the

numbers. "Do you think you can lead me around by the nose? I know all about your agency!"

"We have nothing to hide, Sir," Ziebling answered calmly. "I assumed that you were aware of the nature of our services from the start. You called us, if you remember."

"Dean Carver recommended you, and I put my faith in him," the Ambassador complained bitterly, and added bitingly, "I suppose it was in his interest..."

"I'm not surprised he spoke highly of us," said Ziebling. "We're very good of what we do. I assure you, you will like our show!"

"There won't be any show!" spat Varadin.

"You're cancelling at the last minute?" the Famous Connector shifted uneasily. "Whatever for?"

"Because you expect me to accept a fake Queen, that's why!!" Varadin exploded, "Do you really think we're that stupid?"

Ziebling went red and jumped out of his chair, "My dear man, not for an instant did I expect that you might think that we would actually get hold of Her Majesty herself! That's absurd! Where on earth did you get such a bizarre idea?"

The Ambassador blinked rapidly opposite him. "We'll have to think of something," he mumbled, mostly to himself. "...That she's fallen ill or been called away on important State business. I don't know. We have to think of something!"

"But what about the others?" asked Ziebling, business-like.

"What others?" gaped Varadin. The guest list appeared before his eyes, titles and all.

"I want to inform you that they are only extras, you can't rely on them too much," Ziebling said.

Varadin felt his migraine coming on and massaged his sinuses, without much success. "I should have known," he muttered. "You thought of everything!"

"But of course!" nodded Ziebling. "It wasn't easy, let me tell you! Usually people choose more private scenarios. But you've wanted this concert so much! You obviously have good reasons for it. I don't know. It's not my business to comment on my clients' desires, merely to fulfil them. However, I cannot allow external elements to interfere with the troop. That's unprofessional."

"But they've bought their tickets already, for God's sake!"

"We assumed that this will please you. We included them in the price. Don't worry."

The Ambassador looked up quickly, "You expected me to pay for this masquerade?"

"Amongst other things – that is why I'm here," replied Ziebling cheerfully, "to discuss our fee. I've prepared you an invoice down to the last penny."

"Maybe you didn't understand that I'm turning down your services!"

"Don't rush it, your Excellency," continued Ziebling, paying not slightest attention to his words. "We've already invested in this project and you will be obliged to refund our expenses in any case. Besides which, we all bought our tickets, including myself, see here it is." He pulled a piece of card from his breast pocket, which had the Embassy's seal on it. "And we have no intention of missing the food or the show. I know you've been preparing for this occasion for almost six months. Troubadours and acrobats have been called in all the way from Bulgaria. So it should be worth seeing, shouldn't it?"

"We'll refund the price of the tickets," said the Ambassador gloomily. "I won't let you make fools of us."

"Just don't kill yourself!" Ziebling interrupted. "I am worried about you, you know? Where on earth are you going to find other guests?" He looked at his watch. "You've only got three hours till the concert. I suspect certain people will be unimpressed if the whole room is empty. Especially if they find out why. Where does the buck stop? You can't pass the buck to the small fry. Think of your career!"

Varadin looked at him blankly. What did it matter now? His career was already up the creek. And not a paddle in sight.

"No, nothing is lost, Sir!" shouted Ziebling, as though reading his mind. "You mustn't give up hope. After making one mistake, don't make a second. Let us put on our little show and everything will be all right. They are absolute professionals, especially our Queen. Children have often stopped her in the park to ask her, 'Excuse me, are you Queen Elisabeth II?' You know? And the costumes are simply to die for."

"Are telling me I should try to fool them?"

"I'm offering a way out," Ziebling lowered his voice. "The only one for a man in your position! I'll save you and you simply keep to your contract. There won't be any scandals. Nothing will reach the press. Someone will believe that they've dined with Her Majesty and will be happy. You'll be the hero. And if you want the princess later, you just give me a call. You are quite taken with her, aren't you? We have large discounts for our regular clients."

He had gradually moved closer to Varadin, blocking the faint afternoon light from the window. Suddenly, his figure loomed large and its huge shadow fell across the mass of his desk. His lips were almost kissing his ear, as though they were trying to suck the remains of brain out. Terrible warmth encircled his body.

"You're the Devil himself!" hissed Varadin.

36

At exactly 6.45pm, a pink hat, shaped like a gigantic éclair, passed triumphantly through the Embassy's official entrance. Behind it stepped a neurotic Varadin and the two ladies-in-waiting. The foyer shone as if freshly licked. The crystal chandelier sparkled festively. At the threshold, they were greeted greasily by Mr Kishev. Another two diplomats hovered nearby, looking like coppers. None of them had been honoured with a place at the Concert. Their task consisted of guarding the front-line of the gathering. The technical staff had been pulled back far into the reserve, owing to 'technical incompatibility'.

Devorina Pezantova did not deign to notice the diplomat; she swirled out of her fur cape and deposited it on his arm, as though he were some strange mobile coat rack. Her dress was a sequined nightmare, which instantly caught the light and shone like a garish Christmas display. She was wearing a wide blue band with a medallion at the lower end over one shoulder – a trophy from a visit to some faraway country. She thought that that particular decoration made her look grand, and never passed up an occasion to wear it, especially if said occasion came under the heading 'ceremonial'.

The giant éclair made its way to the main staircase, followed by its entourage. They slowly ascended the stairs, like people making their way to Heaven. The red carpet smelled freshly of lilac. The doors to the reception room had been opened wide; between the tables smartly dressed students hovered, wearing white gloves that had been bought especially for the occasion. An approving smile appeared on Devorina's lips. Then disappeared, far faster.

"What is that stall doing there?" She demanded peevishly.

Her gaze had fallen on a small table to the left of the door. Varadin shrugged. The table was covered with an assortment of articles, each with its own little price tag. He had no idea where the cursed little stand had come from. Only an hour before, when he last did a round to check up on things, it had been nowhere to be seen. The goods gave the general impression of souvenirs everywhere: a catalogue of icons printed way back in 1971 (£7), a pile of CD's of folk songs (£5 each), a few pairs of knitted woollen socks (£5), decorative folk-slippers (£15), towels with folk motifs (£6), plaited straw bag (£10), as well as other odds and ends amongst which the little bronze dog frolicked, its collar showing the respectable sum of £150.

The shady artistic director slid out of the corridor leading to the service area. His long hair was tied back into a ponytail. He was wearing a black, woollen suit and a loose-fitting collarless shirt, which made him look a little like a vicar.

"Did you put this here?" the disapproving voice of Mrs Pezantova greeted his arrival.

"Umm, well, the artists asked me to," he mumbled, looking guiltily at the traditional wooden horse-comb in his hands (£4).

"I don't like it at all, remove it at once!"

The artistic director did not move, however. So timid on an institutional level, he was ready to risk his life for his interests on a domestic level. Mrs Pezantova was not in the habit of paying her artists. Her speciality was spiritual reward. He knew that if no one bought the little dog, he would be going home empty-handed. And the winter heating bills required more than spiritual well-being.

"Can you put those tapes as well," a melodic voice sang. "They are left over from our Argentinean trip."

The voice belonged to one of the singers. She appeared like ghost from the dark corridor, her heavily decorated costume chiming. Her thickly made-up face had playful dimples.

"We were waiting for you, Mrs Pezantova," she said casually. "You don't disapprove of our little display, do you? People like our things, and a few levs on the side will do us good."

At that particular moment a diplomat ran up the stairs and waved his hands, "They're coming" he shouted and ran back.

"Fingers crossed!" exclaimed the singer and disappeared into the dark corridor once more, where the make-up rooms had been improvised.

The artistic director looked all business-like. Pezantova looked at Varadin, who merely raised his eyebrows in philosophical resignation. The others rushed to disappear into the background.

A mysterious silence fell. "It's starting," said Varadin, his stomach in knots. The hard stitches of his tailcoats were digging into his armpits; that halfwit Miladin had obviously got the wrong size. How could he possibly have sent him to hire his outfit! Underneath the hat's brim, Pezantova's eyes were almost popping out of their sockets in anticipation. With a little more luck we might be able to pass off a pig's ear!

"Why is nobody coming?" mumbled Pezantova staring at the empty staircase.

"Here they come!" exclaimed Mitche behind her.

A lone couple made their way across the red carpet.

The man was well built, with an equally well-built gut and a goatee, which made him look older than he was. He was dressed all in black and to judge from his tie and the handkerchief in his breast pocket, he liked to stare at the window displays on Oxford Street. Next to him a strange ostrich-like creature minced, with feathers to match.

"The Halvadjievs!" hissed Pezantova through her teeth. "For once they're not late!"

When the duo reached the landing, however, her face was all sweetness and light. "How nice to see you!" she smiled.

"Thank you for the invitation!" neighed the big man shaking hands with them both. Then he turned to his better half and said,

"Yvonne, let me introduce Mrs Pezantova! And this is Yvonne."
He added with no little pride.

"I am so glad!" the creature smiled. "Brilliant party!"

Her skinny neck was armoured with several rows of pearls.

"Come along!" he put an arm around her waist and towed her away.

Two students rushed to show them to their seats. Pezantova waited for them to be out of earshot and remarked spitefully, "Sponsors, what can you do!?"

How had such a man become so wealthy? In Socialist times, he had just happened to be in charge of a large manufacturing company. When after the fall of the old regime, the Privatization Agency offered the company up, all its records mysteriously disappeared, leaving him as the only shareholder, managing director and president. On the few occasions that he talked of the matter, Halvadjiev liked to use phrases such as: 'saved from bankruptcy' or 'protected from dissolution'. The rumours back in Bulgaria tended to disagree, often vehemently, with his terminology. As a result he tended to sponsor events, especially when members of the government were involved. His buying of indulgences continued, full steam ahead.

At exactly 7pm a huge tourist-like bus pulled up in front of the Embassy. Its doors swooshed open, and, before the ogling eyes of the diplomats, a crowd of people in evening dress poured out. Robert Ziebling led them.

"Here we are!" he shouted and hurried inside.

Pezantova stood stunned.

The guests started to make their way up the stairs. It snowed smiles and titles: Baroness Remoulade, the Duchess Van Der Brayne, Sir Jay, Lady Marx, and Sir De Vilajidioff. She felt like melting in the social whirlpool. The queue extended all the way to the bottom step. Before proceeding into the room, the guests stopped by the little stand, rummaging amongst the displayed items and asking all sorts of questions. Unfortunately, the artistic director spoke not a word of English and was unable to satisfy their curiosity. He could only look at them with growing anger. No one had thought to get their wallet out. Fucking stingy bastards!

Last to appear were the diplomats struggling with the weight of Sir De Fazaposte's wheelchair. His head lolled from side to side and his medals clanked. The severe looking Lady De Viyent fussed around them and was shouting demandingly, "For God's sake, be careful!"

Then a brief moment of silence occurred.

"What if she doesn't come?" fretted Pezantova.

"There's no danger of that," Varadin reassured her, looking at his watch.

Ziebling appeared. "What on earth are you doing here? Why aren't you downstairs already?" he demanded angrily. "Didn't you read the protocol? We are not waiting for a mere countess, you know!"

"Oh my God!" exclaimed Pezantova. "I totally forgot!"

She grabbed the Ambassador by the hand and dragged him down the stairs in a mad rush. Ziebling shook his head disdainfully. Barry Longfellow came over and leaned casually on the balustrade, he was presently the Marquis of Mullet.

"A heavy night awaits, eh Sir?"

"Don't let that rabble out of your sight for an instant!" ordered Ziebling.

"I know my business," the Marquis replied curtly.

The artistic director stared at them with his beady little eyes. The Famous Connector gave him a cheery wave. "Hey, we come in peace!"

The object of this humour entirely failed to understand and raised one eyebrow suspiciously. Fucking stingy so-and-sos!

The Rolls slid silently up to the porch. It lacked all the usual markings: crests, crowns and flags. The vast black automobile was shrouded in secrecy, as though it travelled not in the human reality, but flew on the invisible motorways between worlds. A huge man in a beige raincoat got out of the front seat, opened the back door and offered his hand to the lady inside.

Christ! They could be twins! Varadin was trembling at the thought.

"Your Majesty!" whinnied Mrs Pezantova, forgetting to curtsy and rushing towards the Lady like a hound on the scent.

"Oh, my dear woman," exclaimed Queen Cunningham. "Your little charity brings tears to our eyes! Ah, and so good to see you once again, your Excellency!' she said turning to Varadin. "If you continue to serve your country in this spirit, God himself will reward you."

Witch! he hissed internally, taking her hand in turn and bowing low.

The diplomats buzzed around them like a swarm of wasps, only Varadin's severe look keeping them at a respectable distance. The group wended its way towards the reception room. The Queen leaning on Mrs Pezantova's arm and repeating tirelessly, "Oh, my dear!"

The bodyguard was her shadow.

Blood pounded in Pezantova's ears. My God, what an honour! What an honour! If only Kututcheva and Moustacheva could see me now! What did they know? Pathetic little provincial girls! Here She is, leaning on my arm, speaking to me – the Queen of England, herself! Do you hear over there? Do you see? Do you understand? No, nobody gives a damn about you. Awful yokels, you do not deserve a thing. 'Oh, my dear!' She said it again. Those are signals. She likes me! The carpet beneath her feet had disappeared; she felt she was walking on air. A miraculous light filled her. You can all go to hell, damn peasants! I am on the other side of the divide. I am not what I used to be. I am different. I do not know you.

"Ah, and what is this?" exclaimed Queen Cunningham.

Oh no! That bloody little stand again, Pezantova swore. The magic disappeared. The Queen attached herself to the table and began to examine the display. The little decorative pigskin folk slippers caught her attention.

"What interesting moccasins!" said the Queen holding them up by their laces.

This time the artistic director felt able to say something. "They call tsarvuli," he announced in a serious voice, looking all sweaty, "Natsionalen Kostyoom!"

"Oh, tsarvuli!" she said seemingly respectfully. "How wonderful! Tsarvuli!"

"Tsarvuli, tsarvuli!" everyone around her started to nod enthusiastically.

"How sweet!" she said condescendingly. "Might we try them on?"

The Artistic Director gaped blankly.

"She wants to try them!" translated Pezantova in her iciest tones.

Varadin gave Ziebling a withering look; the latter was observing the scene with unhealthy interest, almost indulgent. The diplomats hurried to bring a chair. She sat and removed her white shoes. The director helped her to do the laces.

"Oh, they are so comfortable, these tsarvuli!" said Queen Cunningham as she walked around. "We'll take them!"

My God, what a lesson She is giving us all, thought Pezantova. Only a Queen could possibly be so diplomatic in such a situation. It is in her blood.

"Your Majesty!" she shouted emotionally. "You look fantastic!"

"Oh, my dear!" Her Majesty waved regally.

Without taking the tsarvuli off, and with a faint slap-slapping sound, she headed into the reception room. All the guests stood up and started to applaud. Then the doors were closed. The faces of the diplomats darkened. Mavrodiev lit a cigarette and put his hands into his pockets. Kishev picked up the Royal shoes from the floor, looked at them with respect and then put them on the table.

"And who is going to pay for the tsarvuli?" the director suddenly remembered.

His question hung in the air. Danailov was prowling in front of the doors, growling like a lion. Sounds of ceremonial pomp were coming from the hall. Kishev, who passed himself off as a classical music buff, listened to it and noted gloomily, "The Ode to Joy."

'The Ode to Joy' was played by a group of Bulgarian students from the Royal College of Music. The guests listened carefully. The waitressing staff rushed quietly between the tables, filling the glasses with wine. When this unique entertainment came to an end and the applause died down, Mrs Pezantova stood up and took a deep breath, filled with scent of power. The world expanded briefly before she brought it back under control, "Your Majesty! Honoured Ladies and Gentlemen!" she started in the bombastic tone of a Girl-Guide Commissioner opening a new camp in the mountains. "It is my great pleasure and honour to welcome you here today. The gathering together of such a large group of so many important people here today is an obvious sign of the worthiness of our charitable cause. I would like to thank you on behalf of the Bulgarian people and to assure you that this historical gesture will be understood and greatly appreciated. This evening you will be given the rare opportunity to scrape only the surface of the eternal cultural values produced by Bulgarian genius. Let me open that priceless spiritual treasure from which radiate the most elevated human ideals, and to convince you that we belong to one and the same cultural family among the realms of Europe. Your Majesty! Ladies and Gentlemen! My heart fills with pride and emotion when I think of the great honour of being the one to present to you the cultural key to my country. I humbly beg you to accept it."

There was a short silence. Ziebling started clapping and all the others followed him. Yes shouted Pezantova in her mind I knew they would be pleased! A professional literary sycophant, who had been taken on by her husband directly from the school of the previous communist leaders, had written her speech. He was good, one had to admit.

"Now I am sure you will join me in the pleasure of welcoming Her Majesty, Elizabeth II," announced Pezantova ceremoniously.

"Thank you," nodded Queen Cunningham in a business-like manner. "The cause of the brown bears has always been close to our heart. That is the reason we think that the present initiative represents a valuable contribution to ecological balance of the continent of Europe."

A shadow of doubt crossed Devorina's face.

"What the Hell is she is on about!" hissed Varadin in Ziebling's ear, "The concert is to raise money for the orphans. It's written on the invitations!"

"What's the difference?" whispered the other. "They are all endangered species, aren't they?"

Behind the mask of not giving a damn, a brutal flow of obscenity filled his mind, that fuck-wit Munroe! How could he screw everything up like that! I will dock his bloody wages!

"The brown bears are our friends," ended Queen Cunningham importantly. "Respectively, the friends of the brown bears are also our friends."

She raised her glass, "To the health of all the bears in the world!"

"Fuck you Munroe!" Ziebling sighed. Frenetic applauses echoed.

"You'll pay me for this!" hissed the Ambassador.

"It's only human to make mistakes!" Ziebling shrugged.

"What is the big deal," thought Mrs Pezantova whilst applauding the Queen's speech. With all those engagements one must get mixed up. She knew it from experience. The words are ephemeral, the facts remain. The main thing is, she is sitting here, at this very table.

The concert opened with the song from the folk singer, Radka Madjurova. The starter was served: chicken livers with a salad of fresh radishes à la Pastricheff.

"Mmm, delicious!" exclaimed Mrs Cunningham, but her compliment remained unheard.

Radka Madjurova was a natural phenomenon, examined many times by physicists. Her voice had a huge drilling power. In order to demonstrate this undeniable fact, a little demonstration was arranged in front of the public. They placed a crystal glass at a metre's distance in front of the singer's mouth, which the singer shattered with several vibratos. Pezantova threw a quick glance at the horrified Queen as though to demand, Do you have such wonders?

The intense frequency of her voice managed to disturb some device in the duty room and it started squeaking. The general stood up and switched off.

"What on earth is going on in there?" he mumbled.

"They are having fun," said Danailov in a bitter voice, whilst chewing a piece of crispy duck skin.

The defence attaché was on duty. He was casually dressed in his tracksuit-bottoms and trainers and feeling far more comfortable than the diplomats, who had been mobilised to fulfil porter's duties. On top of that, he was well provided for the evening: in a strange surge of remarkable generosity and solidarity they had sent him a huge tray, overflowing with dark duck meat and banitsa. He had added to these two bottles of red from Assenovgrad and six cans of Becks. The general was not stingy and he could not manage such a quantity on his own, so he had invited his dejected colleagues to share it with him. The men sat around the low table, stuffing their faces with pieces of meat and drank in a mood that could best be described as 'pissed off with life'. From time to time they threw a distracted glance at the television. At around 8pm Turkeiev and the artist appeared, carrying various flammable materials, and started preparing the foyer for the forthcoming pyrotechnics.

"Look, they are showing the Queen!" exclaimed counsellor Mavrodiev.

The others automatically turned their heads to the screen. BBC1 was showing a report of the Queen's visit to Matrongo. This afternoon Her Majesty Elizabeth II had a meeting with President Dr Michael Sesseto Loko. The visit coincides with the third year celebrations of the first democratic elections in the former British colony. Tomorrow the Queen will be visiting the National park 'Tete' and will have talks with the Head of the Matrongan Anglican Church, Bishop Brian Mega-to-Longo. Next to Queen a tall black man walked importantly, dressed in a traditional handmade golden robe; in the background palm-trees, barefoot children and military men in their parade uniforms could be seen.

"Well, well!" the general opened his eyes wide. "Isn't she here, the Queen?"

Nobody said anything; the television was spewing forth data about the economic development of Matrongo over the last decade, which was not very joyful despite the successes of the democracy.

"Come on, why you are all pretending you don't know!" said Danailov suddenly. "She has her own double, that woman! Like Brezhnev and Yeltsin. They all had their doubles, even our old president, Todor Zhivkov. She's not that stupid, you know!"

"So you think that's a double?" Mavrodiev pointed to the screen unconvinced.

"And what the hell do you think it is?" exploded Danailov, who was a fervent supporter of conspiracy theory. "Do you actually think that they are going to send the real Queen to meet some African? Don't be ridiculous! Why do you think she arrived here incognito without her carriage or any of her official entourage? Why won't they allow any pictures? Because she is officially in Matrongo. If you phone the Palace now and ask them, where the Queen is, the last thing that they are going to tell you is that she is here. They will laugh at you if you confront them!"

"But they are in the shit now because we saw her!" said the general cunningly.

"Like they give a damn!" Danailov waved disparagingly.

He looked at the tray and frowned; the meat had disappeared.

"What about Clinton when he visited Bulgaria," asked Kishev with a guilty expression on his face, whilst cleaning his greasy fingers. "Was that him?"

"Are you nuts?" nodded Danailov. "At that time they wouldn't have let him out of the States at all, because of the Lewinski trial."

An uneasy silence followed.

"Are we gonna watch Leeds-Manchester?" the general prompted cleverly, giving them all a way out.

They all nodded with relief.

Back upstairs, the main course was accompanied by a little musical performance. A pleasant duet, flute and guitar, with its fourteenth century troubadour motifs provided the accompaniment to the prosaic clicking and clacking of cutlery.

"I want to assure you, my dear, that you have an excellent cook!" whispered Queen Cunningham to Pezantova, "The duck is simply delicious!"

Pezantova blushed with pleasure and threw Varadin a glance full of gratitude. She had tasted almost nothing herself. Her senses had gone numb because of the nervous pressure; she had the feeling she was chewing a piece of cardboard. She had no need of this rough material substance, called food! She was more than content with simply absorbing the aristocratic vibrations, which filled the atmosphere of the hall. Varadin, on the other hand, was swallowing her vibrations and his stomach felt full. That was not true of Ziebling though, or of the other guests. Who had said that exquisite people eat very little?

On the other table, Mr Halvadjiev was having an argument in Bulgarian with his wife, "Yvonne, stop playing with your food and eat it!"

"I swallowed something nasty, some little bone, there might be more," she said staring at the plate and not looking up.

"Aah, you're just afraid of getting fat. I know you," he said pointedly.

"Fuck you!"

"You'll never get fat," he said with certain note of disappointment in his voice. "The duck's good, look how that Baroness is stuffing her face! She is not afraid of getting fat!"

"Because she is a Baroness, you wood-head!"

When she heard her title, Baroness Remoulade raised her head and smiled importantly. For the entire evening, she stuck strictly to Barry Longfellow's instructions and avoided opening her mouth with the exception of certain occasions when she stuffed something tasty into it. Only the Bishop of Neverbury had spoilt the good overall impression. He had Barry throwing lightning glances across the room.

"What a funny Holy Father!" thought Halvadjiev feeling some obscure disquiet, whilst watching the Bishop flirting with Yvonne.

At this moment, Sir De Fazaposte decided to pay a visit to the facilities again. For the third time! This was an operation involving quite a lot of effort, because said facilities were downstairs on the ground floor. Four students lifted the wheelchair and started trundling it down the stairs, huffing and puffing, lots of swearwords hidden behind their silent red faces. This time the self-sacrificing Lady De Viyent showed a surprising cold-heartedness. "Aaah, no! That is enough!" she hissed maliciously. "I want to see the next performance. You take care of yourself this time, you clown!"

Sir De Fazaposte, however, could not take care of himself, which led to a lot of additional complications. Samuel Fogg was really having fun.

In the meantime the light in the hall darkened and the table music faded away. More musicians appeared, a big drummer with waxed moustaches amongst them. In the space between the tables, adapted as a stage, some strange woman looking like a Delphic Sybil appeared, "Your Majesty! Ladies and Gentlemen! It gives you great pleasure for me to announce the next performance. It is an ancient ritual, called Molitva za Dusht or Prayer for Rain. This ritual originates the village Kundurli in the South-Eastern part of Bulgaria, and is brought to stage by our famous actress, Larissa Mundeva."

She paused, then started again in a heart-stopping tone, "It is summer, over the drought-filled Thracian plains, and not a single cloud is being. Inside dry and stony sharp riverbeds only snakes and lizards crawling. Worried peasants round their dry lands walking. Even birds are silent singing! Then the wise village men gathering and deciding to turn to old half-forgotten rituals, from their ancestors inheriting, and to the forces of Nature praying. The most beautiful maiden of the village goes to dancing near the river: it is the ritual dancing for the rain summoning."

Her last words faded into the sound of the drum.

A skinny bare-foot girl, dressed in a long white robe, flew onto the stage. Brandishing some non-descript hide stretched across an ancient-looking frame, she threw herself into a threateningly frenzied dance around the tables. 'Bang-bang-bang!' thundered the drum, awakening pagan sensations in the souls of the people present. The flute trilled first, the bagpipe wailed next, than the rest of the instruments entered. The guests stopped eating, in their eyes little flames started to sparkle and soon after that they all, one after the other, started nodding their heads in time to the beat: bang, bang, bang.

"The call of the wild," whispered Mrs Cunningham with respect.

From time to time the girl raised her eyes to look at the ceiling and screamed, "Uuuuh! Uuuuh!" imitating a childbirth push.

An atavistic urge made Mr Halvadjiev put his hand on Yvonne's knee. (My little Yvonne!) Than he shot her a glance out of the corner of his eye, but his action had no visible effect on her. His hand crawled up to the garter of her stocking, swiftly continued over her inner tight and suddenly froze. 'Bang, bang, bang!' continued the drum. Yvonne's face remained still.

The other hand had obviously been there long before his. It was warm and relaxed, soaked in oblivion and pleasure. He squeezed it firmly, before it could escape.

"Yvonne, why are you playing dead?" he whispered in his lowest voice.

She did not react. But the Bishop turned his face in horror. It was the face of a tortured martyr. Halvadjiev had an iron grip. His knuckles cracked and there was no joy in his eyes. What is the world coming to? the big man asked himself bitterly.

"Uuuuh!Uuuuh!" huffed the girl, waving the frame and summoning the elements.

"Aaah!Aaaah!" The Bishop of Neverbury answered and sweat began to stand out on his forehead.

Yvonne, still unmoved by the dramatic action between her legs, dipped her spoon into the dessert.

Outside, important decisions had to be taken.

"The Fire Lady – how does that sound?" asked the artist.

"Good," nodded Turkeiev. "Why not?"

"So, when I say in the end, 'Here comes the Fire Lady!' you light the fuses, understood?" said Spass Nemirov.

"OK, no problem," the intern agreed. He was moved by any close encounter with Modern Art and took his task very seriously.

The Fire Dancer ran up the stairs and threw a last glance inspecting his creation. On the marble floor, exactly 253 metal cups were arranged, each one filled with different flammable liquids and wired up. An extensive imagination was needed to see the contours of a human face in this minefield, but the artist rubbed his hands together contentedly. The bird of luck had finally landed on his shoulder. He had been waiting for this moment for years: years of fire and loneliness, of non-recognition and ridicule. But now – an end to the humiliations! The Queen of England herself was going honour him with Her Royal attention. That could be the turning point of his career. If they liked the demonstration tonight, they could easily throw more orders for new fire performances at him. They would start inviting him to their castles. He licked his dry lips. There was no way they would not like it. He had given everything from himself for this forthcoming illumination. He had calculated everything; he had been experimenting tirelessly for weeks. It was going to be a masterpiece!

"Are you ready Turkeiev!" shouted Spass Nemirov.

The intern sparked his lighter instead of replying.

From the side door the diplomats appeared, well fed and merry. The general accompanied them to the doorstep. Suddenly a worried look appeared on his face. "What are those explosives doing here?" his voice echoed.

"Easy, Sir!" called the Fire Dancer. "The situation is under control."

"Pyrotechnics!" Turkeiev added with a happy face.

"What pyrotechnics? Does the Ambassador know about this?" the General's worried eyes were following the wiring across all the metal cups filled with suspicious powder.

"Those are his personal orders," replied the artist looking down at him.

The three diplomats walked round the installation carefully, tutting. The general continued to stand on the doorstep. He did not like this, at all! He had started his career in the engineering corps of the army and although he had not practiced his speciality for years, he felt now personally disappointed at being left aside. How can he authorise sappers' activity here without a consultation with a specialist? he thought with indignation.

"Turkeiev!" hissed the military man. "Give me that lighter!"

The intern became confused.

"You stay where you are!" the artist threatened him with his finger.

"Don't even think of lighting this up!"

"Don't you dare to screw this up!"

At that moment they all heard the opening of the doors and the guests starting to come out of the hall.

"Lights!" shouted Spass Nemirov dramatically.

Danailov helpfully turned the light switch behind his back and the big chandelier darkened. Soon afterwards, the big staircase was packed with people. In front of everybody Mrs Pezantova and Queen Cunningham importantly stepped out, accompanied by Varadin and Ziebling. Behind them the pale face of the Bishop could be seen, while Sir De Fazaposte was still swaying his body in his wheelchair like a Chinese mandarin.

"Lovely evening!" noted Ziebling casually.

"Hum," muttered the Ambassador and said to himself, When things go too well it's not for the best.

The Fire Dancer greatly appreciated the iconic system of the Wild West. Especially for this occasion he had chosen the best from his wardrobe: a new denim shirt with all sorts of picturesque labels on the pockets and the collar, all in Willy Nelson's style, together with his usual leather trousers and reddish cowboy boots. At his waist a vast buckle sparkled.

The artist waited for the audience to gather, silently standing up in the middle of the foyer with his long hair loose and face down like a shaman reaching into the depths of his soul. He was concentrating on words he had to say in English. Damn words! He was afraid they would run away at the last minute, even though he had spent all morning memorising his speech. Languages were not his strong point. How was the beginning, Respectable guests? damn it! The drummer appeared in the upper part of the stairs and started banging invitingly.

Respectable guests, dear Queen? No, no you couldn't say it like that! But how? In a minute you will witness a unique demonstration conceived in the womb of the most primary element – fire! But how to say all that in English? Fuck my head! How did I end up with all this? I am an artist, not an orator, he concluded in the end. Let my work speak instead of me!

The Fire Dancer raised his head and announced clearly, "Here, The Fire Lady comes!"

Everybody felt sudden strange cold wrapping their senses as they were awaiting the Second Coming. The intern, who did not expect such a sudden beginning, feverishly started looking for the lighter in his pockets. The Fire Dancer strained his ears to hear the familiar hissing of the fuses but nothing of the sort followed.

"Here comes the Fire Lady!" he repeated suggestively.

At that very moment Turkeiev produced the sacred spark. The general instinctively stepped back, closed the door behind his back and ran to the duty room.

The fire spread up to the fuses with its small sparkling flames, hissing maliciously. Then they suddenly disappeared and above the cups thin lines of smoke started to swirl. The smell of sulphur swam in the air. The faces of the guests strained. Varadin and Pezantova exchanged concerned looks. She decided to say something but the words stuck to her mouth like flakes of dry skin on chapped lips. She started chewing her lips. Suddenly a shower of red sparks flew up to the ceiling. The real illumination followed. Within the flames the contours of a human face emerged, which were immediately swallowed by the smoke. The sensors of the smoke alarm reacted instantly. The shrieking of the alarm brought people out of their stupefaction. Confusion reigned. Water poured from the sprinkler system.

"As though Hell opened its gates," remembered old Mrs Cunningham till the end of her life and particularly in her last days, when a devoted priest was coming to give her soul consolation. "Yes, I saw Hell. I know what awaits me, because of my way of life, because I dared to imitate Her Majesty. (Pause) When the flames exploded in front of us, the ugly face of a daemon appeared, calling out to us from Purgatory. And the most sinister thing was that he had the features of the late Princess Diana. Good Lord, I still see it in front of my eyes. In the place of his eyes he had blue flames. Suddenly from his mouth

a purple tongue appeared and licked the chandelier. Then a thick, acrid smoke started spewing from his mouth. The smoke filled the whole foyer! From the ceiling water gushed like rivers, as though the Lord had heard the prayer for rain. Ziebling grabbed my hand and dragged me out. The car was waiting in front of the Embassy. We quickly got inside and drove away. I stopped playing the queen after that incident. I got frightened. I feel the beast near me waiting for me to close my eyes for the last time. What is going to happen to me, Father?"

"But where is everyone?" shouted Pezantova in her screechy voice, as she was looking around with her eyes full of tears. "Your Majesty!!!"

The éclair-hat was as wet as a sponge. A thick, yellowish smoke was still spreading low above the floor level. From the ceiling the sprinklers were still spraying water. Varadin was coughing into his fist. He was trying desperately to hide the malicious satisfaction burning deep inside his soul, *Now You are responsible for the whole mess, you stupid cow!*

The Fire Dancer had disappeared like a spirit from the prairies. The intern Turkeiev was touching his singed eyebrows stupidly. Devorina Pezantova hurried over to him and grabbed him by his collar, "You! You pathetic little worm, you're going to pay me for this!"

"Mitche fainted!" came Veronika's crying voice from the other end, but nobody paid any attention to it.

Mavrodiev and Danailov were running around as though drugged in the foyer, stumbling carelessly over the metal cups. Kishev was crawling to go to the toilet, fumbling in the dark, and groaning helplessly, "My eyes! I can't see..."

"Where is my dog?" exclaimed the artistic director worriedly, after the last patches of smoke cleared away from his stand.

The place of the little sculpture was empty. His glance landed on the Queen's white shoes and did not move from them from a long time. 'Where the hell did those stupid shoes come from?' he desperately tried to remember. Then he looked at the sculpture's place, left empty. Fuck, fuck, fuck! Thieves, everywhere! Then he looked at the shoes again and an acute social protest filled his heart, They didn't even pay for their shoes! Damn it!

Suddenly he realised that he was not the only one looking at the royal shoes. Mr Halvadjiev had his little eyes on these grand royal objects, too.

"Give them to me!" he hissed.

His face was covered with small sweaty drops. Yvonne was coughing and sniffling next to him, her nose was bleeding.

"E-e-e-r!" the director instinctively pulled the shoes to his chest.

"I'll give you twenty quid," said Halvadjiev and his eyes narrowed. Those are royal shoes, one day they will cost millions... his mind had become a calculator.

"Weeeell," the director scratched his head. "Those are Royal shoes....."

"Fifty quid!" Halvadjiev interrupted him.

Wow said the director to himself. You'll not getting them for less than 200!

A wailing noise filled the street outside. Three fire engines with flashing lights stopped in front of the Embassy, which was still shrouded in smoke. Who had called the fire station, nobody knew. The general persistently denied being the one, despite the fact that all the evidence was pointing to the duty room. Despite the late hour, some people came out of the hotel to watch the action.

"Two hundred and not a penny more!" groaned Halvadjiev, his face getting red.

"They are yours," the director looked around and stuffed the shoes into a plastic bag with a Bulgarian advert on it. Halvadjiev's wallet looked like a Christmas piglet.

"Come on Yvonne!" he said and counted ten brand new twenty notes.

The foyer was filled with men in helmets and gasmasks. Pezantova sat on a chair, weeping, her feet trailing in the pool of water that had replaced the usual floor. Nearby a man in yellow protective overalls was speaking some incomprehensible words though his mask. Two others were rescuing Mitche. Varadin was dealing with some enthusiast with a hose, who was insisting on going inside the building.

"Ts, ts, ts," Halvadjiev nodded his head. "We turned this soiree into a total fuck-up, but never mind!"

37

The telephone rang and woke him up at exactly 6.35am. Normally at that time Dale Rutherford was already up drinking his cup of black coffee and watching the repeat of the program 'From a Bird's Eye View' on Animal Planet. But since the duck incident, now widely known as 'The Richmond Catastrophe', his spirit had faded; apathy and melancholia had overtaken him. He did not hurry to drop by and see his favourites with a pocket full of breadcrumbs, but preferred to stay in bed until the last moment, his head buried under the pillow. He started going to work still sleepy and unshaven, and sometimes even late. His colleagues pitied him. In a week's time a new flock of ducks was due to arrive, to replace the missing ones. They all hoped that that would cheer him up. Dale Rutherford knew though that it would never be the same.

The voice rattled in the phone like a mouse in a tin, "Good morning, Dale. Nat Coleway calling. Are you still asleep?"

"No I am not," mumbled Dale.

He had no reason to like Nat Coleway, but it was obvious he despised this case and was completely indifferent to the fate of the ducks. No surprise the investigation had hit a dead end.

"Last night one of the devices called in," said Coleway.

"What?" Dale jumped up.

"We are still not 100% certain," continued the detective. "The signal is not clear. We are comparing it with the recordings of the others. Something tells me though that we have located your bird."

"I thought you had given up?" said Dale not bothering to hide his emotions.

"We had, but not the computer on Astra's board," said Nat flatly.

"Listen Dale, you know the system better than us. Can you come round our way?"

"Of course! When?"

"Wait for us at the upper end of the High Street. In twenty minutes."

The van appeared at around seven. Dale Rutherford was already walking up and down wrapped up in his green parka. Something trembled inside him when he saw the mobile antennae on the roof of the van. Last night one called in, whatever that meant!

"Get in, Dale!" Nat opened the door.

The familiar buzzing of the instruments surrounded him. The dry air was charged with electricity.

"Sir!" called the man with the headphones. "It disappeared again!"

He started twiddling various buttons, but soon after shook his head, "Gone."

"Damn it!" Nat swore.

"What's going on?" Dale was worried.

"That's what I want to know, too," sighed the detective.

The signal had suddenly appeared on the satellite's radar early this morning, just before five. The news shocked Nat Coleway out of his bed and soon after the whole team was on-line. At exactly 5.32am though, the signal mysteriously went silent and they spent more than half an hour immobile in the Chatham area. At 6.20am the signal appeared again.

"And what are we going to do now?" asked Dale.

"Wait," Nat ground his teeth.

In the beginning it had been difficult for him to comprehend the rage and sorrow of the Park's employee. He had thought he was slightly cuckoo. At the end of the day they were only some stupid ducks! But now he did not think so. The Hyde Park case had entered the golden annals of police folklore. Nat was now feeling personally responsible. "Go on, call in again!" he whispered nervously.

Instead of a call from the radar, the popular melody 'Six Little

Ducks' sang from his pocket. Dale gave him an icy look. The detective smiled internally and pulled out his mobile. He had changed the melody whilst they were thinking what to do in Chatham. He hoped subconsciously that the tune would bring him luck. It was Chuck Salinksi from the laboratory of the technical centre. Nat listened to him attentively without interrupting.

"The signal is identical to the others," he said and put the phone back in his pocket. "That much we now know..."

Surprise, surprise the magic had worked!

"But what took it so long?" asked Dale eagerly.

"I have no idea," Nat shrugged. "Maybe something was blocking it. What do you think?"

Dale started to think. During the experiments it had been proven that some of the chips blocked when exposed to temperatures of -20°C and below. This suggestive thought made him shiver.

"If it was deep frozen..." he said in a low voice.

"Of course, I should've thought of that!" exclaimed Coleway. "Nobody can eat 40 ducks at once, can they? They failed to take it out, and then deep froze it!"

The park's employee was silent. Nat put his arm around Dale shoulder. "I think I know what's activated it again..."

"Then we have to hurry up Nat!" Dale said. "Before we find it in the sewers!"

The next hour passed amidst guesses and ominous doubts. The antennae were searching the air in vain, trying to dig out the signal from the universal haystack. The chip was not giving any signs of live. Dale's head bowed in sadness.

"Do you have any idea how it reacts to stomach juices?" asked Nat, trying to cheer up the atmosphere.

9.15. The operator, half asleep with the headphones on his ears, suddenly moved. "Look! The bird's awake!" he said with a note of contempt.

10.30. The car moved down High Street Kensington and stopped in front of Marks & Spencer's.

"Disappeared," the operator reported.

"It will show up again," said Nat.

"Don't you have the impression that all the traces lead to this part of the city?" Dale's voice called out.

"Yes we do," replied the detective.

During the last hour the source had been appearing and disappearing at intervals of about ten minutes. Obviously the device had been partly damaged by the hostile environment, but was continuing to fulfil its duty heroically. Come on, you little beauty, keep it up for another half-hour! Nat was praying.

In the van the atmosphere of expectation lay like a heavy cloud. Every beep could be the last one – the team knew that well. But nobody was in a hurry to celebrate. From a precise control device the instrument had transformed itself into the die of fortune, spinning whilst they all prayed for a six.

"Ooooops! Here we go again!" exclaimed the operator.

The van hesitantly joined the traffic.

"We are close!" Nat Coleway rubbed his hands.

The man in front of the screen nodded. Suddenly his face became worried. "Sir! I'm afraid the source is moving, Sir!" he repeated as he stared at the pulsating light.

"How come!" exploded Nat. "You're not telling me they have an anti-radar device, are you? There are all sorts of hi-tech poachers these days, would you believe it! Follow it!"

```
11.25 AM. Distance 300 yards. We are on M25
West. A traffic jam in the Chiswick area is
blocking all movement. Fortunately, not only
ours...We have every cause to believe that
the chip is in the stomach of an individual,
who is in a car in front of us. Supposed
consumption: - 11 hours. Expected ejection:
+4 hours. We have to catch him before that.
End.
```

Nat switched off the recorder and put it back in his pocket.

"What are you doing that for?" asked Dale with some disgust.

"Making a record of the last phase of the operation," was the gloomy answer.

From the exhaust pipes of the cars, pale smog drifted. The reflections of the dispersing clouds floated across the display widows of the Sega shop, the empire of virtual reality.

"I wonder what that swine looks like?" Dale hissed.

"I don't know," said Nat. "Maybe he didn't have a clue what he was eating?"

"He didn't, didn't he...?!" Dale clenched his fists.

"In any case I expect him to tell us where he ate," added Nat Coleway.

"I want to punch his gluttonous face!" Dale said darkly.

"Question of priorities," shrugged the detective.

```
11.43 AM. We are closely following an olive
green diplomatic Rover 80 with the number
plate 123D001. We have reason to believe that
the individual who has swallowed the source
is in the same car. This makes the situation
considerably difficult. We should not rush.
Possible obstacles of an administrative or
legal nature. I am waiting for instructions
from Central. In the meantime the car is
heading towards Heathrow with us in pursuit.
Mr Rutherford is showing signs of acute
nerves. I'm worried that he might lose control
at any moment and jeopardise the success
of the operation. I have ordered Dale to be
handcuffed. Only temporarily. Sorry, Dale.
End.
```

12.00 AM. No signal. We are entering the area of
the airport. I just spoke with Major Trumble.
The situation is obviously very delicate; there
are consultations with the Foreign Office going
on at the minute. The instructions are vague:
the chase should go on and nothing more...We are
just in the tunnel that leads to Terminals 1, 2
and 3. Speed limit 30 miles per hour.

12.11 PM. Three women and a man got out of
the car. The man is obviously the Bulgarian
Ambassador. They are heading for the VIP
entrance. Mr Rutherford will have to stay
in the van, despite his energetic protests.
Mr Finch, from the technical crew is coming
with me, armed with a portable locator. I'm
wondering which one of those four is the
host of the chip? And what is the extent of
diplomatic immunity...? We have located it
again. We are following their steps, but they
either haven't noticed, or don't care. The
leader of the group is the woman in the red
furs. I don't think Dale's ducks gave her any
particular trouble; she looks like a hardcore
cannibal. They are talking in their own
language and laughing...

"Detective Coleway..." a soft, but powerful voice stopped him.
In front of him stood a well built man in a brown suit and
funereal tie. A badge with VIP was hanging on his lapel. His
blue eyes were like lakes of liquid methane. "Lieutenant Rupert
Everidge!" the man introduced himself. "Please, follow me!"
"But we were just..." Nat tried to object.

"I know," the lieutenant interrupted him. "I have been informed. It is my responsibility to take control of the operation from this moment onwards. We are going to explain everything to you. For Christ sake!" he went on nervously. "Tell your man to remove that stupid device! It's attracting people's attention!"

Nat hesitated. He did not have much choice. He followed the disappearing group with a look full of sorrow.

"Come with me!" Everidge urged them, as though he was afraid that Nat would throw himself after them.

He took them though a good number of corridors and automatic doors, unlocking them softly when he swiped his access card through the readers. Nat had the uneasy feeling that he was walking behind the wings of a big stage. They ended up in a small compartment with a small ceiling, full of monitors. In the middle of the room a man with a beige raincoat and a flat face was sat. The fluorescent lights threw indigo coloured shades over his shoes. MI6...? wondered Nat.

"Good afternoon, gentlemen," he said turning to Nat and Finch without moving from his chair. "Unpleasant situation, eh? We have to decide how to proceed."

"I have the feeling it has already been decided, Sir..." mumbled Nat sourly.

The name of the agent was Bibbit. Michael Bibbit.

"I know how much work and nerves you have thrown into this so far," he started with a slight yawn. "I don't want you to be left with impression that we are acting over your heads."

Why don't you go and shoot yourself! said Nat to himself.

"I just don't get it! Why?" sighed Bibbit, turning his chair toward the monitors. "They look like normal people, almost the same as we are..."

Varadin and Pezantova were having a tête-à-tête, standing near the plate-glass wall overlooking the runway. Her two companions occupied the soft, gold, silk-upholstered armchairs, watching them with curiosity. Mitche was drinking weak tea with lemon, its colour similar to that of her complexion. Veronika was eating fruit pie and washing it down lavishly with sips of black coffee. She looked fresh with a healthy complexion, ready to cross the whole globe from pole to pole.

"And that car, how could it smell like that!" whined Mitche. "I nearly made the same mess again!"

"Oh, you are such a delicate flower!" laughed Veronika. "I know that stench quite well. In the past we had a Trabant and my husband went fishing with it quite often. And when he forgets the fish in the boot, and the sun is up, I cannot describe it. The whole upholstery soaked up that smell; we had real difficulty selling it in the end. Yes, it will take at least a year, before that smell disappears."

"Wow, like cat's piss!" nodded Mitche.

"A-ha, no escape!"

"Why are they going fishing with that expensive car?"

"Like it's theirs!" grunted the other, stabbing another chunk of her pie.

Behind the windows a giant Brazilian Airlines Jumbo Jet took off. Surprised by its close proximity Varadin and Pezantova instinctively stopped waiting for the roar of its massive engines. From behind the thick windows though, only a muted noise came.

"I still cannot believe that She called me after what happened," sighed Pezantova. "Do you think She was being honest?"

"Well, she knows it was not your fault," said Varadin.

"Naturally it isn't!" Pezantova tossed her head and continued thoughtfully "She even apologised for leaving so suddenly. Otherwise She was thrilled with the concert! By the dinner too. She said to congratulate the cook."

"I will congratulate him," he nodded.

"Shame that an accident like that has overshadowed the whole event," she bowed her head and lowered her voice. "You don't think it was accidental, do you? There are some people that are trying to undermine us. They're envious of my success. Pure sabotage, if you ask me. We have to understand who is behind all this."

"We'll do our best," he promised.

"And careful with the media!" she warned him. "No useless information. They are going to re-invent the story anyway."

"And you try to remember who fixed you up with that piss artist," Varadin threw at her cunningly.

"I remember," Pezantova spat. "That is the reason I am in such a hurry to get home. In a week I am opening the 'Days of Bulgarian Culture in Berlin', and a man who was recommended to me by the same people has arranged the program. If it turns out to be another flop I won't be able to bear it!"

"Good luck," said Varadin and squeezed her hand lightly.

"Thank you, anyway, for everything you did for me, I won't forget it," she said instinctively replying to his gesture. "I'll try to drop by again, if I have time, but without those peasants," she stared disdainfully at her companions. "The Halvadjievs are going to cover the expenses, so don't you worry about it. They owe it to us for God's sake!" she concluded in a businesslike voice.

"Those foreigners!" Rupert Everidge shook his head. "I have been working here at this airport for fifteen years and I still can't understand them!"

"Who is the host of the signal?" asked Bibbit looking somewhat disgusted, as though a deadly virus was in question.

"I don't know, Sir," Sergeant Finch said. "They have to go through the scanner one by one. But if you ask me the woman with the furs is the one we are looking for."

"No, that one with the sick-looking face," Lieutenant Everidge nodded his head towards the screen showing the ghastly Mitche.

"I'm putting ten quid on the fat one," said Bibbit. "And you Coleway? What you're going to say about His Excellency?"

"I don't like betting," the detective shook his head, "But I am ready to take on any bets if you let me identify the recipient."

"And, what are you going to do, arrest him?" pressed Michael Bibbit.

"That won't be necessary," replied Nat. "But we'll know how the source ended up in his/her stomach. It must have happened last night. We'll clarify where and what they have eaten exactly…"

"I'll tell you," the agent interrupted him. "They all dined in the Embassy. There was some strange reception. Artists were invited. Unfortunately we don't have many details."

"Then we'll question the cook," Nat continued persistently. "To tell us how he got hold of the ducks. I am sure we'll catch the real criminals in the end!"

He started to babble. Just like Dale. And that wouldn't lead to anything good.

"I do not doubt your logic, Coleway," agreed Bibbit. "You are a good detective. But a bad strategist, which is, of course, not your fault. That is your job. You see the case but you miss its political framework. Can you grasp the political scandal hidden in this case? The situation in the Balkans is complicated enough; probably a military operation will follow. We need the support of the local leaders more than ever. In this very moment what you are proposing is to discredit those people, to paint them as savages! Chaplin's corpse, the umbrella, the Pope, and now this. You know how much effort they put into their new European image! They are almost ill with every negative publication! It'll take us months to calm down public opinion. In the meantime, we have to lead all sorts of delicate discussions. No, no, I cannot allow our national interests to be risked because of a bunch of wild ducks!"

"So the bets are off?" asked Nat Coleway.

"Yes!" the agent said. "I know very well how you feel! I also like to feed the birds in the park and don't think they should be treated as poultry. At the moment though we have other priorities and the ducks are clearly not part of them!"

"Mr Finch," Nat turned to the sergeant. "I think the operation is over. Let's get out of here. Goodbye, gentlemen."

"We are relying on your discretion," the voice of Michael Bibbit followed him.

```
12.55 PM. I just gave orders for Mr Rutherford
to be un-cuffed. I'm afraid he's very cross
with me. The source is leaving the area of
the airport and is flying to the continent.
It is expected to disappear from the
radar's perimeter in five minutes. In a world
dominated by politics the truth will never
reign. End.
```

This time Balkan was flying a Boeing; Varadin had taken his guests to the entrance, waited for the doors to close and come back to the hall. He was content; there were no other people with him. Pezantova thought that some of the diplomats had been involved with the accident. In any case, she was convinced that they were maliciously happy and she did not want to see their faces. Varadin had turned them down with pleasure.

He was not in a hurry. The idea of going back in the stinking Rover was not a very inviting one. He looked at the monitor and saw that the plane to Sofia had already taken off. A wave of relief entered his chest, and his heart beat happily like a cat in front of a mousetrap. He sat at the bar and ordered a small, light Grolsch. Whilst the foam was settling, whispering underneath his nose, and the big white machines were slowly crossing the runways like big white elephants, in his subconscious a door opened. But instead of numbers a light came through the door. He saw his whole four year mandate rolling in front of him like a golden silk carpet covering the mud of life underneath. I'll buy myself a new car! The thought crossed his mind. Maybe a Saab or a Mercedes...? He had not decided yet.

Suddenly from some dark pocket his mobile phone squeaked. He took it out unwillingly.

"Mr Ambassador!" a worried voice sounded. "Major Potty is here with a whole lorry full of bedpans. He wants to unload them into the Embassy's courtyard. He claims that you have promised to transport them to Bulgaria. What shall we do? He's shouting and kicking the staff. I'm afraid he is off his head..."

"What?"

"He got hysterical, when we told him that we have nowhere to put them..."

"What?" Varadin repeated. "I don't hear you very well...Who is calling?"

"He slammed Turkeiev on the head with one bedpan, because he told him it's rusty! He threatens he's going to complain to the President, if we do not accept them. Crazy man! Do you hear him screaming?"

"I can't hear anything!" Varadin ground his teeth. "The connection is bad. I'm at the airport..."

"What are we going to do?"

At that moment someone else grabbed the phone at the other end.

"Excellency! Excellency!" a piercing scream echoed down his phone. "What unheard of insolence! You have no right to reject our help!" It was Major Potty himself. "I insist on speaking with your President personally! We have to solve this problem once and for all. Do you hear me?..."

Varadin instinctively held the phone away from his ear. He had the feeling saliva was dribbling out of it. Then he turned it off.

He felt a sudden urge to slam it on the floor, but then he realised that it would be the second time this week. He swallowed his lager in one go and then ordered another one. He did not move for a while, listening to the whispering of the foam, yet understanding nothing. "I'll survive!" he said. "Whatever happens..."

38

On the 24th of December, Rube Sparks, the jeweller from Regent Street, prepared to enjoy the end of the 20th century. He had been choosing the decoration for weeks, postponing vital deals to the last minute, in order to provide all the available sparkle for Christmas Eve. At exactly eleven p.m., Lady Diana appeared, wrapped in a long fur-coat and an opaque veil, followed by her chauffeur. He gave him twenty quid and sent him back to the car. They made their way to his office, above the shop. The shutters were down. Whilst she was taking her clothes off, Emerald opened the safe behind his desk and started taking all the decorations out. The reflections danced on the ceiling...The Princess was shining in front him with her goddess-like nudity, her breasts moving emotionally as she breathed. He took a diamond necklace from its velvet bed and put it around her neck. This time the decorations were more, both in number and value, than ever before. He continued to dress her up until there was not a single empty spot left on her body. Even on her toes rings sparkled, covered with diamonds! His heart jumped into his throat and his Adam's apple started pulsating like an iguana's.

It was time for photos.

He put a new hypersensitive film in his camera and looked happily through the lenses. Surprisingly, the Princess had put her coat on. In her hand shone a little jewel, which was definitely not part of his collection – a stylish Smith & Wesson, 37 calibre. She pointed it at the petrified jeweller, and made him step back to the window. She put her other hand into the safe and took out a box with photos, which had sealed Rube's ecstasy and happiness.

The last goodbye was dry and businesslike.

Desmond Cook waited in the car with the engine running. Katya threw herself in beside him and took a deep breath. "The Christmas tree is here," she said.

He stepped on the gas and joined the traffic. The car roared up to the brightly lit Regent Street, then turned into some small side street and disappeared into the labyrinth of the city's back alleys.

They were driving in silence. The heating was on fully, blowing hot waves underneath her coat. The stones were stuck to her skin like scales. Small streamlets of sweat were coming out of her armpits. I made it, Christ, I made it!

Desmond turned the radio on: Jazz FM. Relaxing. They crossed Marylebone Road and continued east. Deserted streets, no names, lit in dim yellowish light. Desmond's face was immobile. During all those months he had insisted on not mixing sex with business. That made her feel insecure. Until now they had only had sex (and quite at lot of it, at that!). But she couldn't grasp it, exactly what his plan was. She grasped the gun tightly, Don't even think of cutting me out, you bastard!

Suddenly, he turned towards her and smiled, as though he had read her thoughts. Nice teeth, agile tongue! She tried to think of something more pleasant. In less than 24 hours she would be 10 kilometres above the ocean. Her new Paraguayan passport was issued under the name of Esmeralda Corazon. She could open a private fitness centre in Nassau. She even knew what it was going to be called: 'The Onyx Eye'. She was asking herself how much to send to her parents? Maybe $500 a month would be enough? Or too much? The wheels went cachunk-cachunk as they crossed some old rails, which had sunk deep into the tarmac. There were rows of warehouses on both sides of the road. Their damp arched brick entrances were covered with greenish lichen. Most of the lamps were broken. From time to time a bottle crunched under the wheels. A big cistern blocked the end of the street. Over its blacked metal body a half erased label was still readable, Pooper-scooper. There was a big metal door underneath, covered in bright apocalyptic graffiti.

"We're here," said Desmond and pressed the horn.

"What is this place?" she frowned.

"I don't think that we should spend this particular night in the Ritz," he said, laughing.

The door opened with a muffled shriek. Desmond parked the car in the dark tunnel and switched the lights off.

There was a waft of stale air.

"Come in!" said a powerful voice.

He grabbed her hand. Where he was taking her? The rings that decorated her toes hurt her. He leaned her against some wall and slowly unbuttoned her coat. His lips tenderly started sucking her earring.

"Hey, what are you doing?" she whispered excited.

"I want to see them," purred Desmond.

"Okay, here they are..."

Her coat fell to the floor. He stepped back a little. The priceless stones sparkled in the dark with a clear, deep light.

"They are beautiful," he mumbled after a while.

"But more importantly expensive..." said some other voice cynically.

"Desmond!!!" cried Katya in fear and started looking for her coat.

In the metal tube echoed the clack of a shuttle switch. A dirty white lamp clicked on. She stuck to the wall like a perforated butterfly.

Two automatic machine guns pointed at her bosom – that was the first thing she noticed, of course. Then their faces: three black males, two women and one Chinese. The women held the machine guns. A red band crossed the forehead of one of them. They were all between seventeen and twenty-five and they were wearing combat boots, combat trousers and black jackets. In the middle of the group Desmond himself was standing, his hands in his pockets like Johnny West.

"Desmond!" repeated Katya.

He shook his head.

"I'm not Desmond. I'm sorry I'm only telling you this now. My real name is Moke-le-Ono. The eagle's eye. I'm a fighter."

"What a kind of a fucking fighter are you?" She slid her hand into her pocket.

"Don't do stupid things, Kate!" he warned, stepping towards her, "Easy! These guys are not kidding, give me that here."

He took the gun out of her hand and stuffed it into his pocket. Then wrapped her in her coat, almost with care.

"Bastard!" she hissed.

"Comrades, leave us alone!" Moke-le-Ono turned to the others.

Their shadows quietly disappeared behind the boxes, scattered everywhere in disorder.

"Listen, Kate," he put his hands onto her shoulders. "Listen to me very carefully, you did a really nice job for the Revolution and you should be proud of it."

"Fuck you!" she shouted. "I don't give a damn about your fucking Revolution!"

"I know," he nodded. "You come from Eastern Europe. You screwed up the socialist idea over there. Nothing sacred is left anymore. You compromised with the idea! See what you've become, though. Servants to the West. Slaves. Regardless of whether you are dancing around the pole or typing in front of a computer. Give me dollar, I'll show you my cunt – that is the end of your philosophy. So, do you like showing your cunt to everyone? To let them stuff different things into your ass while you clench your teeth?"

"That is none of your business," she replied still stroppily.

"Naturally. But you don't like it. Otherwise you wouldn't be here with a couple million pounds on top of your body. Because the final moment always comes when you realise you've had enough. And you need a change, isn't that so?"

"Exactly!" she agreed energetically. "That's why I want my share and you can do what the hell you want to with yours. Invest it in any revolution you like, but I have other plans."

"My poor little Kate!" sighed Moko-le-Ono. "She believes she'll get away. She has watched too many American movies. She thinks she's going to disappear like that with £250,000 and make herself a little heaven on the ocean beach. The fantasies of the middle class. Regular income, regular shags. Walks on the beach. If possible, good old Desmond also bathing his ass somewhere nearby. Sorry baby, life is a different movie! Types like your jeweller don't easily get over losses of that size. Maybe you should have killed him after all."

"We have the pictures," she answered after some hesitation. "They'll ruin him if they appear in public..."

"You're not very convinced," he added. "And quite rightly. He is already ruined financially. And when you are broke your reputation is the last thing you worry about. At least, it's like that in this world. You cannot escape Kate; they'll chase you to the last hole. And you know what? They'll get you exactly when you are in your paradise! When you swing into your rubber chair in the middle of your pool and drink piña colada from the coconut shell. Because they have also watched American movies like you, even more than you, and they know exactly where to find you. And if they find you in your inflatable rubber chair, in the middle of your pool, they're not going to be distracted by your tits, no matter how nice they are. If you are there that is. But!" he lifted his finger in front of her face. "You're not going to be there! I promise you that! We'll see to that! They'll never find you!"

"You'll take care of me, huh?" she hissed maliciously like a cornered weasel.

"I'm offering you a way out!" the reflections of the diamonds sparkled in his eyes. "I don't want them to say that I walked over a human being without giving them the possibility to join the cause. The Revolution continues, Kate. We aren't giving up the party only because a bunch of renegades wiped their arses with our flag. The idea, Kate, they cannot touch the idea. Look what is happening! The imperialists are ready to suffocate every sparkle of freedom in the world. The people are turning into herds of cattle, grist to the mill. The individuals – into throats and arses. Crowds of wage-slaves are flooding the towns like rats...The banks are piling up dossiers. But the revolution continues. And it needs fuel. And we have more than we need! Tomorrow we are flying to Columbia. And then we are going to cross the border to Peru, where we are going to join the ranks of our brothers in arms. Are you coming with us?"

"Do I have a choice?" she said sharply.

"Only way out, sorry..." he shook his head. "On a small narrow path which is going to take you to the shining peaks of the fight. I'll stay next to you. We will be comrades."

"Are you going to fuck me from time to time?" asked Katya, licking her lips.

His hand struck her cheek, producing a flat noise. Her earring fell to the floor turning like a spinning top, throwing blinding sparkles all around.

"Cynical bitch," he hissed through his teeth. "Eastern Europeans...!"

CLOSING REMARKS

VARADIN DIMITROV finished his mandate without any particular accidents. After an interruption he went back to the numerical therapy of Dr Pepolen. His regular sex with Doroteya Totomanova helped him maintain a perfect mental balance. And when four years later they offered him the vacant diplomatic post in sunny Nigeria, he accepted it without any fuss.

ROBERT ZIEBLING continues to successfully run 'Famous Connections', but with more vigilance. Three months after Katya's disappearance, he had a visit from a strange man, who wanted to make sure that some diamonds were not in his possession. During the investigation, Ziebling's neck was broken and for some time he had to wear a plaster collar. Since then, the agency avoids employing girls from Eastern Europe.

KOSTA PASTRICHEFF's contract was suddenly terminated four months after the memorable dinner. He is now head chef of a four star restaurant in the foothills of the Vitosha mountain. His speciality is called 'Celtic trotter's jelly'. Many of Sofia's elite go there to taste it.

Soon after his arrival in Sofia, a lucky sequence of coincidences gave **RACHO RACHEV** a mandate in the People's Republic of China. He still lives in the secret department and is saving all his salary.

CHAVDAR TOLOMANOV went through a heavy financial crisis, which resulted in his figure regaining its previous elegance. He stayed in London and is now a street actor. He can be spotted in the area of Covent Garden Market, where he is playing the Green Man. The performance is partly sponsored by Granny's Apple Juice Co.

THE FIRE-DANCER made a huge impression on a group of high-ranking people during his demonstration in Kew Gardens. He is currently working for the Sultan of Brunei and is responsible for the illuminations in the Palace. His net earnings are in the region of $100,000 p.a. and he is thinking of adopting Islam, which would save him some taxes.

DEVORINA PEZANTOVA is still working hard on her society image and is reaping the rewards of successful campaigns everywhere in the EU. At the minute she is organising an Assembly of Bulgarian Talent, which is expected to attract lots of foreign guests.

RUBE SPARKS never filed an official complaint with the police. For some time he has been in the process of delicate negotiations with Viacheslav Levine, an Israeli citizen of Russian origin, who has promised to return the diamonds for a 30% commission. What Rube does not realise is that Levine never works for less that 70% commission. The other 30% he usually donates anonymously to his client's widow, or, if there is no widow, to an Eastern European children's trust.

From the front-line diary of **ESMERALDA CORAZON**:
'12.12.200? Elevation 1200. Bolivia, Nancahuazu gorges.
Today at lunchtime they shot the Eagle's Eye. Some months ago I would've been happy, but the truth is that fighting side-by-side brings people together, even more than sex... We've buried him in the mud and camouflaged his grave with ferns. One day, when the Revolution succeeds, they'll build him a monument for sure, but for now he's waiting for the Second Coming. Fuck it, I still have blood on my fatigues. The fascists have occupied both ends

of the gorge, and are firing mortars (Made in the Czech Republic) at us every hour on the hour. It hasn't stopped raining for the past three days. Everything is falling apart, apart from the laminated biography of Che – a present from Fidel for the Revolution's anniversary. I highly appreciate the gesture, but the photo with chopped hands on the last page somehow makes me nervous... We eat insects. I caught myself a frog and I'm planning to eat it, when they are not watching me. I'll escape from this shit, whatever the price! That which does not kill us, makes us stronger! Whoever said that should go shoot himself!'

Hamam Balkania by Vladislav Bajac (Serbia)
Translated by Randall A. Major
An exploration into the power structures of the Ottoman Empire, juxtaposed with musings on contemporary concepts of identity and faith. A truly ambitious book that rewards the reader with insights into some of the great questions of our time. (January 2014) **ISBN: 978-1-908236-14-2**

Death in the Museum of Modern Art by Alma Lazarevska (Bosnia)
Translated by Celia Hawkesworth
Avoiding the easy traps of politics and blame, Lazarevska reveals a world full of incidents and worries so similar to our own, and yet always under the shadow of the snipers and the grenades of the recent Bosnian war. (June 2014) **ISBN: 978-1-908236-17-3**

False Apocalypse by Fatos Lubonja (Albania)
Translated by John Hodgson
1997, a tragic year in the history of post-communist Albania. This is one man's story of how the world's most isolated country emerged from Stalinist dictatorship and fell victim to a plague of corruption and flawed 'pyramid' financial schemes which brought the people to the edge of ruin. (October 2014) **ISBN: 978-1-908236-19-7**

The Great War by Aleksandar Gatalica (Serbia)
Translated by Will Firth
In the centenary year of the start of WWI, we finally have a Serbian author taking on the themes of a war that was started by a Serb assassin's bullet. Following the destinies of over seventy characters, on all warring sides, Gatalica depicts the destinies of winners and losers, generals and opera singers, soldiers and spies, in the conflict that marked the beginning of the Twentieth Century. (October 2014) **ISBN: 978-1-908236-20-3**

FREEDOM
TO **WRITE**
FREEDOM
TO **READ**

This book has been selected to receive financial assistance from English PEN's Writers in Translation programme supported by Bloomberg and Arts Council England. English PEN exists to promote literature and its understanding, uphold writers' freedoms around the world, campaign against the persecution and imprisonment of writers for stating their views, and promote the friendly co-operation of writers and free exchange of ideas.

Each year, a dedicated committee of professionals selects books that are translated into English from a wide variety of foreign languages. We award grants to UK publishers to help translate, promote, market and champion these titles. Our aim is to celebrate books of outstanding literary quality, which have a clear link to the PEN charter and promote free speech and intercultural understanding.

In 2011, Writers in Translation's outstanding work and contribution to diversity in the UK literary scene was recognised by Arts Council England. English PEN was awarded a threefold increase in funding to develop its support for world writing in translation.

www.englishpen.org

BULGARIA'S ENGLISH MAGAZINE

VAGABOND

EVERYTHING
YOU WANTED
TO KNOW
ABOUT
BULGARIA...

...BUT THERE
WAS NO ONE
TO TELL YOU

www.vagabond.bg